THE
MARQUIS'
SECRET

BETHANY HOUSE PUBLISHERS

Minneapolis, Minnesota 55438

The Novels of George MacDonald Edited for Today's Reader

Edited Title	Original Title

The two-volume story of Malcolm:

| *The Fisherman's Lady* | *Malcolm* |
| *The Marquis' Secret* | *The Marquis of Lossie* |

Companion stories of Gibbie and his friend Donal:

| *The Baronet's Song* | *Sir Gibbie* |
| *The Shepherd's Castle* | *Donal Grant* |

Companion stories of Hugh Sutherland and Robert Falconer:

The Tutor's First Love	*David Elginbrod*
The Musician's Quest	*Robert Falconer*
The Maiden's Bequest	*Alec Forbes of Howglen*

Companion stories of Thomas Wingfold:

The Curate's Awakening	*Thomas Wingfold*
The Lady's Confession	*Paul Faber*
The Baron's Apprenticeship	*There and Back*

Stories that stand alone:

A Daughter's Devotion	*Mary Marston*
The Gentlewoman's Choice	*Weighed and Wanting*
The Highlander's Last Song	*What's Mine's Mine*
The Laird's Inheritance	*Warlock O'Glenwarlock*
The Landlady's Master	*The Elect Lady*
The Minister's Restoration	*Salted with Fire*
The Peasant Girl's Dream	*Heather and Snow*
The Poet's Homecoming	*Home Again*

MacDonald Classics Edited for Young Readers

Wee Sir Gibbie of the Highlands
Alec Forbes and His Friend Annie
At the Back of the North Wind
The Adventures of Ranald Bannerman

George MacDonald: Scotland's Beloved Storyteller by Michael Phillips
Discovering the Character of God by George MacDonald
Knowing the Heart of God by George MacDonald
A Time to Grow by George MacDonald
A Time to Harvest by George MacDonald

HAMPSHIRE BOOKS™

George MacDonald
THE
MARQUIS' SECRET

BETHANY HOUSE PUBLISHERS
MINNEAPOLIS, MINNESOTA 55438

The Marquis' Secret
George Macdonald

Originally published as *The Marquis of Lossie* in 1877 by
J. B. Lippincott and Co.

Cover by Dan Thornberg,
Bethany House Publishers staff artist.

Published by Bethany House Publishers
A Ministry of Bethany Fellowship, Inc.
11300 Hampshire Avenue South
Minneapolis, Minnesota 55438

Printed in the United States of America

Introduction

I like a good story.

Though I read many kinds of books for a variety of reasons, nothing quite conpares with the adventure of finding myself caught up in a compelling piece of fiction.

Discovering an author whose stories create such enjoyment is a treasure indeed.

For me, and for increasing thousands, George MacDonald is such a writer. A Scottish author and personality of great renown in Great Britain and the United States a century ago, his fame gradually diminished as his more than fifty volumes, one by one, ultimately went out of print. Happily, however, his popularity is once more on the upswing, and his books are again delighting readers the world over.

Most of you who are now beginning *The Marquis Secret* (originally published in 1877 as *The Marquis of Lossie*) will already have read the *Fisherman's Lady*, to which it is the sequel. If you haven't, by all means, do so. For maximum reading enjoyment, they should be read in the proper sequence.

Brew yourself a pot of tea, sink into your favorite overstuffed chair, and drift over the miles to MacDonald's Scotland and London with his masterful spinner of tales....

—Michael Phillips

Contents

Characters

Malcolm Colonsay—The Marquis of Lossie
Hector Crathie—The factor of Lossie House
Mr. Stoat—Lossie House groom
Kelpie—Malcolm's mare
Mrs. Courthope—Lossie House housekeeper
Miss Horn—Malcolm's friend
Lizza Findlay—Seaton village girl
Joseph Mair (Blue Peter)—Malcolm's best friend
Annie Mair—Blue Peter's wife
Mr. Soutar—Duff Harbor lawyer
Davy—Young cabinboy
Lady Florimel Gordon (Colonsay)—Malcolm's half sister
Lord Liftore (formerly Lord Meikleham)—Lady Bellair's nephew
Mr. Wallis—London servant of Florimel's
Arnold Lenorme—London painter
John Findlay (Partan)—Lizza's father
Meg Findlay (Partan)—Lizza's mother
Alexander Graham—Malcolm's friend, a schoolmaster
Lady Clementina Thornicroft—Friend of Florimel's
Travers—Yacht's mate
Caley—Florimel's maid
Mrs. Catanach—Portlossie midwife
Griffith—Florimel's groom
Mr. & Mrs. Merton—Portland Place servants
Rose—Portland Place servant girl
Duncan MacPhail—Malcolm's adopted grandfather
Johnny Bykes—Lossie House gatekeeper
Mrs. Crathie—Hector Crathie's wife
Phemy Mair—Blue Peter's daughter
Mr. Morrison—Local magistrate

1 The Stable Yard

It was one of those exquisite days that come in every winter and seem like the beautiful ghost of summer. The loveliness of the morning, however, was but partially visible from the spot where Malcolm Colonsay stood in the stable yard of Lossie House, ancient and roughly paved. He stood on the unleveled stones grooming the coat of a powerful and fidgety black mare. Nothing about him indicated he was anything but an ordinary stable-hand.

The mare looked dangerous. Every now and then she cast back a white glance of the one visible eye; but the youth was on his guard and as wary as fearless in his handling of her. When at length he had finished with her coat, he took from his pocket a lump of sugar and held it for her to bite at with angry-looking teeth. It was a cold, crisp morning, bright with the morning's sun. But for all the cold, there was keen life in the air.

As they stood thus, a man who looked half farmer, half lawyer appeared on the opposite side of the court in the shadow.

"You are spoiling that mare, MacPhail!" he cried.

"I could hardly do that, sir; she couldn't be much worse," returned Malcolm.

"It's whip and spur she needs, not sugar."

"She has had, and shall have both in turn, and I hope they'll do something for her when the time comes, sir."

"Her time shall be short here, anyway. She's not worth the sugar you give her."

"Eh, Mr. Crathie—just look at her," said Malcolm in a tone of expostulation as he stepped back a few paces and regarded her with admiring eye. "Have you ever seen such legs, and such a neck, and such a head, and such hindquarters? She's beautiful in every way except for her temper, and she can't help that like you and I can. She's such a beauty; it's little wonder the marquis bought her the moment he laid eyes on her."

"She'll be the death of somebody someday. The sooner we get rid of her the better. Just look at that!" he added as the mare laid back her ears and made a vicious snap at nothing in particular.

"She was bound to be a favorite of my—master, the marquis," returned Malcolm. "It's only too bad he didn't live long enough to tame and ride her himself. I know he was looking forward to it. Knowing that, sir, I would not want to part with her."

"I'll take any offer within reason for her," said the factor. "You'll just ride her to Forres market next week and see what you can get for her. I do think she's quieter, though, since you took her in hand."

"I'm sure she is, but it won't last a day if she's sold. The moment I leave her she'll be just as bad as ever. She has a kind of liking to me because I give her sugar and she can't throw me, but she's no better in her heart yet. She's an unsanctified brute. I couldn't think of selling her like this."

"Let whoever buys beware," said the factor.

"Oh, yes, let them! I don't object as long as they know what she's like before they buy her," rejoined Malcolm.

The factor burst out laughing. To his judgment, the youth had spoken like an idiot. "We'll not send you to sell," he said. "Stoat shall go with you, and you shall have nothing to do but hold the mare and your own tongue."

"Sir," said Malcolm seriously, "you don't mean what you say? You said yourself she'd be the death of somebody, and to sell her without telling what she's like would be to break the sixth commandment clean to shivers."

"That may be good doctrine in church, my lad, but it's pure heresy in the horse market. No, no! You buy a horse as you take a wife—for better or worse, as the case may be. A woman's not bound to tell her faults when a man wants to marry her."

"Hoot, sir! There's no comparison. Mistress Kelpie here's plenty ready to confess her faults by giving anyone who wants to know a taste of them—she won't even wait to be asked. And if you expect me to hold my tongue about them, Mr. Crathie, I'd as soon think of selling Blue Peter a rotten boat. And, besides, there's the eighth commandment as well as the sixth. There's no exceptions about horseflesh. We must be as honest with that as anything else."

"There's one commandment, my lad," said Mr. Crathie with the dignity of intended rebuke, "you seem to find hard to learn, and that is to mind your own business."

"If you mean catching herring, maybe you're right," said Malcolm. "I know more about that than horse-selling, and it's a mite cleaner."

"None of your impudence," returned the factor. "The marquis isn't here to uphold you in your follies. That they amused him is no reason why I should put up with them. So keep your tongue between your teeth or you'll find it the worse for you."

Malcolm smiled a little oddly, and held his peace.

"You're here to do what I tell you, and make no remarks," added the factor.

"I'm aware of that, sir—within certain limits," returned Malcolm.

"What do you mean by that?"

"I mean within the limits of doing by your neighbor as you would have your neighbor do by you; that's what I mean, sir."

"I've told you already that doesn't apply in horse-dealing. Every man has to take care of himself in the horse market. That's understood. If you had been brought up amongst horses instead of herring, you would have known that as well as any other man."

"I don't doubt I'll go back to the herring, then, for they're likely to prove the more honest of the two. But there's no hypocrisy in Kelpie, and she must have her day's feed whatever comes of it."

At the word "hypocrisy" Mr. Crathie's face grew red. He was an elder in the church and had family worship every night as regularly as his toddy. The word was offensive and insolent to him. He would have turned Malcolm adrift on the spot had he not remembered the favor of the late marquis for the lad, as well as the favor of the present marchioness, as well as his own instructions to deal kindly with him. Choking down, therefore, his rage and indignation, he said sternly, "Malcolm, you have two enemies—a long tongue and a strong conceit. You have little enough to be proud of. I advise you to mind what you're about and show suitable respect to your superiors, or as sure as judgment you'll be back to your fish guts."

While he spoke, Malcolm had been smoothing Kelpie all over with his palm; the moment the factor ceased talking he ceased stroking and with one arm thrown over the mare's back looked him full in the face. "If you imagine, Mr. Crathie," he said, "that I count it any worldly promotion that brings me under the orders of a man less honest than he might be, you're mistaken. I don't think it's pride this time. I'll lay out Blue Peter's long nets for him, but I won't lie for any factor between here and Davy Jones' locker."

It was too much for him. Mr. Crathie's feelings overcame him, and he was a wrathful man to see as he strode up to the youth with clenched fist.

"Keep away from the mare, for Heaven's sake, Mr. Crathie!" cried Malcolm.

But even as he spoke, the gleaming iron of Kelpie's horseshoes opened on the terror-struck factor with a lightning kick. He started back, white with dismay, having by a bare inch of space and a bare moment of time escaped what he called eternity. Dazed with fear, he turned and staggered halfway across the yard before he recovered himself. Then he turned again and with what dignity he could scrape together said, "MacPhail, you go about your business. You are dismissed!"

In his foolish heart he believed Malcolm had made the brute strike out.

"I can't go until Stoat comes home," answered Malcolm.

"If I see you about the place after sunset, I'll horsewhip you," said the factor and walked away.

Malcolm again smiled oddly, but made no reply. He undid the mare's halter and led her into the stable. There he fed her, standing by her while she ate, not once taking his eye off her. Ever since her arrival, just several days after the marquis' death, Malcolm had taken her in hand in the hope of taming her a little. The factor, who still regarded Malcolm as something even lower than a servant under his charge, allowed both him and the horse to remain in the hopes of by-and-by selling her for a greater price than the marquis had paid.

When the mare had finished her oats, Malcolm left her busy with her hay, for she was a huge eater, and went into the house, passing through the kitchen and ascending the spiral stone stairs to the library. As he went along the narrow passage on the second floor, Mrs. Courthope peeped after him from one of the bedrooms and watched him as he went, nodding her head two or three times with decision. He reminded her so strongly, not of his father the late marquis, but of his brother who had preceded him, that she felt all but certain, whoever might be his mother, that he had as much of the Colonsay blood in his veins as any marquis of them all.

Malcolm went straight to a certain corner and from amongst a dingy set of old classics took down a small volume, sat down and began to read. But he could not keep his mind on the words, for he was occupied with other things. He recalled how the late marquis, about three months before, had on his deathbed secretly acknowledged him his son and committed to his trust the welfare of his sister. The memory of this charge was never absent from his heart. His had been an agonizing perplexity these recent months. For to appear as the marquis of Lossie was not merely to take from Florimel the title she supposed her own but to declare her illegitimate, seeing that the marquis' first wife—Malcolm's mother—was still alive when she was born, a fact rendering void his marriage to Florimel's mother. How was he to act so that as little scandal might befall her whom he loved so much?

Despite his own rough education his thoughts were not troubled about his own prospects. Mysteriously committed to the care of a poor blind Highland piper settled amongst the local fishing people of the Seaton, he had, as he grew up, naturally fallen into their ways of life and labor. He had but lately abandoned the calling of a fisherman to take charge of the marquis' yacht, whence by degrees he had, in his helpfulness, become indispensable to him and his daughter and had come to live in the House of Lossie as a privileged servant. He owed his book education mainly to the friendship of the parish schoolmaster.

If he could content himself with Florimel's future and at the same time, in good conscience, remain faithful to the people who were his charge as marquis, it is doubtful Malcolm would ever have seen the need to identify himself as the marquis. He was perfectly content as fisherman, stable-hand, or servant insofar as he could be sure he was in fact serving Florimel's best interests.

But events over which Malcolm exercised no control now seemed to be making such an option impossible. For not only was Florimel gone from Portlossie and therefore out of reach of his ministrations; she was being swept into a circle of acquaintances judged by Malcolm, at the very least, to be more concerned for their own welfare than hers. The marchioness of Lossie, as she was now called—for the family was one of two or three in Scotland in which the title descends to an heiress—had been, since her father's death, under the guardianship of a certain dowager countess. Lady Bellair had taken her first to Edinburgh and then to London. It was with Florimel's potential suitor, Lady Bellair's nephew Lord Meikleham, that Malcolm was most concerned. Malcolm received tidings of her through Mr. Soutar, the late marquis' lawyer of Duff Harbor. The last amounted to this—that as rapidly as the proprieties of mourning would permit, she was circling the vortex of London society. Malcolm found himself almost in despair of ever being the least service to her as a brother. If he might but once more be her skipper, her groom, her attendant, he might at least learn how to reveal to her the bond between them without breaking it in the very act and so ruining the hope of serving her and his charge to their father.

The door to the library opened and in walked Miss Horn. She looked stern, gaunt, hard-featured—almost fierce. She shook Malcolm's hand with a sort of loose dissatisfaction, and dropped into one of the easy chairs with which the library abounded.

"Do you call yourself an honest man, Malcolm?"

"I call myself nothing," he answered, "but I would hope to be what you say, Miss Horn."

"Oh, I don't doubt you wouldn't steal or tell lies about a horse; I've just come from some wagging of tongues about you. Mistress Crathie tells me her man's steaming angry with you that you won't tell a wordless lie about the black mare. But a gentleman mustn't lie, not even by saying nothing. And yet what's your life right now but a lie, Malcolm? You that's the honest marquis of Lossie to waste your time and the strength of your body wrestling with that devil of a horse, when that half sister of yours is going to the very devil of perdition himself among the godless gentry of London! Aren't you letting her live believing a lie? Aren't you allowing her to go on as if she was someone more than mortal when you know she's no more the marchioness of Lossie than you're the son of old Duncan MacPhail? Faith, man! You've lost the truth just like your father, even if you've gained the world in exchange."

"Say nothing against the dead, mem. He's made up with my mother before now I imagine. And anyway, he confessed her his wife and me her son before he died, and what more did he have time to do?"

"It's a fact," returned Miss Horn, "and now look at you. What your father confessed to with the very death throws of his laboring spirit—that same confession you place back in a cloud of secrecy rather than removing the blot from the memory of one who, I believe, I loved more as my third cousin than you do as your own mother."

"There's no blot on her memory, mem," returned Malcolm, "or I would be marquis tomorrow. There's not a soul who knows she was a mother but knows she was wife and whose wife, too."

Miss Horn had neither wish nor power to reply and so changed her front of attack. "And so, Malcolm Colonsay," she said, "you have no less than made up your mind to spend your days in your own stable, neither better or worse than a servant at Lossie Arms? And after all I have done to make a gentleman of you, coming to your father like a very lion in his den and making him confess the thing against every hair upon his stiff neck? Losh, laddie, it was a picture to see him standing with his back to the door like an obstinate bull!"

"Hold your tongue, mem. I can't stand to hear my father spoken of like that. For, you see, I loved him before I knew there was a drop of his blood in me."

"Well, that's very well, but father and mother's man and wife. You didn't come from father alone."

"That's true, mem. And it can't be that I should ever forget the face you showed me in the coffin—the prettiest, saddest face I ever saw," returned Malcolm with a quaver in his voice. "And don't you think, mem, that I'm going to forget the dead because I'm more concerned about the living. I tell you I just don't know what to do. With my father's dying words committing her to my charge and the more than regard I have for Lady Florimel herself, how can I take the very sunshine out of her life? How can I get near enough to her to do any good turn worth doing? And here I am, her own half brother, with nothing in my power but to scar her heart or else lie! Even supposing she was well married first, how would she stand with her husband when he came to know she was no marchioness and had no lawful right to any name but her mother's? And before that, what right could I have to allow any man to marry her without knowing the truth about her? Poor thing! She looks down on me from the top of her pretty head as from the heights of heaven. But I'll let her know yet, if only I can find the right way to do it." He gave a sigh with the words, and a pause followed.

"The truth's the truth," resumed Miss Horn, "not more, not less."

"Yes," responded Malcolm, "but there's a right and a wrong time for the telling of it. It's not as if I had a hand in any long lie. It was nothing of my doing, as you know, mem. To myself I was never anything but a fisherman."

"And what about your own folk? How on earth are you to do

your duty by them if you don't take your power and reign? You have the power and the money to do whatever you like for them that's been settled on your land all around for many a generation. They're honest folk. If a man's a king he's bound to reign over them."

"Ay, mem. I've thought how much I would like to build a big harbor at Scaurnose for the fisher-folk that're my own flesh and blood. But the foundation must be laid in righteousness first, mem. And I'll not set out to do anything until I can do it without ruining my sister."

"Well, one thing's clear: you'll never know what to do so long as you hang about a stable full of four-footed animals with no sense and some two-footed ones with less."

"I don't doubt you're right there, mem, and if I could but take poor Kelpie away with me. For I'm thinking I must go," said Malcolm.

"Where to, then?" asked Miss Horn.

"Oh, to London; where else?"

"And what will your lordship do there?"

"Don't say lordship to me, mem, I beg you. I'm not used to it just yet. I doubt I ever will be."

"I know nothing but that you're bound to be a lord and not a stableman. And I won't let you rest until you rise up and say, 'What next?'"

"I've been asking myself that very question for the last three months," said Malcolm.

"I daresay," said Miss Horn. "But you've been saying it inside and I would have you up and *say* it!"

"If I but knew what to do!" said Malcolm for the thousandth time.

2   The Trouble

When Miss Horn left him—with a farewell kindlier than her greeting—Malcolm went back to the stable, saddled Kelpie, and took her out for an airing. As he passed the factor's house, Mrs. Crathie saw him from the window. She rose and looked after him from the door—a proud woman jealous of her husband's dignity, still more jealous of her own. "The very image of the old marquis!" she said to herself as he passed. "If the brute would but break a bone or two of his! The impudence of the fellow!"

The mare was fresh and the roads hard from the frost. He turned, therefore, toward the Seaton. To its westward side the sand lay smooth, flat, and wet along the edge of the receding tide. He gave Kelpie the rein, and she sprang into a wild gallop. But finding, as they approached the stony part from which rose the Bored Craig, that he could not pull her up in time, he turned her head toward the long dune of sand which, a little beyond the tide, ran parallel with the shore. It was dry and loose and the ascent steep. Kelpie's hoofs sank at every step, and when she reached the top, with side-spread struggling haunches and flared pulsating nostrils, he had her in hand. She stood panting, yet pawing and dancing, making the sand fly in all directions.

Suddenly a young woman with a child in her arms rose, as it seemed to Malcolm, from nearly under Kelpie's head. She wheeled and reared and seemed, whether in wrath or terror, to strain every nerve to unseat her rider.

"Stand back, Lizzy!" cried Malcolm. "She's a mad brute and I might not be able to hold her."

Lizza seemed to pay his words no heed but simply stood with a sad look and gazed at Kelpie as she went on plunging and kicking about on the top of the dune.

"I reckon you wouldn't care if the she-devil knocked out your brains, but you have the child, Lizzy. Have mercy on the child and run to the bottom!"

"I want to talk to you, Malcolm MacPhail," she said in a tone which revealed a depth of trouble.

"I don't think I can listen very well right now," said Malcolm. "But wait a minute." He swung himself from Kelpie's back and, hanging hard on the bit with one hand, searched with the other in the pocket of his coat, saying as he did so, "Sugar, Kelpie, sugar!"

The animal gave an eager snort, settled on her feet, and began sniffing about him. He made haste, for if her eagerness should turn to impatience, she would do her best to bite him. After crunching three or four lumps, she stood rather quiet. Malcolm would have to make the best of it he could.

"Now, Lizzy," he said hurriedly, "speak while you can."

"Malcolm," said the girl—and looked him full in the face for a moment, for agony had overcome shame—"Malcolm, he's going to marry Lady Florimel."

Malcolm was silent—stunned.

Could Lizza have learned more concerning his sister than he yet had?

Lizza had never uttered the name of the father of her child, and all her people knew was that he could not have been a fisherman, for then he would have married her before the child was born. But Malcolm had had a suspicion from the first, and now her words but confirmed it. And was that fellow going to marry his sister? He turned white with dismay, then red with anger and stood speechless.

But he was quickly brought to himself by a sharp pinch under the shoulder blade from Kelpie's long teeth. He had forgotten her, and she had taken the advantage.

"Who told you that, Lizzy?"

"I'm not at liberty to say, Malcolm. But I'm sure it's true and my heart's about to break."

"I'm sorry," said Malcolm. "But is it anybody that knows what he says?"

"Well, I don't really know if she *knows*, but I think she must have good reason or she wouldn't have said it. Oh, me! Malcolm, you're about the only one who doesn't look down on me now. So when I saw you coming up the dune, I just felt I had to tell you."

"I wouldn't want you to tell me anything you promised not to tell," said Malcolm, "but I'll gladly listen to anything you want to tell me."

"I have nothing much to tell, Malcolm, except that my Lady Florimel's going to be married to Lord Meikleham—Lord Liftore, they call him now. Oh, me!"

"Heaven forbid she should be married to any such blackguard!" cried Malcolm.

"Don't call him names, Malcolm. I can't stand it, though I have no right to defend him."

"I won't say a word that'll hurt your sad heart," he returned, "but if you knew all, you'd know I have a fair-sized bone to pick with his lordship myself."

The girl gave a low cry. "You wouldn't hurt him, Malcolm?" she said in terror at the thought of the elegant youth in the clutches of an angry fisherman, even if he were the generous Malcolm MacPhail himself.

"I would rather not," he replied, "but we'll have to see how he carries himself."

"Don't do anything to him for my sake, Malcolm. You can have nothing against him yourself."

The descending darkness made it too dark for Malcolm to see the keen look of wistful regret with which Lizza tried to pierce the gloom and read his face. For a moment the poor girl thought he meant he had loved her himself. But far other thoughts were in Malcolm's mind—one was that she whom he had loved before he knew her of his own blood he would rather see married to any honest fisherman in the Seaton of Portlossie than to such a lord as Meikleham. He had seen enough of him at Lossie House to know what he was. And puritanical, fish-catching Malcolm had ideas above most lords of his day. The thought of the alliance was horrible to him. It was yet possible to be avoided, however; only what could he do and at the same time avoid grievous hurt? "I don't think he'll every marry my lady," he said.

"What makes you say that, Malcolm?" returned Lizza with eagerness.

"I can't tell you just now—" Malcolm was interrupted by Kelpie's sudden lurch to get free of him.

"—the madness is coming back to her, Lizzy. I've got to get her home," he said as he once more jumped on Kelpie's back. "I'll talk to you later, and don't you worry."

Back at the stable, Malcolm heard the factor striding across the stones toward him as he was settling Kelpie into her stall. As the door opened he cried out in exultant wrath, "MacPhail! Come out of there! What right do you have to be on the premises? Didn't I turn you out this morning?"

"Ay, sir, but you didn't pay me my wages," said Malcolm.

"No matter. You're nothing better than a housebreaker if you enter any building about the place."

"I break no lock," returned Malcolm. "I have the key my lord gave me."

"Give it to me; I'm master here now!"

Mr. Crathie was a man who did well under authority, but in wielding it himself was overbearing and far more exacting than the marquis had been. Full of presumed importance and yet doubtful of its adequate recognition by those under him, he had grown imperious and resented with indignation the slightest breach of his orders. Hence, he was in no great favor with the fisher-folk. Now all the day he had been fuming over Malcolm's behavior to him in the morning; and when he went home and learned that his wife had seen him upon Kelpie as if nothing had happened, he became furious and had been wandering about the grounds brooding on the words Malcolm had spoken, waiting for some further opportunity to put the impudent lad in his place. He could not rid himself of the acrid burning of Malcolm's words, for they had contained truth, which stings greater than any poison.

"Indeed, I'll do no such thing, sir. What he gave me I'll keep."

"Give up that key or I'll go at once and get a warrant against you for theft!"

"We'll refer it to Mr. Soutar."

The factor cursed, "What has he to do with my affairs, you

lowbred rascal? Come out of there or I'll horsewhip you for a dirty blackguard!"

"Whip away," said Malcolm.

"Get out of my sight," the factor cried, "or I'll shoot you like a dog!"

"Go and fetch your gun," said Malcolm, "and if you find me waiting here for you, you can have me."

The factor uttered a horrible imprecation.

"Hoots, sir! Be ashamed of yourself. Go home to your mistress and I'll be up in the morning for my wages."

"If you set foot on the ground again, I'll set every dog in the place on you."

Malcolm laughed. "If I was to turn the order the other way, Mr. Crathie, who do you think they'd mind, me or you?"

"Give me that key and go about your business."

"No, no, sir. What my lord gave me I'll keep for all the factors in the world," returned Malcolm. "And as for leaving the place, if I'm not in your service, Mr. Crathie, I'm not under your orders. I'll go when it suits me."

Having finished with Kelpie, he walked past the threatening factor with confident stride toward the sea gate, and thence toward Scaurnose. The door of Blue Peter's cottage was opened by his wife. Malcolm, instead of going in, called to his friend, whom he saw by the fire with Phemy on his knee, to come out and speak to him.

Blue Peter at once obeyed the summons. "There's nothing wrong, I hope, Malcolm," he said as he closed the door behind him.

"Mr. Graham would say," returned Malcolm, "nothing was ever wrong but what you did wrong yourself or wouldn't put right when you had the chance. But I've come to ask your counsel, Peter. Come with me down by the shore and I'll tell you about it."

"You don't want the mistress knowing it?" asked his friend. "I don't like to keep secrets from her."

"You shall judge for yourself and tell her or not tell her as you like. Only she'll have to hold her tongue."

"She can hold her tongue like a gravestone," said Peter.

As they spoke, they reached the cliff that hung over the shattered shore. It was a cold, clear night. Scattered bits of snow lay all about them. The sky was clear and full of stars, for the wind that blew cold from the northwest had dispelled the snowy clouds. Then Malcolm turned to his friend and, laying his hand on his arm, said, "Blue Peter, did I ever tell you a lie?"

"No, never. What makes you ask such a thing?"

"Because I want you to believe me now, and it won't be easy."

"I'll believe anything you tell me—that can be believed," said Joseph.

"Well, I have come to the knowledge that my name's not MacPhail—it's Colonsay, man!—I'm the marquis of Lossie!"

Without a moment's hesitation, Blue Peter pulled off his cap.

"Peter," cried Malcolm, "don't break my heart! Put on your hat."

"The Lord be thanked, my lord," said Blue Peter. "And what'll be your lordship's will."

"First and foremost, Peter, that my best friend after my old daddy and the schoolmaster won't turn against me because I had a marquis instead of a piper or a fisherman for my father."

"That's not likely, my lord," returned Blue Peter, "when the first thing I say is, 'What would you have me do?' Here I am, asking no questions."

"Well, I'd like you to hear the story of it."

"Say on, my lord," said Peter.

Malcolm was silent for a few moments. "I'm thinking, Peter," he said, "that I'd be obliged to you to only say 'my lord' to me when we're alone, and even then I'd prefer you not. I don't want to grow used to it and, between you and me, I don't like it. And now I'll tell you all I know."

When he had ended the tale of what had come to his knowledge and how it had come, Peter said, "Give me the grip of your hand, my lord. May God keep you long in life and honor to rule over us! Now, if you please, what are you going to do?"

"Tell me, Peter, what do you think I ought to do?"

"That would take a heap of thinking," returned the fisherman. "But one thing seems plain: you can't let your sister remain exposed to any temptation you could keep from her. That would not be as you promised your father. I do not think he would like my Lady Florimel to be under the influence of such a one as Lady Bellair—where he is now at least. You must go to her. You have no choice, my lord."

"But what am I to do when I go?"

"That's what you have to go and see."

"And that's what I've been telling myself, and what Miss Horn's been telling me too. But it's another thing to get my own thoughts straight. You see, I'm afraid for hurting her in pride, to bring her down to put myself up."

"My lord," said Peter solemnly, "you know the life of poor fisherfolk. You know these people. Do you count as nothing the providence which has now set you over them? Why would God have given you such an upbringing as no marquis' son ever had, or maybe ever will have, if it isn't that you should take these people in hand and do your best for them? If you forget them, you'll be forgetting Him that made them and you and the sea and the herring."

"You speak the truth, as I have felt in my heart, Peter. But I so badly don't want to hurt her."

A silence followed.

"Now listen," Malcolm said with resolve in his voice, "will you sail with me to London . . . tonight?"

The fisherman was silent a moment, then answered, "I will, my lord, but I must tell my wife."

"Run and fetch her here."

"I'll have her here in a minute," said Joseph as he ran back toward the house.

For a few minutes Malcolm stood alone in the dim starlight of winter, looking out on the dusky sea, dark as his own future. He anticipated its difficulties but never thought of its perils. It was seldom anything oppressed him more than the doubt of what he ought to do. But the first step toward action is the beginning of the death of doubt, and so the tide of Malcolm's feeling ran higher than night as he stood thus alone under the stars waiting to embark for he knew not where.

His thoughts were interrupted by the return of Blue Peter

with his wife. She threw her arms around Malcolm's neck and burst into tears.

"Hoots, my woman," said her husband, "what are you crying about?"

"Peter," she answered, "it's just like a death. He's going to leave us and go home to his own. And I can't stand that he should grow strange to us that have known him so long."

"That'll be an evil day," returned Malcolm, "when I grow strange to any friend. I'll have to be long down the low road before that would be possible. I may not be able to do what you would like. But trust me, I'll be fair to you. And now I want Blue Peter to go with me and help me do what I have to do, if you have no objection."

"No, I've none. I would go myself if I could be of any use," answered Mrs. Mair. "But women are usually in the way."

"Thank you. Now, Peter, we must be off."

"Not tonight, surely?" said Mrs. Mair, a little taken by surprise.

"The sooner the better, Annie," replied her husband, "and we couldn't have a better wind. Just run home and get some food together for us and then come after us to Portlossie."

Malcolm and Blue Peter set off for the Seaton to launch the marquis' cutter while Annie Mair went home to get some oat-cakes, dried fish, and other provisions for the voyage. When the two men reached the Seaton, they found plenty of hands ready to help them with the little sloop. Malcolm said he was going to take her to Peterhead and they asked few questions. Once afloat there was very little to be done, for she had been laid up in perfect condition; and as soon as Mrs. Mair appeared with her basket and they had put a keg of water, some fishing line, and a pan of mussels for bait on board, they were ready to sail and bade their friends a good-bye, leaving them to imagine they were gone but for a day or two, probably on some business of Mr. Crathie's.

With the wind from the northwest, they soon reached Duff Harbor where Malcolm went on shore and saw Mr. Soutar. With a landsman's prejudice he made strenuous objection to such a mad prank as sailing to London at that time of year, but in vain. Malcolm saw nothing mad in it, and the lawyer had to admit he ought to know best. He brought on board with him a lad of Peter's acquaintance and, now fully manned, they set sail again and by the time the sun appeared were not far from Peterhead.

Malcolm's spirits kept rising as they bowled over the bright, cold water. He never felt so capable as when at sea. His energies had first been called out in combat with the elements, and hence he always felt strongest, most at home, and surest of himself on the water. His spirits were also buoyed with the prospect of once more seeing his spiritual guide, Mr. Graham, the late schoolmaster of Portlossie, whom the charge of questionable teaching had ultimately driven from the place shortly after the marquis' death and who was now residing in London.

They put in at Peterhead, purchased a few provisions, and again set sail. Malcolm became increasingly aware that he must soon come to a conclusion as to the steps he must take when he reached London. But think as he would, he could plan nothing beyond finding out where his sister lived and going to look at the house and then getting into it if he might.

They knew all the coast as far as the Firth of Forth; after that they had to be more careful. They had no charts on board, nor could they have made much use of any. But the winds continued favorable and the weather cold, bright, and full of life. Off the Nore they had rough weather and had to stand off and on for a day and a night till it moderated. They spoke to someone on a fishing boat, received directions, and found themselves in smooth water more and more as the channel narrowed. They ended their voyage at length below London Bridge in a very jungle of masts.

3 The City

Leaving Davy to keep the sloop, the two fishermen went on shore. Passing from the narrow precincts of the river, they found themselves at once in the roar of London city. Stunned at first, then excited, then bewildered, then dazed, without any plan to guide their steps, they wandered about until, unused to the hard stones, their feet ached. It was a dull day in March. A keen wind blew round the corners of the streets. They wished themselves at sea again.

"Such a lot of people!" said Blue Peter.

"It's hard to imagine," rejoined Malcolm, "that God can look after them in such a tumult."

The two raw Scotchmen looked very out of place on the London streets. At length a policeman directed them to a Scotch eating house where they fared well and from the landlady gathered directions by which they could guide themselves toward Curzon Street, a certain number in which Mr. Soutar had given Malcolm as Lady Bellair's address.

Having found it, the door was opened to Malcolm's knock by a slatternly charwoman who informed him that Lady Bellair had removed her establishment to Lady Lossie's house in Portland Place. After many curious perplexities, odd blunders, and vain endeavors to understand shop signs and window notices and with the help of many policemen, at length they found their way to the stately region of Portland Place.

The house he sought was one of the largest in the area. He would not, however, yield to the temptation to have a good look at it for fear of attracting some attention from its windows and being recognized. They turned, therefore, into some of the smaller streets lying between Portland Place and Great Portland Street where, searching about, they came upon a decent-looking public house and inquired about lodgings. They were directed to a woman in the neighborhood who kept a dingy little curiosity shop. On payment of a week's rent in advance, she allowed them to occupy a small bedroom. But Malcolm did not want Peter with him that night. He wished to feel perfectly free, and besides, it was more than desirable that Peter should go and look after the boat and the boy.

Left alone, he once more fell to his hitherto futile scheming: how was he to get near his sister? He would not lie, and if he appeared before her with no reason to give, would she not be far too offended with his presumption to retain him in her services? And except he could be near her as a servant, he did not see a chance of doing anything for her without disclosing facts which might make all further service impossible. Plan after plan rose and then passed from his mind. Finally the only resolution he could come to was to write Mr. Soutar, to whom he had committed the protection of Kelpie, to send her up by the first smack from Aberdeen. He did so and also wrote Miss Horn, telling her where he was. Then he went out and made his way back to Portland Place.

Night had closed in, and presently it began to snow. Through the night and the snow went carriages in all directions. The hoofs of the horses echoed from the hard road. Could that house really belong to him? It did, yet he dared not enter. He walked up and down the opposite side of the street some fifty times but saw no sign of vitality about the house. At length a coach stopped at the door and a man got out and knocked. The door opened and he entered. The coach waited. After about a quarter of an hour he came out again, accompanied by two ladies, one of whom Malcolm judged by her figure to be Florimel. They all got into the carriage and Malcolm braced himself for a difficult run. But because of the snow, the coachman drove carefully and he found no difficulty in keeping near them.

They stopped at the doors of a large, dark-looking building which Malcolm judged, but wondered, to be a church of some kind. They went up a great flight of stairs, and still he went after them. When he reached the top, they were just vanishing round a curve, when his advance was checked. A man came up to him, said he could not come there, and gruffly requested him to show his ticket.

"I haven't got one. What is this place?" said Malcolm.

The man gave a look of contemptuous surprise and, turning to another who lounged behind him, said, "Tom, here's a gentleman who wants to know where he is. Can you tell him?"

The man laughed and then said, "You go down there and pay for a pit-ticket, and you'll soon know where you are, mate."

Malcolm went and after a few inquiries and the outlay of two shillings found himself in the pit of one of the largest of the London theaters.

The play was begun and to the lit stage Malcolm's eyes were instantly drawn. He was all but unaware of the multitude of faces about him. However, by degrees he accustomed himself to his surroundings, the strange new place he was in and the silent crowd all about him, and then began a systematic search for his sister amongst the ladies in the boxes. But when he found her he dared not fix his eyes upon her lest his gaze should make her look at him and she should recognize him. Alas! her eyes might have rested on him twenty times without his face once rousing in her mind the thought of the fisher-lad of Portlossie. All that had passed between them in the days already old was virtually forgotten.

As he gathered courage and began to look more closely, he felt that some sort of change had already passed upon her. It was Florimel, yet not the very Florimel he had known. She was more beautiful, but not so lovely in his eyes—much of what had charmed him had vanished. She was more stately, but the stateliness had a little hardness mingled with it. Surely she was not so happy as she had been at Lossie House. She was dressed in black, with a white flower in her hair. Beside her sat the bold-faced Lady Bellair, and behind them was her nephew Lord Meikleham, now Lord Liftore.

A fierce indignation seized the heart of Malcolm at the sight. Behind the form of the earl, his mind's eye saw that of Lizzy Findlay out in the wind on the Boar's Tail dune, her old shawl wrapped about herself and the child of the man who sat there so composed and comfortable. His features were fine and clear-cut, his shoulders broad, and his head well-set; he had much improved in looks since Malcolm offered to fight him with one hand in the dining room of Lossie House. Every now and then he leaned forward between his aunt and Florimel and spoke to the latter. To Malcolm's eyes she seemed to listen with some haughtiness. Now and then she cast him an indifferent glance. Malcolm was pleased. Lord Liftore had apparently not swept her off her feet—not yet, anyway. But he was annoyed to see once or twice a look between them that indicated some sort of intimacy at least.

During the last scene of the play as Malcolm turned to glance at his sister and her companions, his eyes fell on a face near him in the pit which was apparently absorbed in someone in the same direction. It was that of a young man a few years older than himself—a large man with prominent eyebrows and dark penetrating eyes. To Malcolm it seemed that his gaze was also on his sister, but as they were a long way from the boxes he could not be certain. Once he thought he saw her look at him. But of that also he could not tell positively.

The moment the play was over Malcolm rose and made his way through the crowd to the foot of the stairs which Florimel and her companions had gone up earlier. He had stood but a little while when he saw in front of him the same man he had observed in the pit, apparently waiting also. After some time his sister, Lady Bellair, and Liftore came slowly down the stairs in the descending crowd. Her eyes seemed searching the multitude that filled the lobby. Presently an imperceptible glance of recognition passed between the two of them and the young man placed himself so that she would have to pass next to him in the crowd. Malcolm thought they had grasped hands for a second as she passed. She turned her head slightly and seemed to put to him a question, with her lips only. He replied in the same manner. But not a feature had moved nor a word been spoken. Neither of her companions had seen the young man, and he remained where he was until they had left the house. Malcolm stood also, much inclined to follow him. But when his attention was diverted in another direction for a moment, the man had disappeared.

He therefore walked home, but before he had reached his lodging he had resolved on making trial of a plan which had previously occurred to him but which till now had seemed too risky. His plan was to watch the house until he saw some entertainment going on, then present himself as if he had but just arrived from her ladyship's country seat. At such a time no one would acquaint her with his appearance and he would, as if it were but a matter of course, at once take his share in waiting on the guests. By this means he might perhaps get her a little accustomed to his presence before she could be at leisure to challenge it.

The next day Malcolm spent with Blue Peter, sight-seeing mostly and in learning their way about London. Peter was already anxious to get out of the city but agreed to stay at least until Malcolm's way became clear. As soon as Peter was gone to return to the boat late in the afternoon, Malcolm dressed himself in his kilt which he had brought with him to London and, when it was dusk, took his bagpipes under his arm and set out for Portland Place. Since the highland dress was that in which Florimel had been most used to seeing him recently, he felt it might prove his best opportunity to gain entrance into the house. He did not know what purpose the pipes might serve but wanted to be ready for any opportunity. He had hopes for a speedy success of his plan since he fancied he had read on his sister's lips, in the silent communication that passed between her and her friend in the crowd, the words *come* and *tomorrow*. It might have been his imagination, yet it was something.

Up and down the street he walked without seeing a sign of life about the house. But at length the hall light was lit. Then the door opened and a servant rolled out a carpet over the wide pavement which the snow had left wet and miry. The first carriage arrived a few minutes later and was followed by others. It proved to be but a modest dinner party and after some time had elapsed and no more carriages appeared since the last, Malcolm judged the dinner must now be in full swing and therefore rang the bell of the front door.

It was opened by a huge footman. Malcolm would have stepped in at once and told his tale at his leisure, but the servant, who had never seen the dress Malcolm wore except on street beggars, quickly closed the door. Before it reached the post, however, it found Malcolm's foot barring its way.

"Go along, Scotchy! You're not wanted here," said the man

pushing the door hard. "Police is just round the corner!"

One of the weaknesses Malcolm owed his Celtic blood was an utter impatience of rudeness. "Open the door and let me in," he said.

"What's your business?" asked the man on whom Malcolm's fierce tone had its effect.

"My business is with Lady Lossie," said Malcolm.

"You can't see her; she's at dinner."

"Let me in and I'll wait. I've come from Lossie House."

"Take away your foot and I'll go see," said the man.

"No, you open the door," returned Malcolm.

The man's answer was an attempt to kick his foot out of the doorway. If he were to let in a tramp, what would the butler say?

But thereupon Malcolm set his port-vent to his mouth, rapidly filled his bag, and then sent from the instrument such a shriek that involuntarily his adversary pressed both hands to his ears. With a sudden application of his knee, Malcom sent the door wide and entered the hall with his pipes in full cry, but only for a moment. For down the stairs bounded Demon, Florimel's huge Irish staghound, and springing on Malcolm put and instant end to his music. The footman laughed, expecting to see him torn to pieces. But when he saw instead the fierce animal, a foot on each of Malcolm's shoulders licking his face with a long tongue, he began to doubt.

"The dog knows you," he said sulkily.

"So shall you before long," returned Malcolm. "Was it my fault I made the mistake of looking for civility from you?"

"I'll go and fetch Wallis," said the man and, closing the door, left the hall.

Now this Wallis had been a fellow servant of Malcolm's at Lossie House, but he did not know that he had gone with Lady Bellair when she took Florimel away; almost everyone had left at the same time. He was now glad indeed to learn there was one amongst the servants who knew him.

Wallis presently made his appearance, with a dish in his hands, on his way to the dining room, from which came the confused noises of the feast.

"You'll be come to wait on Lady Lossie," he said. "I haven't a moment to speak to you now, for we're serving dinner, and there's a party."

"Never mind me. Give me that dish. I'll take it in; you can go for another," said Malcolm, laying his pipes in a safe spot.

"You can't go into the dining room like that!" said Wallis.

"This is how I waited on my lord," returned Malcolm, "and this is how I'll wait on my lady."

Wallis hesitated. But there was something about the fisher-fellow that was too much for him. As he spoke, Malcolm took the dish from his hands and with it walked into the dining room.

Once there, one reconnoitring glance was sufficient. The butler was at the sideboard opening a champagne bottle. He had his hand on the cork as Malcolm walked up to him.

"I'm Lady Lossie's man from Lossie House. I'll help you to wait," said Malcolm.

To the eyes of the butler he looked a savage. But there he was in the room, with a dish in his hands and speaking intelligibly. He peeped into Malcolm's dish. "Take it round, then," he said.

So Malcolm settled into the business of the hour.

It was some time after he knew where she was before he ventured to look at his sister—he would have her already familiarized with his presence before their eyes met. That crisis did not arrive during dinner.

Lord Liftore was one of the company, and so—to Malcolm's pleasure, for he felt in him an ally against the earl—was Florimel's mysterious friend.

Scarcely had the ladies gone to the drawing room when Florimel's maid, who knew Malcolm, came in quest of him. Lady Lossie desired to see him.

"What is the meaning of this, MacPhail?" she said, when he entered the room where she sat alone. "I did not send for you. Indeed, I thought you had been dismissed with the rest of the servants."

How differently she spoke! And she used to call him Malcolm! The girl Florimel was gone. She had forgotten the half friendship that had been between them, that much was certain. And it appeared to Malcolm she had even forgotten his service that had once been such a part of her daily life.

But Florimel had not so entirely forgotten the past as Malcolm thought—not so entirely at least, but that his appearance, and certain difficulties in which she had begun to find herself, brought something of it again to her mind.

"I thought," said Malcolm, "your ladyship might not choose to part with an old servant at the will of a factor and so took upon me to appeal to your ladyship to decide the question."

"But how is that? Did you not return to your fishing when the household was broken up?"

"No, my lady. Mr. Crathie kept me to help Stoat and do odd jobs about the place."

"And now he wants to discharge you?"

Then Malcolm told her the whole story, in which he gave such a description of Kelpie that Florimel expressed a strong wish to see her, for she was almost passionately fond of horses.

"You may soon do that, my lady," said Malcolm. "Mr. Soutar is not of the same mind as Mr. Crathie and is going to send her here. It will be but the cost of the passage from Aberdeen, and she will fetch a better price here if your ladyship should revolve to part with her. She won't fetch a third of her value anywhere, though, on account of her bad temper and ugly tricks."

"But as to yourself, MacPhail, what are you going to do?" said Florimel. "I don't like to have to part with you, but if I keep you I don't know what to do with you. No doubt you could serve in the house, but that is not at all suitable to your education and previous life."

"If your ladyship should wish to keep Kelpie, you will have to keep me too, for she will let no one else near her."

"And pray tell me what use, then, can I make of such an animal?"

"Your ladyship, I should imagine, will want a groom to attend you when you are out on horseback, and the groom will need a horse. So here we are, Kelpie and me!" answered Malcolm.

Florimel laughed. "I see," she said. "You contrive I shall have a horse nobody can manage but yourself." She rather liked the idea of a groom mounted on such a fine animal and had too much well-justified faith in Malcolm to anticipate dangerous results.

"My lady," said Malcolm, appealing to her knowledge of his character for his last means of persuasion, "my lady, did I ever tell you a lie?"

"Certainly not, Malcolm, so far as I know."

"Then," continued Malcolm, "I'll tell your ladyship something that you may find hard to believe, and yet is as true as that I loved your ladyship's father. Your ladyship knows he had a kindness for me?"

"I do know it," answered Florimel, gently, moved by the tone of Malcolm's voice and expression.

"Then I make bold to tell your ladyship that on his deathbed, your father desired me to do my best for you—took my word that I would be your ladyship's true servant."

"Is it so, indeed, Malcolm?" returned Florimel with a serious wonder in her gaze. She had loved her father, and it sounded in her ears almost like a message from the tomb.

"It's as true as I stand here, my lady," said Malcolm.

Florimel was silent for a moment. Then she said, "How is it that only now you come to tell me?"

"Your father never desired me to tell you, my lady; only he never imagined you would want to part with me, I suppose. But when you did not care to keep me and never said a word to me when you went away, I could not tell how to do as I had promised him. It wasn't that one hour I forgot his wish, but that I feared to presume; for if I should displease your ladyship, my chance was gone. So I kept about Lossie House as long as I could, hoping to see my way to some plan or another. But when at length Mr. Crathie turned me away, what was I to do but come to your ladyship? And if your ladyship will let things be as before—in the way of service, I mean—I can't doubt, my lady, but that it'll be pleasant in the sight of your father whenever he may come to know of it."

Florimel gave a strange, half-startled look. Hardly more than once since her father's funeral had she heard him alluded to, and now this fisher-lad spoke of him as if he were still at Lossie House.

Malcolm understood the look. "I know what you're thinking,

my lady. But I can't help it. To love anything is to know it immortal. He's living to me, my lady. And why not? Didn't he turn his face to the light before he died? And Him that rose from the dead said that whoever believed in Him should never die."

Florimel continued a moment looking at him fixedly in the face. She remembered how strange he had always been, yet at the same time she caught the glimmering idea that in this young man's simplicity was an incorruptible treasure.

Malcolm seldom made the mistake of stamping down on any seeds of truth which might have been planted. He knew when to say no more, and for a time neither spoke. For all the coolness of her upper crust, Lady Florimel's heart was warmed with the possession of such a strong, devoted, disinterested squire.

"I wish you to understand," she said at length, "that I am not at present mistress of this house, although it belongs to me. I am but the guest of Lady Bellair, who has rented it of my guardians. I cannot, therefore, arrange for you to be here. But you can find accommodations in the neighborhood and come for me at one o'clock every day for orders. Let me know when your mare arrives; I shall not want you till then. You will find room for her in the stables. You had better consult the butler about your groom's livery."

Malcolm was astonished at the womanly sufficiency with which she gave orders, yet he left her with the gladness of one whose righteous desire had been fulfilled. He spoke with the butler and went home to his lodging. There he sat down and meditated.

A yearning pity arose in his heart. He feared his sister's stately composure was built mainly on her imagined position in society rather than her character. Would it be cruel to destroy that false foundation? At present, however, he need not attempt to answer the question. Familiarity with her surroundings, even as a groom, would probably reveal much. Meantime, it was enough that he would now be so near her that no important change could take place without his knowledge and without his being able to interfere if necessary.

4 The Painter

The next day Wallis came to see Malcolm and take him to the tailor's. They talked about the guests of the previous evening.

"There's a great change in Lord Meikleham," said Malcolm.

"There is that," said Wallis. "I consider him much improved. But he's succeeded to the title. He's the earl now, and Lord Liftore. And a big, strong man he's become."

"Is there no news of his marriage?" asked Malcolm. "They say he has great property."

"But she's just a lassie yet," said Wallis, "though she's changed quite as much as he."

"Who are you speaking of?" asked Malcolm, anxious to hear the talk of the household on the matter.

"Why, Lady Lossie, of course. Anybody with half an eye can see as much as that."

"It's settled, then?"

"That would be hard to say. Her ladyship is too much like her father. No one can tell what may be in her mind to do the next minute. But he's ever hovering about her. And I think my lady, too, has set her mind on it. And I can't see how she could do better. I can see no possible objection to the match."

"We used to think he drank too much," suggested Malcolm. "And besides, he's not worthy of her."

"Well, I confess, his family won't compare with hers. There's a grandfather in it somewhere that was a banker or brewer or soap boiler, or something of the sort, and she and her people have been earls and marquises ever since they walked arm-in-arm out of the ark. But that doesn't seem to matter as much as it used to. Mrs. Tredger, that's our ladyship's maid—only this is secret—says it's all settled. She knows it for certain fact, only there's nothing to be said about it yet. She's so young, you know."

"Who was that man that sat nearly opposite my lady, on the

other side of the table?" asked Malcolm.

"I know who you mean. Didn't look like the rest of them, did he? Odd-and-end sort of people, like he is, never do. He's some fellow that's painting Lady Lossie's portrait. Why he should be asked to dinner because of that, I don't know. But London's a strange place! There's no such thing as respect of persons here. I declare to you, Malcolm MacPhail, it makes me quite uncomfortable at times to think who I may have been waiting on without knowing it. That painter-fellow—Lenorme they call him—makes me downright angry. To see him stare at Lady Lossie as he does!"

"A painter must want to get a right good hold of the face he's got to paint," said Malcolm. "Is he here often?"

"He's been here five or six times already," answered Wallis. "I'm sure there's been time to finish the picture by now! And if she's been once in his studio, she's been twenty times—to give him sittings, as they call it. He's making a pretty penny of it, I'll be bound."

Wallis liked the sound of his own voice, and a great deal more talk of similar character followed before they got back from the tailor's. Malcolm was tired enough of him by the time he set out for a walk with Blue Peter, whom he found waiting at his lodgings.

That night, Florimel's thoughts were full. Already life was not what it had been to her, and the feeling of a difference is often what sets one thinking. While her father lived she had been supplied with a more than sufficient sense of well-being. Since his death, too, there had been times when she fancied an enlargement of life in the sense of freedom and power which came with the consciousness of being a great lady with an ancient title. But she had soon found she had less the feeling of freedom within as before. She was very lonely, too. Lady Bellair had always been kind, but there was nothing about her to make a home for the girl's heart. She felt in her no superiority, and for a spiritual home that is essential. She was not one in whom she could place genuine confidence. The innocent nature of the girl had begun to recoil from what she saw in the woman of the world. And yet she had in herself worldliness enough to render her freely susceptible of her influences.

On the morning after she had taken Malcolm into her services, Florimel awoke between three and four and lay awake, weary yet sleepless. It was not, however, the general sense of unfitness in the conditions of her life that kept her mind occupied and thus awake. Nor was it dissatisfaction with Lady Bellair or the loneliness in the sterile waste of fashionable life or its weariness with the same shows and people and parties. But instead her thoughts rested on the young painter Malcolm had twice seen near her.

Some few weeks ago she had accompanied a friend to his study for which she was sitting for her portrait. The moment she entered, the appearance of the man and his surroundings laid hold of her imagination. Although on the verge of popularity, he was young, not more than twenty-five. His movements were graceful, his address manly, and he displayed confident modesty and unobtrusive humility. Pictures stood on easels, leaned against chairbacks, glowed from the wall—each contributing to the atmosphere of the place. Lenorme was seated, not at his easel, but at a piano half hidden in a corner. They had walked straight in with no announcement and thus came upon him in the midst of a bar of a song in a fine tenor voice. He stopped immediately and came to meet them from the farther end of the study. He shook hands with Florimel's friend and turned with a bow to her. As their eyes met the blood rose to Florimel's face.

While Mrs. Barnardiston sat, Florimel flitted about the room like a butterfly, looking at one thing after another and asking now the most ignorant, now the most penetrating question—disturbing the work, but sweetening the temper of the painter. For the girl had bewitched him at first sight. Sooner than usual he professed himself content with the sitting and then proceeded to show the ladies some of his sketches and pictures. As he did so, Florimel happened to ask to see one standing in disgrace with its front to the wall. He put it, half reluctantly, on an easel and disclosed what was to be the painting of the goddess of nature being gazed upon enraptured by a youth below with outstretched arms. But on the great pedestal where should have sat the goddess there was no form visible. Florimel asked why he had left it so long unfinished, for the dust was thick on the back of the canvas.

"Because I have never seen the face or figure," the painter answered, "that claimed the position."

As he spoke his eyes seemed to Florimel to lighten strangely, and then as if by common consent they turned away and looked at something else. Presently Mrs. Barnardiston, who could sing a little and cared more for sound than form or color, began to glance over some music on the piano, curious to find what the young man had been singing, whereupon Lenorme said to Florimel hurriedly, almost in a whisper with a sort of hesitating assurance, "If *you* would give me a sitting or two—I know I am presumptuous—but if you would, I . . . I would have the picture finished in a week."

"I will," said Florimel, flushing and looking up in his face. "It would have been selfish," she said to herself as they drove away, "to refuse him."

The first interview followed and all the interviews that followed now passed through her mind as she lay awake in the darkness preceding the dawn. One of the feelings now of concern to her was the sense of lowered dignity she felt because of the relation in which she stood to the painter. Her rank had already grown to seem to her so identified with herself that she was hardly capable of the analysis that should show it distinct from her being. Yet even though in the circle in which she now moved she repeatedly heard, on all sides, professions, arts and trades alluded to with implied contempt, she nevertheless never entered the painter's study but with trembling heart, uncertain foot, and fluttering breath. It was at once an enchanted paradise and a forbidden garden. Though the woman in her was drawn to Lenorme, the marchioness in her could not overcome his lowly station. She was excited to be with him, yet afraid of being seen at the same time. And by this time things had gone far enough between them to add greatly to Florimel's inward strife.

She knew Lady Bellair was set upon her marriage with her nephew. Now she recoiled from the idea of marriage and dismissed it into the indefinite future. She had no special desire to please Lady Bellair from the point of gratitude, for she was perfectly aware that the relation between them was not without its advantage to that lady's position. Neither could she persuade herself that Lord Liftore was at all the sort of man she could become genuinely proud of as a husband. Yet, she felt destined to be his wife. On the other hand, she had no great dislike of him. He was handsome, well-informed, capable—a gentleman, she thought, of good regard in the circles in which they moved. To be sure, he was her inferior in rank, and she would rather have married a duke. But she was by no means indifferent to the advantages of having a husband with money enough to restore the somewhat tarnished prestige of her family to its former brilliancy. She had never said a word to encourage the scheming of Lady Bellair; neither had she ever said a word to discourage her hopes or give her ground for doubt. Hence, Lady Bellair had naturally come to regard the two as nearly engaged. But Florimel's aversion to the idea of marriage grew as did her horror at the thought of the slightest whisper of what was between her and Lenorme.

There were times when she asked herself whether she had been altogether above reproach in the encouragement she was giving the painter. She never once had visited him without a companion, though that companion was sometimes only her maid; but her real object was covered by the pretext of sitting for a portrait, which Lady Bellair pleased herself to imagine would one day be presented to Lord Liftore. But she could not fail to occasionally doubt whether the visits she paid and the liberties she allowed him could be justified on any ground other than that she was prepared to give him all and become his wife. All, however, she was not prepared to give him.

With such causes for uneasiness in her young heart and brain, it is no wonder that to such an unexperienced and troubled heart the assurance of one absolutely devoted friend should come with healing and hope. Even if that friend should be but a groom altogether incapable of understanding her position. A clumsy, ridiculous fellow, she said to herself, from whom she could never disassociate the smell of fish, and who could not be prevented from uttering unpalatable truths at uncomfortable moments, yet whose thoughts were as chivalrous as his person was powerful. She actually felt stronger and safer to know he was near and at her beck and call.

5   The Factor

Mr. Crathie, seeing nothing more of Malcolm, believed himself at last well rid of him; but it was days before his wrath ceased to flame, and then it went on smoldering. Nothing occurred to take him to the Seaton, and no business brought any of the fisher-people to his office during that time. Hence, for some time he heard nothing of the mode of Malcolm's departure. When at length, in the course of ordinary talk the news reached him that Malcolm had taken the yacht with him, he was enraged beyond measure at the impudence of the theft, as he called it, and rushed to the Seaton in a fury. He had this consolation, however: the man who accused him of dishonesty and hypocrisy had proved but a thief.

He found the boathouse indeed empty and went storming from cottage to cottage, but came upon no one from whom his anger could draw nourishment. At length he reached the Partan's and commenced abusing him as an aider and abettor of the felony. But Meg Partan was at home also, as Mr. Crathie soon learned to his cost. She returned his tongue-lashing as only she was capable of.

"Hold your tongue, woman," said the factor. "I have nothing to say to you."

"Ah, it's a pity you wasn't foreordained to be marquis yourself! It must be a sore vex to you that you're nothing but a lowly factor!"

"If you don't mind your manners, Mistress Findlay," said Mr. Crathie in glowing indignation, "perhaps you'll find that the factor is as much as the marquis when he's all there is for one."

"Lord save us, listen to the man!" cried the Partaness. "Who would have thought it of him? His father, honest man, would never have spoken like that to Meg Partan, but then he was an honest man."

"I've a great mind to take out a warrant against you, John Findlay," resumed the factor, doing the best his wrath would allow to ignore the outbursts from the wife present, "for your part in stealing the marchioness of Lossie's pleasure boat. And as for you, Mistress Findlay, I would have you remember that this house—as far, at least, as you are concerned—is mine, although I am but the factor and not the marquis; and if you don't keep that unruly tongue of yours a little quieter in your head, I'll turn you right out on the street. For there's not a house in all the Seaton that belongs to another than her ladyship. And I run her affairs around here now!"

"Indeed, Mr. Crathie," returned Meg Partan, a little sobered by the threat, "you would have more sense than to run the risk of an uprising of the fisher-folk. They would hardly stand to see me and my man mistreated like that, not to say that her ladyship herself would never allow any of her own folk to be turned out for doing nothing wrong!"

"Her ladyship would give herself small concern over it," returned the factor. "And as for the town, the folk would like the quiet too much to lament the loss of you!"

"The devil's in the man!" cried Meg in high scorn.

"You see, sir," interposed the mild Partan, "we didn't know there was anything out of the ordinary in it. If we had but known that he was out of your good graces—"

"Hold your tongue before you lie, man," interrupted his wife. "You know well enough that you would have done whatever Malcolm MacPhail asked of you for any factor in Scotland!"

"You *must* have known," said the factor, apparently heedless of the last outbreak of evil temper and laying a cunning trap for the information he sorely wanted, "else why was it that not a soul went with him? He could hardly manage the boat alone."

"What put such a thing into your head?" rejoined Meg, defiant of the hints her husband sought to convey to her. "There's many that would have been only too ready to go; only who should have gone but him that went with him and his lordship from the first?"

"And who was that?" asked Mr. Crathie.

"Who but Blue Peter!" answered Meg.

"Hmm!" said the factor in a tone that, for almost the first time in her life, made the woman regret that she had spoken, and therewith he rose and left the cottage.

"Oh, mother!" cried Lizza, appearing from the back of the cottage. "You've brought ruin on the earth. He'll have Peter and Annie out of their house by midsummer now!"

"I *dare* him!" cried her mother in the impotence and self-despite of a mortifying blunder. "I'll raise the town upon him!"

The factor ran half the way home, flung himself trembling in anger on his horse, vouchsafing his anxious wife scarce any answer to her inquiries and galloped to Duff Harbor to Mr. Soutar. I will not occupy my tale with their interview. Suffice it to say that the lawyer succeeded at last in convincing the demented factor that it would be prudent to delay measures for the recovery of the yacht and the arrest and punishment of its abductors until he knew what Lady Lossie would say to the affair. She had always had a liking for the lad, Mr. Soutar said, and he would not be in the least surprised to hear that Malcolm had gone straight to her ladyship and put himself under her protection. No doubt by this time the boat was at its owner's disposal; it would be just like the fellow. He always went the nearest road anywhere, and to prosecute him for a thief would, in any case, but bring down the ridicule of the whole coast upon the factor and breed him endless annoyance in the getting of his rents, especially amongst the fishermen. The result was that Mr. Crathie went home—not indeed a humbler or wiser man than he had gone, but a thwarted man and therefore the more dangerous in the channels left open to the outrush of his angry power.

The result of his submerged anger made itself known to Blue Peter's wife within the week: they had till midsummer to leave the premises. Annie asked that, with her husband away, couldn't this wait until he could discuss it with the factor personally? Mr. Crathie replied coolly, however, that it was his very absence which made him guilty in the matter, and he hoped, therefore, that Peter would be home soon to make their arrangements for new quarters. Annie replied that she had no way of knowing when he would be home but expected him within a week or two. And with that the factor bid her good-day.

6 The Suitor

The chief cause of Malcolm's anxiety had been, and still was, Lord Liftore. Knowing what he knew of his character, Malcolm's whole nature revolted against the thought of him marrying his sister. At Lossie he had made himself agreeable to her, and now, if not actually living in the same house, he was there at all hours of the day.

It took nothing from his anxiety to see that his lordship was even more fine looking than before. His admiration of Florimel had been growing as well, and if he had said nothing definite, it was only because his aunt represented the importunity declaring of himself just yet; she was too young. Still, all the time she had been under his aunt's care, he had had abundant opportunity for paying her all sorts of attention and compliments and for recommending himself, and he had made use of the privilege. For one thing, assured that he looked well in the saddle, he had constantly encouraged Florimel's love of riding and desire to become a thorough horsewoman, and they had ridden a good deal together.

For a long time Lady Bellair had had her mind set on a match between the daughter of her old friend, the marquis of Lossie, and her nephew. And it was with this in view that, when invited to Lossie House, she had begged leave to bring Lord Meikleham with her. The young man was from the first sufficiently taken with the beautiful girl to satisfy his aunt and would, even then, have shown greater attention to her had he not met Lizza Findlay and found her more than pleasing. He had not purposed to do her wrong from the beginning. But even when he had seen plainly to what their mutual attraction was tending, he had given himself no trouble to resist it. And through the whole unhappy affair he had not had one small struggle with himself for the girl's sake. To himself he was all in all. What was the shame and humiliation of the girl herself compared to the honor of having been shone upon for a brief period by his honorable countenance? Since he left her at last with many promises, not one of which he had had any intention of fulfilling, he had never taken the least further notice of her either by gift or letter. He had taken care also that it should not be in her power to write to him, and now he did not even know that he was a father.

Lizza was a good girl and had promised to keep the matter secret until she heard from him, whatever might be the consequences, and surely there was fascination enough in the holding of a secret with such as he to enable her to keep her promise. He would requite her when he was lord of Lossie. Meantime, although it was even now in his power to make rich amends, he would prudently leave things as they were and not run the risk that must lie in opening communications.

And so the young earl held his head high, looked as innocent as may be desirable for a gentleman and had many a fair, clean hand laid in his, while Lizza flitted about half an alien amongst her own, with his child wound in her old shawl of Lossie tartan—wandering frequently at dusk over the dunes with the wind blowing keen upon her from the regions of eternal ice. There were many who made Lizza keenly aware of her disgrace, but there was one man who showed her even greater kindness than before. That man, strange to say, was the factor. With all his faults he had some chivalry, and he showed it to the fisher-girl. This was all the more remarkable in that since Malcolm's departure he had grown all the more bitter against his friends and against the fisher-folk in general. It was sore proof to Mr. Crathie that his discharged servant was in favor with the marchioness when the order came from Mr. Soutar to send Kelpie to London. She had written to him herself for her own horse; now she sent for this brute through her lawyer. It was plain Malcolm had been speaking against him.

Since Malcolm's departure the factor had twice been on the point of poisoning the mare. It was with difficulty he found two men to take her to Aberdeen. But it had been done, and Malcolm was waiting for her at the wharf in the gray of a gurly dawn when at length the smack arrived in London. They had had a rough passage and the mare was considerably subdued by sickness. But after pacing for a little while in relative quietness, the evil spirit in her began to awake, and before he reached the mews Malcolm was very near wishing he had never seen her. But when he led her into the stable, he was encouraged to find that she had not forgotten Florimel's horse and they greeted each other with an affectionate neigh. This, along with all the feed she could devour, quieted her considerably.

Before noon Lord Liftore came round to the mews: his riding horses were there. Malcolm was not at the moment in the stable.

"What animal is that?" he asked of his own groom, catching sight of Kelpie in her loose box.

"One just in from Scotland for Lady Lossie, my lord," answered the man.

"Lead her out and let me see her."

"She's not in a good temper, my lord, the groom that brought her says. He told me not to go near her till she's got used to the sight of me."

"Oh, you are afraid, are you?" said Liftore, whose breeding had not taught him courtesy to his inferiors.

At such a challenge, the man proceeded to walk into her box. He was careful, but it was in vain. In a moment she had wheeled, jammed him against the wall, and taken his shoulder in her teeth. He gave a yell of pain. His lordship caught up a stable broom and attacked the mare with it over the door but she still kept hold of her man. Luckily Malcolm was not far off and, hearing the noise, rushed in just in time to save the groom's life. He jumped the partition and seized the mare with a mighty grasp and soon compelled her to open her mouth. The groom staggered and just managed to open the door before he fell on the stones. Lord Liftore called for help and they carried him into the saddle room while one ran for a doctor.

Meantime Malcolm was putting a muzzle on Kelpie, and while he was thus occupied his lordship came from the saddle room and approached the box. "Who are you?" he asked. "I think I've seen you before."

"I was servant to the late marquis of Lossie, my lord, and am now groom to her ladyship."

"What a fury you've brought here. She'll never do for London!"

"I told the man not to go near her, my lord."

"What's the use of her if no one can go near her?"

"I can, my lord. She'll do for me to ride after my lady well enough. If only I had room to exercise her a bit."

"Take her into the park early in the morning and gallop her round. Only mind she doesn't break your neck. What can have made Lady Lossie send for such a creature?"

Malcolm held his peace.

"I'll try her myself some morning," his lordship went on, who thought himself a better horseman than he was.

"I wouldn't advise that, my lord."

"Who the devil asked your advice?"

"Ten to one she'd kill you, my lord."

"That's for me to watch out for then," said Liftore, noticeably perturbed at Malcolm's insolence, and went into the house.

As soon as Malcom had finished with Kelpie, he went to tell his mistress of her arrival. She told him to bring the mare around in half an hour. He went back, took off her muzzle, fed her, and while she ate her corn put on the spurs he had prepared expressly for use with her. Then he saddled her and rode her around.

Having had her fit of temper she was to all appearance going to be fairly good for the rest of the day. And she looked splendid! She was a large mare, an animal most men would have been pleased to possess and proud to ride. Florimel came to the door to see her, accompanied by Liftore, and was so delighted with the very sight of her that she sent at once to the stable for her own horse that she might ride out attended by Malcolm. His lordship also ordered his horse.

They went straight to the park for a little gallop, and Kelpie was behaving very well.

"What did you have two such savages, horse and groom, brought here from Scotland for, Florimel?" asked his lordship as they cantered gently along.

Florimel looked back and cast an admiring glance on the two. "Do you know I am rather proud of them," she said.

"He's a clumsy fellow, the groom; and, for the mare, she's downright wicked," said Liftore.

"At least neither is a hypocrite," returned Florimel, with Malcolm's account of his quarrel with the factor in her mind. "The mare is just as wicked as she looks, and the man is good. That man you call a savage, my lord, never told a lie in his life."

"I know what you mean," he said. "You don't believe my professions." As he spoke he edged his horse close up to hers. "But," he went on, "if I know that I speak the truth when I swear that I love—confound the fellow! What's he about now with his horse-devil?"

For at that moment his lordship's horse, a high-spirited but timid animal, had sprung away from the side of Florimel's, and as he did, suddenly there stood Kelpie on her hind legs pawing the air to keep him from bolting. Florimel, whose old confidence in Malcolm was now more than revived, was laughing merrily at the discomfiture of his lordship's attempt at lovemaking. Her behavior and his own frustration put him in such a rage that, wheeling quickly around, he struck Kelpie with his whip across the haunches. She plunged and kicked violently, came within an inch of breaking his horse's leg, and flew across the rail into the park. Nothing could have suited Malcolm better. He did not punish her as he would have done had she been to blame but took her a great round at racing speed, while his mistress and companion looked on. Finally, he hopped her over the rail again and brought her up, dripping and foaming, to his mistress. Florimel's eyes were flashing and Liftore looked still angry. "Don't do that again, my lord," said Malcolm. "You're not my master, and if you were, you would have no right to break my neck."

"No fear of that. That's not how your neck will be broken, my man," said his lordship with an attempted laugh; for, though he was all the angrier than he was ashamed of what he had done, he dared not further wrong the servant before his mistress.

A policeman came up and laid his hand on Kelpie's bridle.

"Take care what you're about," said Malcolm; "the mare's not safe. There's my mistress, the marchioness of Lossie."

The man saw an ugly look in Kelpie's eye, withdrew his hand, and turned to Florimel.

"My groom is not to blame," she said. "Lord Liftore struck his mare."

The man gave a look at Liftore, seemed to take his likeness, touched his hat, and withdrew.

"You'd better ride the jade home," said Liftore.

Malcolm only looked at his mistress. She moved on and he followed.

Malcolm was not so innocent in the affair as he had seemed. The expression on Liftore's face as he drew nearer to Florimel was to him so hateful that he interfered in a very literal fashion. Kelpie had been doing no more than he made her until the earl struck her.

"Let us ride to Richmond tomorrow," said Florimel, "and have a good gallop in the park. Did you ever see a finer sight than that animal on the grass?"

"The fellow's too heavy for her," said Liftore. "I should very much like to try her myself."

Florimel pulled up and turned to Malcolm. "MacPhail," she said, "have that mare of yours ready whenever Lord Liftore chooses to ride her."

"I beg your pardon, my lady," returned Malcolm, "but would your ladyship make a condition that he not mount her anywhere on the stones?"

"By Jove!" said Liftore scornfully, "you fancy yourself the only man that can ride!"

"It's nothing to me, my lord, if you break your neck, but I am bound to tell you I do not think your lordship will sit my mare. Stoat can't, and I can only because I know her as well as my own palm."

The young earl made no answer and they rode on, Malcolm nearer than his lordship liked.

"I can't think, Florimel," he said, "why you should want that fellow about you again. He is not only awkward, but insolent as well."

"I should call it straightforward," returned Florimel.

"My dear Lady Lossie! See how close he is riding to us now."

"He is anxious, I daresay, as to your lordship's behavior. He is like some dogs that are a little too careful of their mistresses—touchy as to how they are addressed: not a bad fault in a dog—or groom either. He saved my life once, and he was a great favorite with my father. I won't hear anything against him."

"But for your own sake, just consider. What will people say if you show any preference for a man like that?" said Liftore, who had already become jealous of the man who he feared could ride better than himself.

"My lord!" exclaimed Florimel, with a mingling of surprise and indignation in her voice and, suddenly quickening her pace, dropped him behind.

Malcolm was after her so instantly that it brought him abreast of Liftore. "Keep your own place," said his lordship with stern rebuke.

"I keep pace to my mistress," returned Malcolm.

Liftore looked at him as if he would strike him. But he thought better of it, apparently, and rode after Florimel.

———

By the time Malcolm had put Kelpie up after the ride, he had to hurry to the wharf. Since he was again in Florimel's service, and it appeared his stay in London would be a lengthy one, Blue Peter had made preparations to return home on the same smack which had brought Kelpie from Aberdeen and was scheduled to depart that same afternoon. On the way, Malcolm reflected on what had just passed and was not altogether pleased with himself. He had nearly lost his temper with Liftore. And to attract attention to himself was almost to insure frustration to his plan.

When he reached the wharf, he found they had nearly got her freight on board the smack. Blue Peter stood on the deck.

"I hardly know you in those riding clothes," he said.

"Nobody in London would look twice at me now," returned Malcolm. "But you remember how we were stared at when we first came!"

That same moment came the command for all but passengers

to go ashore. The men grasped hands, looked each other in the eyes, and parted—Blue Peter down the river and to Scaurnose and Annie, and Malcolm to the yacht lying still in the Upper Pool. He saw it taken properly in charge and arranged for having it towed up the river and anchored in the Chelsea Reach.

When Malcom at length reached his lodging, he found there a letter from Miss Horn containing information where the schoolmaster was to be found in the London wilderness. It was now getting rather late, and the dusk of a spring night had begun to gather; but little more than the breadth of the Regent's Park lay between him and his only friend in London, and he set out immediately for Camden Town.

The relation between him and his late schoolmaster was indeed of the strongest and closest. Long before Malcolm was born and ever since had Alexander Graham loved Malcolm's mother, but not until within the last few months had he learned that Malcolm was the son of Griselda Campbell. The discovery was to the schoolmaster like the bursting out of a known flower on an unknown plant. He knew then, not why he had loved the boy—for he loved every one of his pupils—but why he had loved him with such a peculiar affection.

An occasional preacher in his younger days, he had accepted the vacant position of schoolmaster at Portlossie where he made the acquaintance of Griselda Campbell who was governess to Lady Annabel, the only child of the late marquis' elder brother, at that time himself marquis. A love for her began to consume him, though it was hopeless from the first. Silence was the sole armor of his privilege. So long as he was silent he might love on, nor be grudged the bliss of his visions. And Miss Campbell thought of him more kindly than he knew. But before long the late marquis fell in love with her and persuaded her to a secret marriage. She became Malcolm's mother at a time when her husband was away. But the marquis of the time, jealous for the succession of his daughter and fearing his brother might yet make public his marriage, contrived, with the assistance of the midwife, to remove the infant and persuade the mother that he was dead and also to persuade his brother of the death of both mother and child. After this time, imagining herself willfully deserted by her husband, yet determined to endure shame rather than break the promise of secrecy she had given him, the poor young woman accepted the hospitality of her distant relative, Miss Horn, and continued with her till she died. Though Mr. Graham lived for twenty years in friendly relations with Miss Horn and Miss Campbell, neither suspected his innermost feelings, and it was not until Miss Campbell's death that he came to know the strange fact that the object of his calm, unalterable devotion had been a wife all those years and the mother of his favorite pupil. About the same time he was dismissed from the school on the charge of heretical teaching, founded on certain religious conversations he had had with some of the fisherpeople who sought his advice, and thereupon he had left the place and gone to London. He hoped there to earn a meager income through tutoring and with the assistance of what occasional preaching opportunities might come his way.

It was a lovely evening. There had been rain in the afternoon, but before the sun had set it had cleared up and the ethereal, sweet scents of buds and grass and ever-pure earth moistened with the waters of heaven was all about Malcolm as he walked through the park.

After not a few inquires, he found himself at a stationer's shop, a poor little place, and learned that Mr. Graham lodged over it and was then at home. He was shown up into a shabby room with an iron bedstead, a chest of drawers, a table, a few bookshelves in a recess over the washstand, and two chairs. On one of these, by the side of a small fire in a neglected grate, sat the schoolmaster reading his Plato.

He looked up as the door opened and, notwithstanding his strange dress, recognized at once his friend and pupil, rose hastily, and welcomed him with hand and eyes and countenance, but without a word spoken. For a few moments the two stood silent, holding the other's hand and gazing in the other's eyes, then sat down on each side of the fire.

They looked at each other again; then the schoolmaster rose, rang the bell and, when it was answered by a rather careworn young woman, requested her to bring tea.

"I'm sorry I cannot give you cakes or fresh butter, my lord," he said with a smile. "The former are not to be had, and the latter is beyond my means."

He was a man of middle height, but so thin that notwithstanding a slight stoop in the shoulders he looked rather tall—on the young side of fifty but apparently a good way on the other, partly since the little hair he had was gray. About Portlossie he had been greatly respected in certain circles and much loved by his students; and when the presbytery dismissed him, there had been many tears on the part of his pupils.

"You look fine, my friend," said Malcolm.

"Thank you," returned Mr. Graham. "The Lord provides for my every need. I have students to keep me busy and midweek preaching at Hope Chapel."

After their tea followed a long talk, Malcolm first explaining his present position and then answering many questions of the master as to how things had gone since he had left. Next followed anxious questions on Malcolm's side as to how his friend found himself in London.

It was late before Malcolm left.

7 The Park

The next day at noon, mounted on Kelpie, Malcolm was in attendance upon his mistress, who was eager for a gallop in Richmond Park. Lord Liftore, who had intended to accompany her, had not made his appearance yet, but Florimel did not seem any less desirous of setting out at the time she had appointed Malcolm. The fact was that she had said one o'clock to Liftore, intending twelve, that she might get away without him. Kelpie seemed on her good behavior, and they started quietly enough. By the time they got out of the park upon the Kensington road, however, the evil spirit had begun to wake in her. Still, whatever her escapades, they caused Florimel nothing but amusement, for her confidence in Malcolm—that he could do whatever he believed he could— was unbounded. They were hardly into the park when Lord Liftore, followed by his groom, came suddenly up behind them at such a rate as quite destroyed the small stock of equanimity Kelpie had to go on. She bolted.

Florimel was a good rider and knew herself quite mistress of her horse, and if she now followed, it was at her own will. She wanted to make the horses behind her bolt also, if she could. His lordship came flying after her and his groom after him, but she kept increasing her pace until they were all at full stretch, thundering over the grass, upon which Malcolm had at once turned Kelpie, giving her little rein and plenty of spur. Gradually, Florimel slackened speed and at last pulled up suddenly. Liftore and his groom went past her like the wind. She turned at right angles and galloped back to the road. There on a gaunt thoroughbred sat Lenorme, whom she had already passed and signaled to remain thereabout. They drew alongside each other. The three riders were now far away over the park, and still Kelpie held on and the other horses after her.

"I little expected such a pleasure," said Lenorme.

"I meant to give it to you, though," said Florimel with a merry laugh. "Bravo, Kelpie! take them with you!" she cried, looking after the still-retreating horses. "I have got a groom since I saw you last, Arnold," she went on. "See if I don't get some good for us out of him. I want to tell you all about it. I did not mean Liftore to be here when I sent you word, but he has been too much for me."

Lenorme replied with a look of gratitude, and as they walked their horses along she told him all concerning Malcolm and Kelpie.

"Liftore hates him already," she said, "and I can hardly wonder; but you must not, for you will find him useful. He is one I can depend on. You should have seen the look Liftore gave him when he told him he could not sit his mare! It would have been worth gold to you.

"He thinks no end of his riding," Florimel continued; "but if it were not so improper to have secrets with another gentleman, I would tell you that he rides just average. He wants to ride Kelpie, and I have told my groom to let him have her. Perhaps he'll break his neck."

Lenorme smiled grimly.

"You wouldn't mind, would you, Arnold?" added Florimel with a roguish look.

"Would you mind telling me, Florimel, what you mean by the impropriety of having secrets with another gentleman? Am I the other gentleman?"

"Why, of course. You know Liftore imagines he has only to name the day."

"And you allow an idiot like that to cherish such a degrading idea of you?"

"Why, Arnold! What does it matter what a fool like him thinks?"

"If you don't mind it, I do. I feel it an insult that he should dare think of you like that."

"I don't know. I suppose I shall have to marry him someday."

"Lady Lossie, do you want to make me hate you?"

"Don't be foolish. It won't be tomorrow nor the next day."

"Oh, Florimel! What is to come of this? Do you want to break my heart? I hate to talk rubbish. You won't kill me; you will only ruin my work and possibly drive me mad."

Florimel drew close to his side, laid her hand on his arm, and looked in his face with a witching entreaty. "We have the present, Arnold," she said.

"So has the butterfly," answered Lenorme, "but I had rather be the caterpillar with a future. Why don't you put a stop to the man's lovemaking? He can't love you or any woman. He doesn't know what love means. It makes me ill to hear him when he thinks he is paying you irresistible compliments. They are so silly! So mawkish! I want to help you grow as beautiful as God meant you to be when He first thought of you."

"Stop, stop, Arnold! I'm not worthy of such love," said Florimel, again laying her hand on his arm. "I do wish for your sake I had been born a village girl."

"If you had been, then I might have wished for your sake that I had been born a marquis. As it is, I would rather be a painter than any nobleman in Europe; that is, with you to love me."

"This won't do at all," said Florimel with the authority that should belong only to one in the right. "You will spoil everything! I dare not come to your studio if you are going to behave like this. It would be very wrong of me. And if I am never to come and see you, I shall die. I know I shall!"

The girl was so full of the delight of the secret love between them that she cared only to live in the present as if there were no future beyond. Lenorme wanted to make the future better than the present. The word "marriage" put Florimel in a rage. She thought herself superior to Lenorme because he, in the dread of losing her, would have her marry him at once, while she was more than content with the bliss of seeing him now and then. Often her foolish talk stung him with bitter pain—worst of all when it compelled him to doubt whether there was that in her to be loved as he was capable of loving. At one moment she would reveal herself in such a sudden rush of tenderness as seemed possible only to one ready to become his altogether and forever; the next, she would start away as if she had never meant anything.

They rode in silence for some hundred yards. At length he spoke. "What, then, can you gain, my lady marchioness," he said with soft seriousness and a sad smile, "by marrying one of your own rank? I should lay new honor and consideration at your feet. I am young; I have done fairly well already. And you know, too, that the names of great painters go down with honor from generation to generation when my lord this or my lord that is remembered only as a label to the picture that makes the painter famous. I am not a great painter yet, but I will be one if you will be good to me. And men shall say, when they look on your portrait in ages to come, 'No wonder he was such a painter when he had such a woman to paint!'"

"When shall the woman sit for you again, painter?" said Florimel—sole reply to his rhapsody.

The painter thought a little. Then he said, "I don't like that servant woman of yours. She has two evil eyes—one for each of us. I have again and again caught their expression when they were upon us and she thought none were upon her. I can see without lifting my head when I am painting, and my art has made me quick at catching expressions and, I hope, interpreting them."

"I don't altogether like her myself," said Florimel. "Of late I am not so sure of her as I used to be. But what can I do? I must have somebody with me, you know. And Caley is the most available. A thought strikes me, but—yes! You shall see what I will dare for you, faithless man."

She set off at a canter, turned onto the grass, and rode to meet Liftore, whom she saw in the distance returning, followed by the two grooms. "Come on!" she cried, looking back; "I must account for you. He sees I have not been alone."

Lenorme joined her, and they rode along side by side.

The earl and the painter knew each other; as they drew near, the painter lifted his hat and the earl nodded.

"You owe Mr. Lenorme some acknowledgment, my lord, for taking charge of me after your sudden desertion," said Florimel. "Why did you gallop off in such a mad fashion?"

"I am sorry," began Liftore, a little embarrassed.

"Oh, don't trouble yourself to apologize," said Florimel. "I have always understood that great horsemen find a horse more interesting than a lady. It is a mark of their breed, I am told."

She knew Liftore would not be ready to confess he could not hold his hack.

"If it hadn't been for Mr. Lenorme," she added, "I should have been left without a squire, subject to any whim of my four-footed servant here."

As she spoke she patted the neck of her horse. The earl, on his side, had been looking the painter's horse up and down with a would-be humorous expression of criticism. "I beg your pardon, marchioness," he replied, "but you pulled up so quickly that we shot past you. I thought you were close behind, and preferred following.—Seen his best days, eh, Lenorme?" he said, turning to the painter, willing to change the subject.

"I fancy he doesn't think so," returned the painter. "I bought him out of a butterman's cart three months ago. He's been coming to himself ever since. Look at his eye, my lord."

"Are you knowing in horses, then?"

"I can't say I am, beyond knowing how to treat them something like human beings."

Malcolm was just near enough, on the pawing and foaming Kelpie, to catch what was passing. "The fellow will do," he thought to himself. "He's worth a score of such earls!"

"Ha, ha!" said his lordship. "I don't know about that. He's not the best of tempers, I can see. But look at that demon of Lady Lossie's—that black mare there! I wish you could teach her some of your humanity. By the way, Florimel, I think now we are upon the grass," he said loftily, as if submitting to injustice, "I will presume to mount the reprobate."

The gallop had communicated itself to Liftore's blood, and besides, he thought after such a run Kelpie would be less extravagant in her behavior.

"She is at your service," said Florimel.

He dismounted, his groom rode up, he threw him the reins, and called Malcolm, "Bring your mare here, my man."

Malcolm rode her up halfway and dismounted. "If your lordship is going to ride her," he said, "will you please get on her here? I would rather not take her near the other horses."

"Well, you know her better than I do. You and I must ride about the same length, I think."

So saying, his lordship carelessly measured the stirrup leather against his arm and took the reins.

"Stand well forward, my lord. Don't mind turning your back to her head. I'll look after her teeth; you mind her hind hoof," said Malcolm, with her head in one hand and the stirrup in the other.

Kelpie stood rigid as a rock, and the earl swung himself up cleverly enough. But hardly was he in the saddle, and Malcolm had just let her go, when she plunged and lashed out. Then, having failed to unseat her rider, she stood straight up on her hind legs.

"Give her her head, my lord!" cried Malcolm.

She stood swaying in the air, Liftore's now-frightened face half hidden in her mane, and his spurs stuck in her flanks.

"Come off her, my lord, for heaven's sake! Off with you!" cried

Malcolm as he leaped at her head. "She'll be on her back in a moment!"

Liftore only clung the harder. Malcolm caught her head just in time; she was already falling backward.

"Let all go, my lord. Throw yourself off!"

Malcolm swung her toward him with all his strength, and just as his lordship fell off behind her, she fell sideways to Malcolm and clear of Liftore.

As Malcolm was on the side away from the little group, and their own horses were excited, those who had looked breathlessly on at the struggle could not tell how he had managed it; but when they expected to see the groom writhing under the weight of the demoness, there he was with his knee upon her head while Liftore was gathering himself up from the ground, only just beyond the reach of her iron-shod hoofs.

"Thank God," said Florimel, "there is no harm done! Well, have you had enough of her yet, Liftore?"

"Pretty nearly, I think," said his lordship, with an attempt at a laugh as he walked rather feebly and foolishly toward his horse. He mounted with some difficulty and looked very pale.

"I hope you're not much hurt," said Florimel kindly as she moved toward him.

"Not in the least—only disgraced," he answered almost angrily. "The brute's a perfect Satan. You must part with her. With such a horse and such a groom you'll get yourself talked of all over London. I believe the fellow himself was at the bottom of it. You really must sell her."

"I would, my lord, if you were my groom," answered Florimel, whom his accusation of Malcolm had filled with angry contempt.

Malcolm was seated quietly on her head. She had ceased sprawling, and lay nearly motionless but for the heaving of her sides with her huge inhalations. She knew from experience that struggling was useless.

"I beg your pardon, my lady," said Malcolm, "but I daren't get up."

"How long do you mean to sit there?" she asked.

"If your ladyship wouldn't mind riding home without me, I

would give her a good half hour of it. I always do when she throws herself over like that."

"Do as you please," said his mistress. "Let me see you when you get home. I should like to know you are safe."

Florimel returned to the gentlemen, and they rode homeward.

In about two hours Malcolm reported himself. Lord Liftore had gone home, they told him. The painter-fellow, as Wallis called him, had stayed to lunch but was gone also, and Lady Lossie was alone in the drawing room.

She sent for him. "I am glad to see you are safe, MacPhail," she said. "It is clear your Kelpie—don't be alarmed; I am not going to make you part with her—but it is clear she won't always do for you to attend me upon. Suppose now I wanted to dismount and make a call or go into a shop?"

"There is a sort of friendship between your Abbot and her, my lady. She would stand all the better if I had him to hold as well."

"Well, but how would you put me up again?"

"I never thought of that, my lady. Of course I daren't let you come near Kelpie."

"Could you trust yourself to buy another horse to ride after me about town?" asked Florimel.

"No, my lady, not without a ten days' trial. But there's Mr. Lenorme. If he would go with me, I fancy between us we could do pretty well."

"Ah! a good idea!" returned his mistress. "But what makes you think of him?" she added, willing enough to talk about him.

"The look of the gentleman and his horse together and what I heard him say," answered Malcolm.

"What did you hear him say?"

"That he knew he had to treat horses something like human beings. I've often fancied, within the last few months, that God does with some people something like as I do with Kelpie."

"I know nothing about theology," she said, and went to write a note to the painter.

"Maybe not, my lady, but this concerns biography rather than theology. No one could tell what I meant except he had watched his own history and that of people he knew."

"And horses too?"

"It's hard to get at their insides, my lady, but I suspect it must be so. I'll ask Mr. Graham."

"What Mr. Graham?"

"The schoolmaster of Portlossie."

"Is he in London, then?"

"Yes, my lady. He believed too much to please the presbytery and they turned him out."

"I should like to see him. He was very attentive to my father on his deathbed. Next time you see him give him my compliments, and ask if I can be of any service to him."

"I'll do that, my lady. I'm sure he will take it very kindly."

Florimel sat down at her writing table and wrote a note. "There," she said, "take that note to Mr. Lenorme. I have asked him to help you in the choice of a horse."

"What price would you be willing to go, my lady?"

"I leave that to Mr. Lenorme's judgment—and your own," she added.

"Thank you, my lady," said Malcolm, and went to find the painter.

8   The Request

The address on the note Malcolm had to deliver took him to a house in Chelsea—one of a row of beautiful old houses fronting the Thames, within sight of the spot where Malcolm had put up the cutter, with little gardens between them and the road. The servant who took the note returned immediately and showed him up to the study, a large back room looking over a good-sized garden, with stables on one side. There sat Lenorme at his easel. "Ah!" he said, "I'm glad to see that wild animal has not quite torn you to pieces. Take a chair. What on earth made you bring such an incarnate fury to London?"

"I see well enough now, sir, she's not exactly the one for London use, but if you had once ridden her, you would never quite enjoy another between your knees."

"Here your mistress tells me you want my assistance in choosing another horse."

"Yes, sir—to attend upon her in London."

"I don't profess to know horses. What made you think of me?"

"I saw how you sat your own horse, and I heard you say you bought him out of a butterman's cart and treated him like a human being. That was enough for me. 'That gentleman and I would understand one another,' I said to myself."

"I'm glad you think so," said Lenorme, with entire courtesy. Although so much more a man of the world, he was able in a measure to look into Malcolm and appreciate him, both as a result of his nature and his art.

"You see, sir," Malcolm went on, encouraged by the simplicity of Lenorme's manner, "if they were nothing like us, how should we be able to get on with them at all, teach them anything, or come a hair nearer them, do what we might? For all her wickedness, I firmly believe Kelpie has a sort of regard for me: I won't call it affection, but perhaps it comes as near that as may be possible to one of her temper."

"Now I hope you will permit me, Mr. MacPhail," said Lenorme, who had been paying more attention to Malcolm than to his words, "to give a violent wrench to the conversation, and turn it upon yourself. You can't be surprised, and I hope you will not be offended, if I say you strike one as not altogether like your calling. No London groom I have ever spoken to in the least resembles you. How is it?"

"I hope you don't mean to imply, sir, that I don't know my business?" returned Malcolm.

"Anything but that. Come now," said Lenorme, growing more and more interested in his new acquaintance, "tell me something about your life. Account for yourself. If you will make a friendship of it, you must do that."

"I will, sir," said Malcolm, and with the word began to tell him most things he could think of as bearing upon his mental history up to and after the time also when his birth was disclosed to him. In omitting that disclosure he believed he had without it quite accounted for himself.

"Well, I must admit," said Lenorme when he had ended, "that you are no longer unintelligible, not to say incredible. You have had a splendid education, in which I hope you give the herring and Kelpie their due share, as well as Mr. Graham, of whom you speak so fondly." He sat silently regarding him for a few moments. Then he said, "I'll tell you what, now; if I help you buy a horse, you must help me paint a picture."

"I don't know how I'm to do that," said Malcolm; "but if you do, that's enough. I shall be only too happy to do what I can."

"Then I'll tell you. But you're not to tell anybody: it's a secret. I have discovered there is no suitable portrait of Lady Lossie's father. It is a great pity. His brother and his father and grandfather are all in Portland Place, in Highland costume, as chiefs of their clan; only his place is vacant. Lady Lossie, however, has in her possession one or two miniatures of him which, although badly painted, I should think may give the outlines of his face and head with tolerable correctness. From the portraits of his predecessors and from Lady Lossie herself, I have gained some knowledge of what is common to the family; and from all together I hope to gather and paint what will be recognizable by her as a likeness of her father, which afterward I hope to better by her first remarks. These remarks I hope to get first from her feelings unadulterated by criticism, through the surprise of coming upon the picture suddenly; afterward from her judgment at its leisure. Now, I remember seeing you wait at table—the first time I saw you—in the Highland dress. Will you come to me so dressed, and let me paint from you?"

"I'll do better than that, sir!" cried Malcolm eagerly. "I'll get up from Lossie House my lord's very dress that he wore when he went to court—his jeweled dirk and broadsword with the hilt of real silver. That'll greatly help your design upon my lady, for he dressed up in them all more than once just to please her."

"Thank you," said Lenorme very heartily; "that will be of immense advantage. Write at once!"

"I will. Only I'm bigger than my late master, and you must mind that."

"I'll see to it. You get the clothes and all the rest of the accouterments."

"I'll go write to Mrs. Courthope, the housekeeper, tonight, to send the things at once. When would it be convenient for you to go look at some horses with me, Mr. Lenorme?" he said.

"I shall be at home all tomorrow," answered the painter, "and ready to go with you any time you'd like to come for me."

As he spoke he held out his hand and they parted like old friends.

The next morning Malcolm took Kelpie into the park and gave her a good breathing. He was turning home with her again when one of her evil fits began to come upon her, beginning as always with the straightening of her muscles and the flaming of her eyes. He well knew it would soon end in a wild paroxysm of rearing and plunging. He had more than once tried the exorcism of patience, sitting sedately upon her back; but on these occasions the tempest that followed had been of the very worse description, so that he concluded it better to confront her attacks head-on by using his spiked heels with vigor. And since he had adopted this procedure they had become, if no less violent, certainly fewer.

Upon this occasion he had a stiff tussle with her but as usual had gained the victory and was riding slowly along, Kelpie tossing up now her head, then her heels in indignant protest against obedience in general. Suddenly a lady on horseback came galloping up with her groom behind her; she had seen something of what had been going on. As she pulled up, Malcolm reined in. But Kelpie was now as unwilling to stop as she had been before to proceed and the fight began again, the spurs once more playing a free part.

"Man! Man!" cried the lady in reproof, "do you know what you are about?"

"It would be a bad job for her and me if I did not, my lady," said Malcolm, and as he spoke he smiled in the midst of the struggle. He seldom got angry with Kelpie.

But the smile only made his conduct appear in the lady's eyes more cruel. "How is it possible you can treat the poor animal so unkindly? Why, her poor sides are actually . . ." A shudder and look of distress completed the sentence.

"You don't know what she is, my lady, or you would not think it necessary to intercede for her."

"But if she is naughty, is that any reason why you should be cruel?"

"No, my lady; but it is the best reason why I should try to make her good."

"You will never make her good that way!"

"Improvement gives ground for hope," said Malcolm.

"But you must not treat a poor dumb animal as you would a responsible human being."

"She's not so very poor, my lady. She has all she wants and does nothing to earn it—nothing at all with goodwill. For her dumbness, that's a mercy. If she could speak she wouldn't be fit to live amongst decent people. But for that matter, if someone hadn't taken her in hand, dumb as she is, she would have been shot long ago."

"Better that than live with such usage."

"I don't think she would agree with you, my lady. My fear is that, for as cruel as it looks to your ladyship, she enjoys the fight. In any case, I am certain she has more regard for me than any other being in the universe."

"Who *can* have any regard for you," said the lady very gently, in utter mistake of his meaning, "if you have no command of your temper? You must learn to rule yourself first."

"That's true, my lady; and so long as my mare is not able to be a law to herself, I must be a law to her too."

"But have you never heard of the law of kindness? Surely you could do so much more without the severity."

"With some natures I grant you, my lady, but not with such as she. Horse or man—they never know kindness till they have learned to fear. Kelpie would have torn me to pieces before now if I had taken your way with her. But unless I can do a good deal more with her yet, she will be nothing better than a natural brute beast made to be taken and destroyed."

All this time Kelpie was trying hard to get at the lady's horse to bite him; but she did not see that. She was too much distressed and was growing more and more so. "I wish you would let my groom try her," she said. "He's an older and more experienced man than you. He has two children. He would show you what can de done by gentleness."

"It would be a great satisfaction to my old Adam to let him try her," said Malcolm. "But it would be murder, not knowing myself what experience he has had."

"I see," said the lady to herself, but loud enough for Malcolm to hear, for her tenderheartedness had made her both angry and unjust, "his self-conceit is equal to his cruelty—just what I might have expected."

With those words she turned her horse's head and rode away, leaving a lump in Malcolm's throat. It added hugely to the bitterness of being thus rebuked that he had never seen such a beautiful face in his life. She was young—not more than twenty—tall and with a stately grace. It tried Malcolm sorely that such gentleness and beauty should be so unreasonable. Was he never to have the chance of convincing her how mistaken she was concerning his treatment of Kelpie?

Malcolm gazed after her long and earnestly. "It's an awful thing to have a woman like that angered at you," he said to himself, "—as pretty as she is angry. It's a painful thing to be misjudged. But it's no more than God puts up with every hour of the day. But He's patient. So long as He knows He's in the right, He lets folk think what they like—till He has time to make them know better. Lord, make my heart clean within me, and then I'll care little for any judgment but yours!"

For the lady, she rode away, sadly strengthened in her notion that Malcolm was, in fact, the beast and Kelpie the higher creature of the two.

Malcolm rode home and put the demoness in her stall.

9   The Boy

It was a lovely day, but Florimel would not ride; she would not go out again until she could have a choice of horses to follow her. Malcolm must go at once to Mr. Lenorme, "Your Kelpie is all very well in Richmond Park—and I wish I were able to ride her myself, Malcolm—but she will never do in London."

His name sounded sweet on her lips. "Who knows, my lady," he answered his mistress, "but you may ride her someday? Give her a bit of sugar every time you see her—on your hand so that she may take it with her lips and not catch your fingers."

"You shall show me how," said Florimel. "But in the meantime here is a note for Mr. Lenorme. I do so want to ride again."

Malcolm left immediately. The moment his arrival was announced to Lenorme, he came down and went with him, and in an hour or two they had found very much the sort of horse they wanted. Malcolm took him home for trial, and Florimel was pleased with him. The earl's opinion was not to be had, for he had hurt his shoulder when he fell from the rearing Kelpie the day before and was confined to his room in Curzon Street.

In the evening, Malcolm put on his yachter's uniform and set out again for Chelsea. There he took a boat and crossed the river to the yacht, which lay near the other side in the charge of an old salt whose acquaintance Blue Peter had made when lying below the bridges. On board he found all tidy and shipshape. He dived into the cabin, lighted a candle, and made some measurements: all the little luxuries of the next—carpets, cushions, curtains, and other things—were at Lossie House, having been removed when the *Psyche* was laid up for winter. He was going to replace them, and he was anxious to see whether he could not fulfill a desire he had once heard Florimel express to her father—that she had a bed on board and could sleep there. He found it possible and had soon contrived a berth: even a tiny stateroom was within the limits of construction.

Returning to the deck, he was consulting Travers about a carpenter when, to his astonishment, he saw young Davy, the boy they had brought from Duff Harbor and whom he understood to have gone back with Blue Peter, gazing at him from before the mast.

"How do you come to be here?" said Malcolm. "Peter was to take you home with him."

"If you please, Mister MacPhail," said Davy, "I made him think I was going."

"I gave him your wages," said Malcolm.

"Ay, he told me that, but I let them go and gave him the slip and returned ashore, close behind you yourself, sir. I couldn't go without a word with you to see whether you wouldn't let me stay, sir. I'm not too smart, they tell me, but I could do what you'd tell me and keep from doing anything you told me not to do."

The words of the boy pleased Malcolm, more than he judged it wise to show. He looked hard at Davy. There was little to be seen in his face except the best and only thing—truth.

"But," said Malcolm, almost satisfied, "how is this, Travers? I never gave you any instructions about the boy."

"I seed the boy aboard before," answered the old man, "and when he come aboard again, just after you left, I never as much as said to mysel', 'Is it all right?' I axed him no questions and he told me no lies."

"Look here, Davy," said Malcolm, turning to him, "can you swim?"

"Ay, I can, sir," answered Davy.

"Jump overboard, then, and swim ashore," said Malcolm, pointing to the Chelsea bank.

The boy made two strides to the side of the larboard gunwale and would have been over the next instant, but Malcolm caught him by the shoulder. "That'll do, Davy; I'll give you a chance."

"Thank you, sir," said Davy. "I'll do what I can to please you, sir."

"Well, I'll write to your mother and see what she says," said Malcolm. "Now I want to tell you, both of you, that this yacht belongs to the marchioness of Lossie, and I have command of her, and I must have everything on board shipshape and clean. If there's the head of a nail visible, it must be as bright as silver."

He then arranged that Travers was to go home that night and bring with him the next morning an old carpenter friend of his. He would himself be down by seven o'clock to set him to work.

The result was that before a fortnight was over, he had the cabin thoroughly fitted up with all the luxuries it had formerly possessed and as many more as he could think of to compensate for the loss of the space occupied by the daintiest little state-room—a very jewel box for softness and richness and comfort. In the cabin, amongst the rest of his additions, he had fixed in a corner a set of tiny bookshelves and filled them with what books he knew his sister liked and some that he liked for her. By that time also he had arranged with Travers and Davy a code of signals.

The day after Malcolm had his new hack, he rode him behind his mistress in the park. When they left the park Florimel went down Constitution Hill, and, turning westward, she stopped and said to Malcolm, "I am going to run in and thank Mr. Lenorme for the trouble he has been about the horse. Which is the house?"

She pulled up at the gate. Malcolm dismounted, but before he could get near to assist her she was already halfway up the walk, flying, and he was but in time to catch the rein of Abbot, already moving off, curious to know whether he was actually trusted alone. In about five minutes she came out again, glancing about her all ways but behind—with a scared look, Malcolm thought. But she walked more slowly and stately than usual down the path. In a moment Malcolm had her in the saddle, and she cantered away past the hospital into Sloan Street and across the park home. "She knows the way," he thought.

Florimel had found her daring visit to Lenorme stranger and more fearful than she had expected; her courage was not quite so masterful as she had thought. The next day she got Mrs. Barnardiston to meet her at the studio. But she contrived to be there first by some minutes, and her friend found her seated and the painter looking as if he had fairly begun his morning's work. When she apologized for being late, Florimel said she supposed her groom had brought round the horses before his time; being ready, she had not looked at her watch. She was sharp on other people for telling stories, but of late had ceased to see any great harm in telling one to protect herself.

Malcolm found it dreary waiting in the street while she sat for the painter. He would not have minded it on Kelpie, for she was occupation enough, but with only a couple of quiet horses to hold, it was dreary. One thing he had by it, however, and that was a good lesson in waiting—a grand thing for any man, and most of all for those in whom the active is strong.

The next day Florimel did not ride until after lunch but took her maid with her to the studio, and Malcolm had a long morning with Kelpie.

At length the parcel he had sent for from Lossie House arrived. He had explained to Mrs. Courthope what he wanted the things for, and she had made no difficulty of sending them to the address he gave her. Lenorme had already begun the portrait, had indeed been working at it very busily and was now quite ready for him to sit. The early morning being the only time a groom could contrive to spare—and that involved yet earlier attention to his horses—they arranged that Malcolm should be at the study every day by seven o'clock until the painter's object was gained. So he mounted Kelpie at half-past six of a fine breezy spring morning, rode across Hyde Park and down Grosvenor Place and so reached Chelsea, where he put up his mare in Lenorme's stable.

As soon as he arrived he was shown into the painter's bedroom, where lay the portmanteau he had carried thither himself the night before. Out of it, with a strange mingling of pleasure and sadness, he now took the garments of his father's vanished state. He handled each with the reverence of a son. Having dressed in them, he drew himself up with not a little of the Celt's pleasure in fine clothes and walked into the painting room. Lenorme started with admiration of his figure and wonder at the dignity of his carriage. He almost sprang at his palette and brushes: whether or not he succeeded with the likeness of the late marquis, it would be his own fault if he did not make a good picture. He painted eagerly and they talked little, and only about trivialities.

"Confound it!" he cried suddenly, and sprang to his feet, but without taking his eyes from his picture. "What have I been doing all this time but making a portrait of you, MacPhail, and forgetting what you were there for! And yet," he went on, hesitating and catching up the miniature for a closer look, "I have got a certain likeness! Yes, it must be so, for I seen in it also a certain look for Lady Lossie. Well, I suppose a man can't altogether help what he paints anymore than what he dreams.—That will do for this morning, anyhow, I think, MacPhail. Make haste and put on your own clothes, and come into the next room to breakfast. You must be tired with standing so long."

"It is about the hardest work I ever tried," answered Malcolm, "but I doubt if I am as tired as Kelpie. I've been listening for the last half hour to hear the stalls flying."

10 The Eavesdropper

Florimel was beginning to understand that the shield of the portrait was not large enough to cover many more visits to Lenorme's studio. Still, she must and would venture, and should anything be said, there, at least, was the portrait. For some weeks it had been all but finished, was never off its easel, and always showed wet paint somewhere. He kept the last of it lingering, ready to prove itself almost, yet not altogether, finished. What was to follow its absolute completion neither of them could tell. The worst of it was that their thoughts about it differed. It must be remembered that Florimel had had no mother since her childhood, that she was now but a girl, and that of genuine love she had little more than enough to serve as salt to the passion. In Florimel's case, there was much of the childish in it. Definitely separated from Lenorme, she would have been merry again in a fortnight; and yet, though she half knew this herself and at the same time was more than half ashamed of the whole affair, she did not give it up—would not—only intended by and by to let it go. It was no wonder, then, that Lenorme, believing, hoping she loved him, should find her hard to understand.

The painter was not merely in love with Florimel; he loved her. I will not say that he was in no degree dazzled by her rank, but such thoughts were only changing hues on the feathers of his love.

A day or two passed before Florimel went again to the studio, accompanied, notwithstanding Lenorme's warning and her own doubt, yet again by her maid, a woman, unhappily, of Lady Bellair's finding. At Lossie House, Malcolm had felt a repugnance to her, both moral and physical. When first he heard her name, one of the servants speaking of her as Miss Caley, he took it for Scaley; and if that was not her name, yet it was her nature.

This time Florimel rode to Chelsea with Malcolm, having directed Caley to meet her there. And, the one designing to be a little early and the other to be a little late, two results naturally followed—first, that the lovers had a few minutes alone; and second, that when Caley crept in, noiseless and unannounced as a cat, she had her desire and saw the painter's arm round Florimel's waist and her head on his chest. She crept out again as quietly as she had entered. Through the success of her trick it came about that Malcolm, chancing to look up from his horses to the room where he always breakfasted with his new friend, saw in one of the windows a face radiant with the expression of evil discovery.

Caley was of the common class of servants in this, that she considered service servitude and took her amends in selfishness. Her one thought was to make the most of her position. She was clever, greedy, cunning. She rather liked her mistress, but watched her in the interests of Lady Bellair. She had a fancy for the earl, a natural dislike to Malcolm, which she concealed in distant politeness, and for all the rest of the house, indifference.

The look on Caley's face gave Malcolm something to think about. Clearly she had a triumph. What could it be? The nature of the woman had by this time become clear to him as a result of his interaction with her in the house; it was clear the triumph was not

75

in good. It was plain, too, that it was in something which had that very moment occurred, and could hardly have to do with anyone but her mistress. She had gone into the house but a moment before, a minute or two behind her mistress, and he knew with what a catlike step she went about. She had undoubtedly surprised them—discovered how matters stood between her mistress and the painter. He pieced together everything almost as it had taken place. She had seen without being seen and had retreated with her prize! Florimel was then in the woman's power. What was he to do? He must clearly tell her somehow.

Once arrived at a resolve, Malcolm never lost time. They had turned but one corner on their way home when he rode up to her. "Please, my lady," he began, "I must tell you something I happened to see while I waited with the horses," he said.

The earnestness of his tone struck Florimel. She looked at him with eyes a little wider and waited to hear.

"I happened to look up at the drawing-room windows, my lady, and Caley came to one of them with such a look on her face! I can't exactly describe it to you, my lady, but—"

"Why do you tell me?" interrupted his mistress with absolute composure and hard, questioning eyes. Then, before he could reply, a flash of thoughts seemed to cross her face with a quick single motion of her eyebrows, and it was instantly altered and thoughtful. She seemed to have suddenly perceived some cause for taking a mild interest in his communication. "But it cannot be, Malcolm," she said in quite a changed tone. "You must have taken someone else for her. She never left the studio all the time I was there."

"It was immediately after her arrival, my lady. She went in about two minutes after your ladyship, and could not have had much more than time to go upstairs when I saw her come to the window. I felt bound to tell you."

"Thank you, Malcolm," returned Florimel kindly. "You did right to tell me, but it's of no consequence. Mr. Lenorme's housekeeper and she must have been talking about something."

But her eyebrows were now thoughtfully contracted over her eyes.

"There had been no time for that, I think, my lady," said Malcolm.

Florimel turned again and rode on. Malcolm saw that he had succeeded in warning her and was glad. But had he foreseen to what it would lead, he would hardly have done it.

Florimel was indeed very uneasy. She could not help strongly suspecting that she had betrayed herself to one who, if not an intentional spy, would yet be ready enough to make a spy's use of anything she might have picked up. What was to be done? It was now too late to think of getting rid of her: that would be but her signal to disclose whatever she had seen and so not merely enjoy a sweet revenge, but account with clear satisfactoriness for her dismissal. What would not Florimel have now given for someone who could sympathize with her and yet counsel her! She was afraid to venture another meeting with Lenorme. Besides, she was not a little shy of the advantage the discovery would give him in pressing her to marry him. And now first she began to feel as if her sins were going to find her out.

A day or two passed. She watched her maid, but discovered no change in her manner or behavior. Weary of observation, she was gradually settling into her former security when Caley began to drop hints that alarmed her. Might it not be the safest thing to take her into confidence? It would be such a relief, she thought, to have a woman she could talk to! The result was that she began to lift a corner of the veil that hid her trouble. The woman encouraged her, and at length the silly girl threw her arms round the scaly one's neck, much to that person's satisfaction, and told her she loved Mr. Lenorme. She said she knew, of course, that she could not marry him. She was only waiting a fit opportunity to free herself from a connection which, however delightful, she was unable to justify. Could Lenorme have known her capable of unbosoming herself to such a woman, it would almost have slain the love he bore her.

Caley first comforted the weeping girl and then began to insinuate encouragement. She must indeed give him up—there was no help for that—but neither was there any necessity for doing so all at once. Mr. Lenorme was a beautiful man, and any woman might be proud to be loved by him. She must take her time to it. She could trust her.

The first result was that, on the pretext of bidding him farewell and convincing him that he and she must meet no more, Florimel arranged with her woman one evening to go the next morning to the studio. She knew the painter to be an early riser and always at his work before eight o'clock. But although she tried to imagine she had persuaded herself to say farewell, certainly she had not yet brought her mind to any resolve in the matter. At seven o'clock in the morning the marchioness, habited like a housemaid, slipped out by the front door, turned the corners of two streets, found a hackney-coach waiting for them and arrived in due time at the painter's abode.

When the door opened and Florimel glided in, the painter sprang to his feet to welcome her, and she flew softly into his arms; for, the study being large and full of things, she was not aware of the presence of Malcolm who was there for an early morning sitting. From behind a picture of an easel he saw them meet, but shrinking from being an open witness to their secret, and also from being discovered in his father's clothes by the sister who knew him only as a servant, he instantly sought escape. Nor was it hard to find, for near where he stood was a door opening into a small intermediate chamber next to the drawing room, and by it he fled, intending to pass through to Lenorme's bedroom and change his clothes. With noiseless stride he hurried away but could not help hearing a few passionate words that escaped his sister's lips before Lenorme could warn her they were not alone—words which, it seemed to him, come only from a heart whose very pulse was devotion.

"How can I live without you, Arnold?" said the girl as she clung to him.

Lenorme gave an uneasy glance behind him, saw Malcolm disappear, and answered, "I hope you will not try, my darling."

"Oh, but you know this can't last," she returned with playfully affected authority. "It must come to an end. They will interfere."

"Who can? Who will dare?" said the painter with confidence.

"People will. We had better stop it ourselves—before it all

comes out and we are shamed," said Florimel, with perfect seriousness.

"Shamed!" cried Lenorme. "Well, if you can't help being ashamed of me—and perhaps, as you have been brought up you can't—do you not then love me enough to encounter a little shame for my sake? I should welcome worlds of such for yours."

Florimel was silent. She kept her face hidden on his shoulder, but was already halfway to a quarrel.

"You don't love me, Florimel," he said after a pause.

"Well, suppose I don't!" she cried, half defiantly. Drawing herself from him, she stepped back two paces and looked at him with saucy eyes, in which burned two little flames of displeasure that seemed to shoot up from the red spots glowing upon her cheeks. Lenorme looked at her. He had often seen her like this before and knew that the shell was charged and the fuse lighted. But within lay a mixture even more explosive than he had suspected, for she was conscious of having now been false to him. That rendered her temper dangerous. Lenorme had already suffered severely from the fluctuations of her moods. They had almost been too much for him. He could endure them, he thought, to all eternity if he had her to himself, safe and sure; but this confidence often failed him. If, after all, she should forsake him, he knew he would survive it; but he knew also that life could never be the same again, that for a season work would be impossible. It was no wonder, then, if her behavior sometimes angered him. And now a black fire in his eyes answered the blue flash in hers. A word of indignant expostulation rose to her lips, but a thought came that repressed it. He took her hand and led her—her hand lying dead in his. It was but to the other end of the room he led her, to the picture of her father, now all but finished.

Malcolm stepped into the drawing room, where the table was laid as usual for breakfast. There stood Caley helping herself to a spoonful of honey. At his entrance she started violently, and her sallow face grew earthy. For some seconds she stood motionless, unable to take her eyes off the apparition, as it seemed to her, of the late marquis, in wrath at her encouragement of his daughter in disgraceful courses. Malcolm, supposing she was ashamed of herself, took no further notice of her and walked deliberately toward the other door. Before he reached it she knew him. Burning with the combined ires of fright and shame, conscious also that by the one little contemptible act of greed in which he had surprised her she had justified the aversion which her woman instinct had from the first recognized in him, she darted to the door, stood with her back against it, and faced him flaming. "So!" she cried, "this is how my lady's kindness is abused! The insolence! Her groom goes and sits for his portrait in her father's court dress! My lady shall know this," she concluded, with a vicious clenching of her teeth and two or three small nods of her neat head.

Malcolm stood regarding her with a coolness that yet inflamed her wrath. He could not help smiling at the reaction of shame and indignation. Had her anger been but a passing flame, that smile would have turned it into enduring hate. She hissed in his face.

"Go and have the first word," he said, "but leave that door and let me pass."

"Let you pass, indeed! What would you pass for—the son of old Lord James and a married woman? I don't care *that* for you," and she snapped her fingers in his face.

Malcolm turned from her and went to the window, taking a newspaper from the breakfast table as he passed and there sat down to read until the way should be clear. Carried beyond herself by his utter indifference, Caley darted from the room and went straight into the study.

Lenorme led Florimel in front of the picture. She gave a great start and turned and stared pallid at the painter. The effect upon her was such as he had not foreseen, and the words she uttered were not such as he could have hoped to hear. "What would he think of me if he knew?" she cried, clasping her hands.

That moment Caley burst into the room, her eyes like a cat's. "My lady!" she shrieked, "there's MacPhail the groom, my lady, dressed up in your honored father's bee-utiful clothes as he always wore when he went to dine with the prince! And please, my lady, he's so rude, I could hardly keep my hands off him."

Florimel flashed a dagger of question in Lenorme's eyes. The painter drew himself up. "It was at my request, Lady Lossie," he said.

"Indeed!" returned Florimel, in high scorn, and glanced again at the picture. "I see," she went on. "How could I be such an idiot! It was my groom's, not my father's likeness you meant to surprise me with!" Her eyes flashed as if she would annihilate him.

"I have worked hard in the hope of giving you pleasure, Lady Lossie," said the painter with wounded dignity.

"And you have failed," she adjoined cruelly.

The painter took the miniature after which he had been working from a table near, handed it to her with a proud obeisance, and the same moment dashed a brushful of dark paint across the face of the picture.

Florimel turned away and walked from the study. The door of the drawing room was open, and Caley stood by the side of it. Florimel, too angry to consider what she was about, walked in. There sat Malcolm in the window in her father's clothes and his very attitude, reading the newspaper. He did not hear her enter. He had been waiting till he could reach the bedroom unseen by her, for he knew from the sound of the voices that the study room was open. Her anger rose yet higher at the sight. "Leave the room," she said.

He started to his feet, and now perceived that his sister was in the dress of a servant.

"Take those clothes off instantly," said Florimel slowly, replacing wrath with haughtiness as well as she might.

Malcolm turned to the door without a word. He saw that things had gone wrong where most he would have wished them to go right.

"I'll see that they're well aired, my lady," said Caley, with sibilant indignation.

Malcolm went to the study. The painter sat before the picture of the marquis, with his elbows on his knees and his head between his hands. "Mr. Lenorme," said Malcolm, approaching him gently.

"Oh, go away," said Lenorme without raising his head. "I can't bear the sight of you just yet."

Malcolm obeyed. He was in his own clothes, booted and belted, in two minutes. Three sufficed to replace his father's garments in the portmanteau, and in three more he and Kelpie went plunging past his mistress and her maid as they drove home in their lumbering vehicle.

"The insolence of the fellow!" said Caley, loud enough for her mistress to hear notwithstanding the noise of the rattling windows. "A pretty pass we are come to!"

But already Florimel's mood had begun to change. She felt that she had done her best to alienate men on whom she could depend, and that she had chosen for a confidante one whom she had no ground for trusting.

She got safe and unseen to her room, and Caley believed she had only to improve the advantage she had now gained.

Things had taken a turn that was not to Malcolm's satisfaction, and his thoughts were as busy all the way home as Kelpie would allow. He had ardently desired that his sister should be thoroughly in love with Lenorme, for that seemed to open a clear path out of his worst difficulties. Now they had quarreled and were both angry with him. The main fear was that Liftore would now make some progress with her. Things looked dangerous. Even his warning against Caley had led to a result the very opposite of his intent and desire. And now it recurred to him that he had once come upon Liftore talking to Caley and giving her something that shone like a sovereign.

When Florimel returned from her unhappy visit and had sent her attendant to get her some tea, she threw herself upon her bed. She was yet tossing in her own disharmony when Malcolm came for orders. To get rid of herself and Caley both, she desired him to bring the horses round at once.

It was more than Malcolm had expected. He ran: he might yet have a chance of trying to turn her in the right direction. He knew that Liftore was neither in the house nor at the stable. With the help of the earl's groom he was round in ten minutes. Florimel was all but ready. She sprang from Malcolm's hand to the saddle and led as straight northward as she could go, never looking behind her till she drew rein on the top of Hampstead Heath. When he rode up to her, Florimel said, half ashamed, "Malcolm, I don't think my father would have minded you wearing his clothes."

"Thank you, my lady," said Malcolm. "At least he would have forgiven anything meant for your pleasure."

"I was too hasty," she said. "But the fact was, Mr. Lenorme had irritated me, and I foolishly mixed you up with him."

"When I went into the studio after you left it this morning, my lady," Malcolm ventured, "he had his head between his hands and would not even look at me."

Florimel turned her face aside, and Malcolm thought she was sorry; but she was only hiding a smile. She had not yet gotten beyond the kitten stage of love and was pleased to find she gave pain.

"If your ladyship never had another true friend, Mr. Lenorme is one," added Malcolm.

"What opportunity can you have had for knowing?" said Florimel.

"I have been sitting for him every morning for a good many days," answered Malcolm. "He is something like a man!"

Florimel's face flushed with pleasure. She liked to hear him praised, for he loved her.

"You should have seen, my lady, the pains he took with that portrait. He would stare at the little picture you lent him of my lord for minutes, as if he were looking through it at something behind it; then he would go and gaze at your ladyship on the pedestal, as if you were the goddess herself, about to tell him everything about your father; and then he would hurry back to his easel and give a touch or two to the face, looking at it all the time as if he loved it. It must have been a cruel pain that drove him to smear it as he did."

Florimel began to feel a little motion of shame somewhere in the mystery of her being. But to show that to her servant would be to betray herself—all the more that he seemed the painter's friend.

"I will ask Lord Liftore to go and see the portrait, and if he thinks it good I will buy it," she said. "Mr. Lenorme is certainly very clever with his brush."

Malcolm saw that she said this not to insult Lenorme but to blind her groom, and made no answer.

"I will ride there with you tomorrow morning," she added in conclusion and moved on.

Malcolm touched his hat and dropped behind. But the next moment he was by her side again. "I beg your pardon, my lady, but would you allow me to say one word more?"

She bowed her head.

"That woman Caley, I am certain, is not to be trusted. She does not love you, my lady."

"How do you know that?" asked Florimel, speaking steadily but writhing inwardly with the knowledge that the warning was too late.

"I have tried her spirit," answered Malcolm, "and know that it is of the devil. She loves herself too much to be true."

After a little pause Florimel said, "I know you mean well, Malcolm, but it is nothing to me whether she loves me or not. We don't look for that nowadays from servants."

"It is because I love you, my lady," said Malcolm, "that I know Caley does not. If she should get hold of anything your ladyship would not wished talked about—"

"That she cannot," said Florimel, but with an inward shudder. "She may tell the whole world all she can discover."

She would have cantered on as the words left her lips, but something in Malcolm's look held her. She turned pale, she trembled. Her father was looking at her as only once had she seen him—in doubt whether his child lied. The illusion was terrible. She shook in her saddle. The next moment she was galloping along the grassy border of the heath in wild flight from her worst enemy, whom yet she could never by the wildest of flights escape; it was the self which had just told a lie to the servant of whom she had so lately boasted that he never told one in his life. Then she grew angry. What had she done to be thus tormented? She, a marchioness, thus pestered by her own menials—pulled opposing directions by a groom and a maid! She would turn them both away and have nobody about her either to trust or suspect.

She turned and rode back, looking the other way as she passed Malcolm.

When they reached the top of the heath, riding along to meet them came Liftore—this time to Florimel's consolation and comfort; she did not like riding unprotected with a good angel at her heels. So glad was she that she did not even take the trouble to wonder how he had discovered the road she went. She never suspected that Caley had sent his lordship's groom to follow her until the direction of her ride should be evident, but took his appearance without question as a lover-like attention and rode home with him, talking the whole way and cherishing a feeling of triumph over both Malcolm and Lenorme. Had she not a protector of her own kind? Could she not, when they troubled her, pass from their sphere into one beyond their ken? For the moment the poor, weak lord who rode beside her seemed to her foolish heart a tower of refuge. She was particularly gracious and encouraging as they rode, and fancied again and again that perhaps the best way out of her troubles would be to encourage and at last accept him.

Malcolm followed, sick at heart that she should prove herself so shallow.

When she went to her room, there was Caley taking from a portmanteau that had been delivered the Highland dress which had occasioned so much. A note fell, and she handed it to her mistress. Florimel opened it, grew pale as she read it and asked Caley to bring her a glass of water. No sooner had her maid left the room than she sprang to the door and bolted it. Then the tears burst from her eyes; she sobbed despairingly and but for the help of her handkerchief would have wailed aloud. When Caley returned she answered to her knock that she was lying down and wanted to sleep. She was, however, trying to force further communication from the note. In it the painter told her that he was going to set out the next morning for Italy, and that her portrait was at the shop of certain carvers and gilders, being fitted with a frame for which he had made drawings. Three times she read it, searching for some hidden message to her heart. She held it up between her and the light, then before the fire till it crackled like a bit of old parchment; but all was in vain. By no device, intellectual or physical, could she coax the shadow of a meaning out of it beyond what lay plain on the surface. She must—she would—see him again.

That night she was merrier than usual at dinner, and after it, sang ballad upon ballad to please Liftore; then went to her room and told Caley to arrange for yet another visit to Mr. Lenorme's studio. She positively must, she said, secure her father's portrait ere the ill-tempered painter—all men of genius were hasty and unreasonable—should have it destroyed utterly, as he was certain to do before leaving, and with that she showed her Lenorme's letter. Caley was all service, only saying that this time she thought they had better go openly. She would see Lady Bellair as soon as Lady Lossie was in bed and explain the thing to her.

11 The Confrontation

The next morning the two drove to Chelsea in the carriage. When the door opened Florimel walked straight up to the study. There she saw no one, and her heart, which had been fluttering strangely, sank and was painfully still, while her gaze went wandering about the room. Again the tears gushed from the heart of Florimel. As she choked down a cry, suddenly arms were around her. Never doubting whose the embrace, she leaned her head against his bosom, and slowly opening her tearful eyes, lifted them to the face that bent over hers.

It was Liftore's!

She was dumb with disappointment and dismay. It was a hateful moment. He kissed her forehead and eyes and sought her mouth. She shrieked aloud. In her very agony at the loss of one to be kissed by another! And there! It was too degrading, too horrid!

At the sound of her cry someone started up at the other end of the room. An easel with a large canvas on it fell, and a man came forward with great strides. Liftore let her go, with a muttered curse on the intruder, and she darted from the room into the arms of Caley, who had had her ear against the other side of the door. That same instant Malcolm received from his lordship a well-planted blow between the eyes, which filled them with flashes and darkness. The next the earl was on the floor. The ancient fury of the Celt had burst up into the nineteenth century and mastered a noble spirit. All Malcolm could afterward remember was that he came to himself dealing Liftore, still on the floor, repeated blows. His lordship, struggling to rise, turned up a face white with hate and impotent fury. "You flunkie!" he cursed. "I'll have you shot like a mangy dog!"

"Meantime I will chastise you like an insolent nobleman," said Malcolm, who had already almost recovered his self-possession. "You dare to touch my mistress!" Liftore sprang to his feet and rushed at him. Malcolm caught him by the wrist with a fisherman's grasp. "My lord, I don't want to hurt you. Take a warning and let it be, for fear of worse," he said and threw his hand from him with a swing that nearly dislocated his shoulder.

The warning sufficed. His lordship cast him one scowl of concentrated hate and revenge, and hurried from the house.

At the usual morning hour Malcolm had ridden to Chelsea, hoping to find his friend in a less despairing and more companionable mood than when he left him. To his surprise and disappointment he learned that Lenorme had sailed by the packet for Ostende the night before. He asked leave to go into the study. There on its easel stood the portrait of his father as he had last seen it—disfigured with a great smear of brown paint across the face. He knew that the face was dry, and he saw that the smear was wet. He would see whether he could, with turpentine and a soft brush, remove the insult. In this endeavor he was so absorbed, and by the picture itself was so divided from the rest of the room that he neither saw nor heard anything until Florimel cried out.

Naturally, those events made him yet more dissatisfied with his sister's position. Evil influences and dangers were on all sides of her, the worst possible outcome being that loving one man, she could marry another—and him such a man as Liftore! Whatever he heard in the servant's hall, both tone and substance, only confirmed the unfavorable impression he had of the bold-faced countess from the first. The oldest of her servants had, he found, the least respect for their mistress, although all had a certain liking for her, which gave their disrespect the heavier import. He must get Florimel away somehow. While all was right between her and the painter, he had been less anxious about her immediate surroundings, trusting that Lenorme would before long deliver her. But now she had driven him from the very country, and he had left no clue to follow him by. His housekeeper could tell nothing of his purposes. The gardener and she were left in charge as a matter of course. He might be back in a week or a year; she could not even conjecture.

Seeming possibilities, in varied mingling with rank absurdities, kept passing through Malcolm's mind as, after Liftore's punishment, he lifted the portrait, set it again upon its easel and went on trying to clean the face of it with no small promise of success. But as he made progress, he grew anxious lest with the defilement he should remove some of the color as well. The painter alone, he concluded at length, could be trusted to restore the work he had ruined.

He left the house, walked across the road to the riverbank, and gave a short, sharp whistle. In an instant Davy was in the dinghy, pulling for shore. Malcolm went on board the yacht, saw that all was right, gave some orders, went ashore again, and mounted Kelpie.

In pain, wrath, and mortification Liftore rode home. What would the men at his club say if they knew he had been thrashed by a scoundrel of a groom for kissing his mistress? The fact would soon be out. He must do his best to have it taken for what it ought to be—fiction. It was the harder upon him that he knew himself no coward. He must punish the rascal somehow—he owed it to society to punish him—but at present he did not see how, and the first thing was to have the first word with Florimel. He must see her before she saw the ruffian.

Mistress and maid road home together in silence. The moment Florimel heard Malcolm's voice she had left the house. Caley, following, had heard enough to know that there was a scuffle at least going on in the study, and her eye witnessed against her heart that Liftore could have no chance with the detested groom. Would MacPhail thrash his lordship? If he did, it would be well she should know it.

As to Florimel, she was enraged at the liberties Liftore had taken with her. But alas, was she not in some degree in his power? He had found her there and in tears! How did he come to be there? If Malcolm's judgment of her was correct, Caley might have told him. Was she already false? She pondered within herself and cast no look upon her maid until she had concluded how best to carry herself toward the earl. Then glancing at the hooded cobra beside her, she said, "What an awkward thing that Lord Liftore, of all moments, should appear just then! How could it be?"

"I'm sure I haven't an idea, my lady," returned Caley. "My lord has always been kind to Mr. Lenorme, and I suppose he has been in the way of going to see him at work. Who would have thought my lord was such an early riser? There are not many gentlemen like him nowadays, my lady. Did your ladyship hear the noise in the studio after you left it?"

"I heard high words," answered her mistress, "nothing more. How on earth did MacPhail come to be there as well? From you, Caley, I will not conceal that his lordship behaved indiscreetly; in fact, he was rude. And I can quite imagine that MacPhail thought it his duty to defend me. It is all very awkward for me. Who could have imagined him there and sitting behind amongst the pictures! It almost makes me doubt whether Mr. Lenorme be really gone."

"It seems to me, my lady," returned Caley, "that the man is always just where he ought not to be, always meddling with something he had no business with. I beg your pardon, my lady," she went on, "but wouldn't it be better to get some staid elderly man for a groom—one who has been properly bred up to his duties and taught his manners in a gentlemen's stable? It is so odd to have a groom from a rough seafaring set—one who behaves like the rude fisherman he is, never having had to obey orders of lord or lady! The want of it is, your ladyship will soon be the town's talk if you have such a groom on such a horse after you everywhere."

Florimel's face flushed. Caley saw she was angry and held her peace.

Breakfast was hardly over when Liftore walked in slowly, looking pale. Florimel threw herself back in her chair and held out her left hand to him in an expansive, benevolent sort of way. "How dare you come into my presence looking so well pleased with yourself, my lord, after giving me such a fright this morning?" she said. "You might at least have made sure that there was—that we were—" She could not bring herself to complete the sentence.

"My dearest girl," said his lordship, not only delighted to get off so pleasantly, but profoundly flattered by the implied understanding, "I found you in tears. How could I think of anything else? It may have been stupid, but I trust you will think it pardonable."

Caley had not fully betrayed her mistress to his lordship, and he had, entirely to his own satisfaction, explained the liking of Florimel for the society of the painter as mere fancy.

"It was no wonder I was crying," said Florimel. "Anyone would have cried to see the state my father's portrait was in."

"You father's portrait?"

"Yes. Didn't you know? Mr. Lenorme has been painting one from a miniature I lent him—under my supervision of course; and just because I let fall a word that showed I was not altogether satisfied with the likeness, what should the wretched man do but catch up a brush full of filthy black paint and smudge the face all over!"

"Oh, Lenorme will soon set it to rights again. He's not a bad fellow. I will go about it this very day."

"You'll not find him, I'm sorry to say. There's a note I had from him yesterday. And the picture's quite unfit to be seen—utterly ruined. But I can't think how you could miss seeing it."

"To tell you the truth, Florimel, I had a bit of a scrimmage after you left me in the studio." Here his lordship did his best to imitate a laugh. "Who should come rushing upon me out of the back regions of paint and canvas but that mad groom of yours! I don't suppose you knew he was there?"

"No. I saw a man's feet, that was all."

"Well, there he was, for what reason the devil knows, and when he heard your little startled cry—what should he fancy but that you were frightened and he must rush to the rescue! And so he did with a vengeance. I don't know when I shall quite forget the blow he gave me." And again Liftore laughed, or thought he did.

"He struck you!" exclaimed Florimel, rather astonished, but hardly able for inward satisfaction to put enough indignation into her tone.

"He did, the fellow! But don't say a word about it, for I thrashed him so unmercifully that, to tell the truth, I had to stop because I grew sorry for him. I am sorry now. So I hope you will take no notice of it. In fact, I had begun to like the rascal. You know I was never favorably impressed with him. By Jove! it's not every mistress that can have such a devoted attendant. But he is hardly, with all his virtues, the proper servant for a young lady to have about her. He has had no proper training at all, you see. But you must let the villain nurse himself for a day or two anyhow. It would be torture to make him ride after what I gave him."

Florimel knew that her father had on one occasion struck Malcolm and that he had taken it with the utmost gentleness, confessing himself in the wrong. The blow Malcolm struck Liftore was for her, not himself. Therefore, while her confidence in Malcolm's courage remained unshaken, she was yet able to believe that Liftore had done as he said and supposed that Malcolm had submitted. In her heart she pitied without despising him.

Caley herself took him the message that he would not be wanted. As she delivered it, she smiled an evil smile and dropped a mocking curtsey, with her faze fixed on his two black eyes and the great bruise between them.

When Caley returned to her mistress and reported the condition of his face, Florimel informed her of the chastisement he had received from Liftore and desired her to find out for his condition, whether he had any broken ribs or the like, for she was anxious about him. But preferably from someone else, possibly the wife of his lordship's groom to whom he would undoubtedly have gone with anything like a serious injury. Florimel felt sorrier for him than she could well understand, seeing he was but a groom—

a great lumbering fellow, all his life used to hard knocks, which probably never hurt him.

That her mistress should care so much about him added yet an acrid touch to Caley's spite, but she put on her bonnet and went to the mews. She had begun to fear Malcolm a little as well as hate him. And indeed he was rather a dangerous person to have about when it came to her own schemes.

"Merton's wife knows nothing, my lady," she said on her return. "I saw the fellow in the yard going about much as usual. He will stand a good deal of punishment I fancy, my lady, like that brute of a horse he makes such a fuss with. I can't help wishing, for my lady's sake, we had never set eyes upon him. He'll do us all mischief yet before we're rid of him."

But Florimel was not one to be talked into an opinion she did not choose. Neither would she render to her maid her reasons for not choosing. She had repaired her fortifications, strengthened herself with Liftore, and was confident.

"The fact is, Caley," she said, "I have fallen in love with Kelpie and never mean to part with her—at least till I can ride her—or she kills me. So I can't do without MacPhail. The man must go with the mare. Besides, he is such a strange fellow; if I turned him away, I should quite expect him to poison her before he left."

The maid's face grew darker. That her mistress had the slightest intention of ever mounting that mare she did not find herself fool enough to believe, but of other reasons she could think plenty. And such there certainly were, though none of the sort which Caley's low imagination now supplied. Caley had no faculty for understanding the kind of confidence she reposed in her groom and was the last sort of person to whom her mistress could ever impart the fact of her father's leaving her in charge to his young henchman. And to the memory of her father she faithfully clung, so that no matter how unpleasant Malcolm from time to time became, she yet regarded him not the less confidently.

When later that afternoon Liftore mounted to accompany Lady Lossie, it took all the pluck that belonged to his high breed to enable him to smile, with twenty counselors in different parts of his body persuading him that he was at least a liar. As they rode,

Florimel asked how he came to be at the studio that morning. He told her that he had wanted very much to see her portrait before the final touches were given to it. He could have made certain suggestions, he believed, that no one else could. He had indeed, he confessed, heard from his aunt that Florimel was to be there that morning for the last time. It was, therefore, his only chance. But he had expected to be there hours before she was out of bed. For the rest he hoped he had been punished enough, since her rascally groom—and here once more his lordship laughed peculiarly—had but just failed of breaking his arm. It was, in fact, all he could do to hold the reins.

12   The Daydream

As the days passed and Florimel heard nothing of Lenorme, the uneasiness that came with her thoughts of him gradually diminished. Her imagination began to work on her concerning the person and gifts and devotion of the painter. When lost in her blissful reveries she often imagined herself—while not exactly marrying Lenorme in the flushed face of an outraged London society—fleeing with him from the judgment of all to some blessed isle of the southern seas. But this mere fancy, as lacking in courage as it was in realism, she was far from capable of carrying into effect. But even the poorest dreaming has its influences, and the result of hers was that the attentions of Liftore became again distasteful to her. And no wonder, for indeed his lordship's presence made a poor show beside that of the painter in the ideal world of the woman who, though she could not in truth be said to love him, certainly had a strong fancy for him.

The pleasure of her castle-building was but seldom interrupted by any thought of the shamefulness of her behavior to him. That did not matter much. Her selfishness closed her eyes to her own falsehood. Meantime, as the past with its trembling joys glided away, widening the space between her and her false fears and shames, she gathered courage to resist Liftore's attentions, and his lordship began to find her as uncertain and variable as ever. Assuredly, as his aunt said, she was yet a girl incapable of knowing even her own mind, and he must not press his suit. Nor was there any jealousy or fear to urge him on, for society regarded her as his.

There was one good process, unknown to her, going on in Florimel. Despite the discomfort often occasioned her by Malcolm, her confidence in him was increasing. And now that the kind of danger threatening her seemed altered, she leaned upon him by degrees more and more, even more than she could have accounted for on the ground that he was a loyal attendant authorized by her father. In a matter of imagined duty, he might make presumptions, but that was a small thing beside the sense of safety his very presence brought with it.

If only Lenorme would come back and allow her to be his friend—his only young lady friend—leaving her at perfect liberty to do just as she liked, then all would be well, perfectly comfortable! In the meantime, life was endurable without him and would be, provided Liftore did not make himself disagreeable. If he did, there were other gentlemen who might be induced to keep him in check. She would punish him; she knew how. She liked him better, however, than any of those.

It was out of pure kindness to Malcolm, upon Liftore's representation of how he had punished him, that for the rest of the week she dispensed with his attendance. But he, unaware of the lies Liftore had told her and supposing she resented the liberty he had taken in warning her against Caley, feared the breach would go on widening. Everything seemed to be going counter to his desires. A whole world of work lay before him—a harbor to build, a numerous fisher-clan to house as they ought to be housed, justice to do on all sides, righteous servants to appoint in place of oppressors, mortgages, and debts to pay off. He had Miss Horn to thank, he wanted to see the schoolmaster again, and he especially had his first friend and father, Old Duncan, to find and minister

to. Not a day passed without these and many other concerns pressing upon him. Yet to set his sister free from the dangers he felt
threatened her was his first business, and that business as yet refused to be done. He was hemmed in, shut up, in stubborn circumstances from a long-reaching range of duties which called aloud
upon his conscience. What made it all the more disheartening was
that having discovered, as he hoped, how to gain his first end, his
sister's behavior to and the consequent disappearance of Lenorme
had swept the whole possibility from him, leaving him more re-
sourceless than ever.

When Sunday evening came he made his way to Hope Chapel,
as was his occasional practice, not a long walk from his lodgings,
where many Scots gathered for prayer and worship services and
the site of Mr. Graham's intermittent preaching. Walking in, he
was shown to his seat by a grimy-faced pew-opener. It was with a
mind full of varied thoughts that he sat there thinking of the past
and what would become of his future. But his thoughts would have
been stranger still had he seen who sat several pews behind him
watching him like a cat watching a mouse, or rather like a half-
grown kitten watching a rat, for she was a little frightened of him,
even while resolving to have him. And how could she doubt her
final success when her plans were already affording her so much
more than she had expected and so soon? He was large game,
however, not to be stalked without care and due foresight.

She had been seeking some means for drawing her net around
him without his knowledge for some time and had been frequent-
ing the little chapel regularly since stumbling into a service con-
ducted by Sandy Graham some weeks before. "The old heretical
schoolteacher become a preacher!" she said to herself as she sat
in the shadows of the last row. "Bless me! Will wonders never
cease? Who knows what birds may come to gather around the
scarecrow Sandy Graham?" And she laughed an oily, contemptuous laugh in the depths of her profane person.

Since then her incognito attendance had in mind the hope of
crossing Malcolm's path to subtly gain some advantage over him.
She was one to whom intrigue, founded on the knowledge of private history, was as the very breath of her being. Her one passion

was to exercise wherever she could whatever measure of control she could gain over those in high places. Her calling as a midwife had at various times in the past led her into certain relationships which afforded her this very sort of grip on unwilling lords and ladies who unknowingly sought her assistance, and the scope of influence of her profession was even now the foundation for her hoped-for advantage over Malcom and, possibly, Lady Florimel as well.

Mrs. Catanach had followed Florimel from Portlossie to Edinburgh and then to London, but not yet had seen how to approach her with probable advantage. In the meantime she had renewed old relations with a certain herb doctor in Kentish Town, at whose house she was now accommodated. Through him she had been able to acquire certain poison weeds of occult power but had, as yet, discovered no possibility of making use of them. But she bade her time, depended on the fortuitous falling of circumstances as one thread was knotted to another until all together had made a clue to guide her straight through the labyrinth to the center, to lay her hand on the collar of the demon of the House of Lossie. It was the biggest game of her life and had been its game for many long, patient years of waiting. Now, however, she sensed the time of her fulfillment drawing nigh.

When the congregation was dismissed, Malcolm saw no trace of the watchful eyes that had been glued to his back. She had slipped out noiselessly some moments before. And as he walked home, he was followed by a little boy far too young to excite suspicion, who had come with Mrs. Catanach to watch her horse. He was the grandson of her friend the herb doctor. When she learned that he was lodged so near Portland Place, she concluded that he was watching his sister and chuckled over the idea of his being watched in turn by herself.

Every day for weeks after her declaration concerning the birth of Malcolm, her evil mind had exercised itself to the utmost to invent some way of undoing her own testimony. She would have had no moral scruples in eating her words, but a magistrate and a lawyer had been present and she feared the risk. Malcolm's behavior to her after his father's death had embittered the unfriendly feelings she had cherished toward him for years. While she had believed him baseborn, and was even ignorant as to his father, she had long tried to secure power over him for the annoyance of the old blind man to whom she had committed him and whom she hated with the hatred of a wife with whom for the best of reasons he had refused to live. But she had found in the boy Malcolm a rectitude over which she could gain no influence. And it even added to her vile indignation that she regarded him as owing her gratitude for not having murdered him at the instigation of his uncle. When at length, to her endless chagrin, she had herself unwittingly supplied the only lacking link in the testimony that should raise him to rank and wealth, she imagined that she had enlarged the obligation infinitely and might henceforth hold him in her hand as a tool for her further operations. When, therefore, he banished her from Lossie House and bound her in silence, she hated him with her whole huge power of hating.

And now she must make speed. For his incognito person in a great city whose ways would still be largely unfamiliar to him afforded a thousandfold facility for doing him mischief. And first she saw that she must draw closer a certain loose tie she had already placed between herself and the household of Lady Bellair. This tie was an influence with the credulous confidence of a certain ignorant and utterly romantic scullery maid, whom she had spied coming and going from the house and had by degrees managed to make acquaintance. She gradually secured a power over her through her imagination by revealing some of the most secretive of disclosures. Among her other favors she had promised to compound for her a mixture—some of whose disgusting ingredients, as potent as hard to procure, she named in her awe-stricken hearing—which when administered under certain conditions and with certain precautions would infallibly secure for her the affections of any man she desired.

This same girl the cat lady now sought and from her learned all she knew about Malcolm, for which Mrs. Catanach supplied a new portion of the love potion—only slightly altered—with some further instructions on its use. Pursuing her inquiries into the composition of the household, however, Mrs. Catanach soon discovered a far more capable and indeed less-scrupulous associate and instrument in Caley. I will not introduce my reader to any of their evil counsels except to say that Mrs. Catanach assumed and retained the upper hand and gathered from Caley much valuable information for her schemes. Doubtless she saw that the very similarity of their designs must cause an eventual rupture between herself and Caley. For neither could expect the other to endure such a rival near her hidden throne of influence. For the aim of both was power in a great family, with consequent money and consideration and midnight counsels and the wielding of all the weapons of hint and threat and insinuation. There was one difference, indeed, since in Caley's eye money was the chief thing, while raw power itself was the midwife's bliss.

13   The Lady

Florimel and Lady Clementina Thornicroft—the same who in the park rebuked Malcolm for his treatment of Kelpie—had met several times during the spring and had been mutually attracted. Left an orphan like Florimel, but at yet an earlier age, Lady Clementina had been brought up with a care that had gone over into severity, against which her nature had revolted with an energy that gathered strength from her own repression of its signs. The lack of discipline in her goodness came out at times amusingly; she would always side at first with the lower or weaker or worse. If a dog had torn a child and was going to be killed in consequence, she would not only intercede for the dog, but absolutely side with him, mentioning that and that provocation which the naughty child must have given him ere he could have been goaded to the deed. Once, when the schoolmaster in her village was going to cane a boy for cruelty to a cripple, she pleaded for his pardon on the ground that it was worse to be cruel than to be a cripple and therefore more to be pitied. Everything painful was, to her, cruel.

Lady Clementina was drawn to the young marchioness, over whom was cast the shadow of a tree that gave but baneful shelter. She liked her frankness, her activity, her daring, and fancied that, like herself, she was at noble feud with that infernal parody of the kingdom of heaven called Society. She did not well understand her relation to Lady Bellair, concerning whom she was in doubt whether or not she was her legal guardian, but she saw plainly enough that the countess wanted to secure her for her nephew. She saw too that, being a mere girl and having no scope of choice in the limited circle of their visitors, she was in great danger of yielding without a struggle. She longed to take Florimel in charge like a poor little persecuted kitten, for the possession of which each of a family of children was contending. What if her father had belonged to a rowdy set, was that any reason why his innocent daughter should be devoured, body and soul and possessions, by those of the same set who had not yet perished in their sins?

With her passion for redemption, therefore, she seized every chance of improving her acquaintance with Florimel; and it was her anxiety to gain such a standing in her favor as might further her coveted ministration that had prevented her from bringing her charge of brutality against Malcolm as soon as she discovered whose groom he was. When she had secured her footing on the peak of her friendship, she would unburden her soul, and meantime the horse must suffer for her mistress.

Happily for Florimel, she had by this time made progress enough to venture a proposal that Florimel should accompany her to a small estate she had on the south coast, with a little ancient house upon it—a strange place altogether, she said—to spend a week or two in absolute quiet. Only she must come alone, without even a maid; she would take none herself. This she said because, with the instinct, if not quite insight, of a true nature, she could not endure the woman Caley.

"Will you come with me there for a fortnight?" concluded Clementina.

"I shall be delighted," returned Florimel without a moment's hesitation. "I am getting quite sick of London. There's no room in it. And there's the spring all outside, and it can't get in here. I shall be only too glad to go with you!"

"And on those hard terms—no maid, you know?" insisted Clementina.

"The only thing wanted to make the pleasure complete. I shall be happy to be rid of her."

"I am glad to see you so independent."

"You don't imagine me such a baby as not to be able to get on without a maid! You should have seen me in Scotland! I hated having a woman about me then. And indeed, I don't like it a bit better now. Only everybody has one, and your clothes need looking after," added Florimel, thinking what a weight it would be off her if she could get rid of Caley altogether. "But I *should* like to take my horse," she said. "I don't know what I should do in the country without Abbot."

"Of course, we must have our horses," returned Clementina. "And, yes, you had better bring your groom."

"Oh, you will find him very useful. He can do anything and everything and is so kind and helpful."

"Except to his horse," Clementina was on the point of saying, but thought again. She would first secure the mistress and bide her time to attack the man.

Before they had parted, the two ladies had talked themselves into ecstasies over the anticipated enjoyments of their scheme. It must be carried out at once.

"Let us tell nobody," said Lady Clementina, "and set off tomorrow."

"Enchanting!" cried Florimel in full response.

Then her brow clouded. "There is one difficulty, though," she said. "No man could ride Kelpie with a led horse, and if we had to employ another, Liftore would be sure to hear where we had gone."

"That would spoil all," said Clementina. "But how much better it would be to give that poor creature a rest and bring the other I see him on sometimes."

"And by the time we came back there would not be a living creature, horse or man, anything bigger than a rat, about the stable. Kelpie herself would de dead of hunger, if she hadn't been shot. No, no. Where Malcolm goes Kelpie must go. Besides, she's such fun—you can't think."

"Then I'll tell you what," said Clementina after a moment's pause of perplexity: "we'll *ride* down. It's not a hundred miles, and we can take as many days on the road as we please."

"Better and better!" cried Florimel. "We'll run away with each other. But what will dear old Bellair say?"

"Never mind her," rejoined Clementina. "She will have nothing to say. You can write and tell her as much as will keep her from being really alarmed. Order your man to get everything ready, and I will instruct mine. He is such a staid old fellow, you know, he will be quite enough for protection. Tomorrow morning we will set out together for a ride in Richmond Park, that lying in our way. You can leave a letter on the breakfast table, saying you are gone with me for a while."

So the thing was arranged. They would start quite early the next morning and, that there might be no trouble in the streets, Malcolm should go before with Kelpie and await them in the park.

Malcolm was overjoyed at the prospect of an escape to the country, and yet more to find that his mistress wanted to have him with her—more still to understand that the journey was to be kept a secret. Perhaps now, far from both Caley and Liftore, he might say something to open her eyes; yet how should he avoid the appearance of a talebearer?

It was a sweet, fresh morning late in the spring. He had set out an hour before the rest and now a little way within the park, was coaxing Kelpie to stand, that he might taste the morning in peace. As he thought, he realized how sorely he missed the adventure of the herring fishing. Kelpie, however, was as good as a stiff gale. If only all were well with his sister! Then he would go back to Portlossie and have fishing enough. But he must be patient and follow as he was led. By the time the two ladies with their attendant appeared, he felt such a masterdom over Kelpie as he had never felt before. They rode twenty miles that day with ease, putting up at the first town. The next day they rode about the same distance. The next they rode nearly thirty miles. On the fourth, with an early start and a good rest in the middle, they accomplished a yet greater distance, and at night arrived at Wastbeach.

Florimel scarcely cast a glance around the dark old-fashioned room into which she was shown, but went at once to bed, and when the old housekeeper carried her something from the supper table at which she had been expected, she found her already fast asleep. By the time Malcolm had put Kelpie to rest, he also was a little tired and lay awake no moment longer than his sister.

14   The Horse

With rats and mice, cats and owls and creaks and cracks, there was no quiet about the place from night to morning; and with swallows and rooks, cocks and kine, horses and foals, dogs and pigeons, turkeys and geese, and every farm creature but pigs—which, with all her zootrophy, Clementina did not like—no quiet from morning to night. But if there was no quiet, there was plenty of calm, and the sleep of neither brother nor sister was disturbed.

When Florimel awoke, the sun was shining into the room by a window far off at the farther end. It must have been shining for hours, so bright and steady did it shine. She sprang out of bed refreshed and strong. A few aching remnants of stiffness was all that was left of the old fatigue. It was a heavenly joy to think that no Caley would come knocking at her door. She glided down the long room to the sunny window, drew aside the rich old faded curtain, and peeped out. Nothing but pines and Scotch firs all about and everywhere. They came within a few yards of the window. She threw it open. The air was still, the morning sun shone hot upon them and the resinous odor exhaled from their bark and their needles and their fresh buds filled the room—sweet and clean. There was nothing, not even a fence, between this wing of the house and the wood.

All through his deep sleep Malcolm heard the sound of the sea—whether of the phantom sea in his soul or of the world sea to whose murmurs he had listened with such soft delight as he fell asleep, matters little. The sea was with him in his dreams. But when he awoke, it was to no musical crushing of waterdrops, no half-articulated tones of animal speech, but to tumult and outcry from the stables. It was but too plain that he was wanted. Either Kelpie had waked too soon, or he had overslept himself; she was kicking furiously. Hurriedly induing a portion of his clothing, he rushed down and across the yard, shouting to her as he ran, like a nurse as she runs up the stairs to a screaming child. She stopped once to give an eager whinny and then fell to again. Griffith, the groom, and the few other men about the place were looking on appalled. He darted to the cornbin, got a great pottleful of oats, and shot into her stall. She buried her nose in them like the very demon of hunger, and he left her for the few moments of peace that would follow. He must finish dressing as fast as he could. Already, after four days of travel, which with her meant anything but a straightforward jogtrot struggle with space, she needed a good gallop. When he returned he found her just finishing her oats and beginning to grow angry with her own nose for getting so near the bottom of the manager. While there was yet no worse sign, however, than the fidgeting of her hindquarters, and she was still busy, he made haste to saddle her. But her unusually obstinate refusal of the bit and his difficulty in making her open her unwilling jaws gave unmistakable indication of coming difficulty. Anxiously he asked the bystanders about some open place where he might let her go—fields or tolerably smooth heath or sandy beach. He dared not take her through the trees, he said, while she was in such a humor: she would dash herself to pieces. They told him there was a road straight from the stables to the shore and there miles of pure sand without a pebble. Nothing could be better. He mounted and rode away.

Florimel was yet but half dressed when the door of her room opened suddenly and Lady Clementina darted in. With a glide like the swoop of an avenging angel, she pounced upon Florimel, caught her by the wrist, and pulled her toward the door. Florimel was startled, but made no resistance. She half led, half dragged her up a stair that rose from a corner of the hall gallery to the battlements of a little square tower, whence a few yards of the beach, through a chain of slight openings amongst the pines, was visible. Upon that spot of beach a strange thing was going on, at which afresh Clementina gazed with indignant horror.

There was Kelpie rearing on end, striking out at Malcolm with her forehoofs, and snapping with angry teeth, then upon those teeth receiving such a blow from his fist that she swerved and, wheeling, flung her hind hoofs at his head. But Malcolm was too quick for her; she spent her heels in the air and he had her by the bit. Again she reared, and would have struck at him, but he kept well by her side and with the powerful bit forced her to rear to her full height. Just as she was falling backward, he pushed her head from him and, bearing her down sideways, seated himself on it the moment it touched the ground. Then first the two women turned to each other. An arch of victory bowed Florimel's lip. Her eyebrows were uplifted; the blood flushed her cheek and darkened the blue in her wide-opened eyes. Lady Clementina's forehead was gathered in vertical wrinkles over her nose, her eyes were contracted, while her teeth and lips were firmly closed. When Clementina's gaze fell upon her visitor, the fire in her eyes burned more angry still. Her soul was stirred by the presence of wrong and cruelty, and here, her guest, and looking her straight in the eyes, was a young woman—one word from whom would stop it all—actually enjoying the sight!

"Lady Lossie, I am ashamed of you!" she said with reproof, and turning from her, she ran down the stairs.

Florimel turned again toward the sea. Presently she caught sight of Clementina as she sped swiftly to the shore and after a few short minutes of disappearance saw her emerge upon the space of sand where sat Malcolm on the head of the demoness.

"MacPhail, are you a man?" cried Clementina, startling him so that in another instant the floundering mare would have been on her feet.

"I hope so, and a bold one," was on Malcolm's lips for reply, but he bethought himself in time. "I am sorry that what I am compelled to do should annoy your ladyship," he said.

With indignation and breathlessness—she had run so fast—Clementina had exhausted herself in that one exclamation and stood panting and staring. The black bulk of Kelpie lay outstretched on the yellow sand, giving now and then a sprawling kick.

As Malcolm spoke he cautiously shifted his position and, half rising, knelt with one knee where he had sat before, looking observantly at Lady Clementina.

The champion of oppressed animality soon recovered speech. "Get off the poor creature's head instantly," she said with dignified command. "I will permit no such usage of a living thing on my ground."

"I am very sorry to seem rude, my lady," answered Malcolm, "but to obey you might be to ruin my mistress' property. If the mare were to break away, she would dash herself to pieces in the wood."

"You have goaded her to madness."

"I am the more bound to take care of her, then," said Malcolm. "But indeed it is only temper—such temper, however, that I almost believe she is at times possessed of a demon."

"The demon is in yourself. There is none in her but what your cruelty has put there. Let her up, I command you."

"I dare not, my lady. If she were to get loose, she would tear your ladyship to pieces."

"I will take my chance."

"But I will not, my lady. I know the danger and have to take care of you who do not. There is no occasion to be uneasy about the mare. She is tolerably comfortable. I am not hurting her—not much. Your ladyship does not reflect how strong a horse's skull is. And you see what great powerful breaths she draws."

"She is in agony!" cried Clementina.

"Not in the least, my lady. She is only balked of her own way and does not like it."

"And what right have you to balk her of her own way? Has she no right to a mind of her own?"

"She may of course have her mind, but she can't have her way. She has got a master."

"And what right have you to be her master?"

"That my master, my Lord Lossie, gave me charge of her."

"I don't mean that sort of right. That goes for nothing. What right in the nature of things can you have to tyrannize over any creature?"

"None, my lady. But the higher nature has the right to rule the lower in righteousness. Even you can't have your own way always, my lady."

"I certainly cannot now, so long as you keep in that position. Pray, is it in virtue of your being the higher nature that you keep *my* way from *me*?"

"No, my lady. But it is in virtue of right. If I wanted to take your ladyship's property, your dogs would be justified in refusing me my way. I do not think I exaggerate when I say that if my mare here had *her* way, there would not be a living creature about your house by this day next week."

Lady Clementina had never yet felt upon her the power of a stronger nature than her own. She had had to yield to authority, but never to superiority. Hence her self-will had been abnormally developed. Her very compassion was self-willed. Now for the first time, she continuing altogether unaware of it, the presence of such a nature began to operate upon her. The calmness of Malcolm's speech and the immovable decision of his behavior told.

"But," she said, more calmly, "your mare has had four long journeys, and she should have rested today."

"Rest is just the one thing beyond her, my lady. There is a volcano of life and strength in her you have no conception of. I could not have dreamed of a horse like her. She has never in her life had enough to do. I believe that is the chief trouble with her. What we all want, my lady, is a master—a real, right master. I've got one myself, and—"

"You mean you want one yourself," said Lady Clementina. "You've only got a mistress, and she spoils you."

"That is not what I meant, my lady," returned Malcolm. "But one thing I know is that Kelpie would soon come to grief without me. I shall keep her here till her half hour is out and then let her take another gallop."

Lady Clementina turned away. She was defeated. Malcolm knelt there on one knee, with a hand on the mare's shoulder, so calm, so imperturbable, so ridiculously full of argument, that there was nothing more for her to do or say. Indignation, expostulation, were powerless upon him as mist upon a rock. He was the oddest, most incomprehensible of grooms.

Going back to the house, she met Florimel and turned again with her to the scene of discipline. Ere they reached it Florimel's delight with all around her had done something to restore Clementina's composure. The place was precious to her, for there she had passed nearly the whole of her childhood. After a moment Clementina interrupted Florimel's ecstasies by breaking out in fresh accusation of Malcolm, not untempered, however, with a touch of dawning respect. At the same time, her report of his words was anything but accurate, for, as no one can be just without love, so no one can truly report without understanding. But there was no time to discuss him now, as Clementina insisted on Florimel's putting an immediate stop to his cruelty.

When they reached the spot, there was the groom again seated on his animal's head. "Malcolm," said his mistress, "let the mare get up. You must let her off the rest of her punishment this time."

Malcolm rose again to his knee. "Yes, my lady," he said. "But perhaps your ladyship wouldn't mind helping me to unbuckle her girths before she gets to her feet. I want to give her a bath. Come to this side," he went on, as Florimel advanced to do his request, "round here by her head. If your ladyship would kneel upon it, that would be best. But you mustn't move till I tell you."

"I will do anything you bid me, exactly as you say, Malcolm," responded Florimel.

"There's the Colonsay blood! I can trust that!" cried Malcolm, with a pardonable outbreak of pride in his family.

Clementina was shocked at the insolent familiarity of her poor little friend's groom, but Florimel saw none and kneeled, as if she had been in church, on the head of the mare, with the fierce crater of her fiery brain blazing at her knee. Then Malcolm lifted the flap of the saddle, undid the buckles of the girths and, drawing them a little from under her, laid the saddle on the sand, talking all the time to Florimel lest a sudden word might seem a direction and she should rise before the right moment had come.

"Please, my Lady Clementina, will you go to the edge of the wood? I can't tell what she may do when she gets up. And please, my Lady Florimel, will you run there, too, the moment you get off her head?"

When he had gotten rid of the saddle, he gathered the reins together in his bridle-hand, took his whip in the other, and softly and carefully straddled across her huge barrel without touching her.

"Now, my lady," he said, "run for the wood."

Florimel rose and fled, heard a great scrambling behind her and, turning at the first tree which was only a few yards off, saw Malcolm, whom the mare had lifted with her, sticking by his knees on her bare back. The moment her forefeet touched the ground he gave her the spur severely and after one plunging kick, off they went westward over the sands, away from the sun, nor did they turn before they had dwindled to such a speck that the ladies could not have told by their eyes whether it was moving or not. At length they saw it swerve a little. By and by it began to grow larger, and after another moment or two they could distinguish what it was, tearing along toward them like a whirlwind, the lumps of wet sand flying behind like an upward storm of clods. What a picture it was!

As he came in front of them, Malcolm suddenly wheeled Kelpie and dashed her straight into the sea. The two ladies gave a cry—Florimel of delight, Clementina of dismay, for she knew the coast, and that there it shelved suddenly into deep water. But that was only the better to Malcolm; it was the deep water he sought, though he got it with a little pitch sooner than he expected. He had often ridden Kelpie into the sea at Portlossie, even in the cold autumn weather when first she came into his charge, and nothing pleased her better or quieted her more. He was a heavy weight to swim with, but she displaced much water. She carried her head bravely, he balanced sideways, and they swam splendidly. To the eyes of Clementina the mare seemed to be laboring for her life.

When Malcolm thought she had had enough of it, he turned her head to the shore. But then came the difficulty. So steeply did the shore shelve that Kelpie could not get a hold with her hind hoofs to scramble up into the shallow water. The ladies saw the struggle, and Clementina, understanding it, was running in an agony right into the water with the vain idea of helping them. Malcolm threw himself off, drawing the reins over Kelpie's head as he fell and, swimming but the length of them shoreward, felt the ground with his feet and stood. Kelpie, relieved of his weight, floated a little farther on to the shelf, got a better hold with her forefeet, some hold with her hind ones, and was beside him in a moment. The same moment Malcolm was on her back again, and they were tearing off eastward at full stretch. So far did the lessening point recede in the narrowing distance that the two ladies sat down on the sand and started talking about Florimel's more uncategorical groom, as Clementina, herself the most uncategorical of women, to use her own scarcely justifiable epithet, called him. She asked if such persons abounded in Scotland. Florimel could but answer that this was the only one she had met with.

"It's a pity he is such a savage. He might be quite an interesting character. Can he read?"

"He reads Greek," said Florimel.

"Ah, but I meant English," returned Clementina, whose thoughts were a little astray. Then laughing at herself, she explained: "I mean, can he read aloud? I put the last of the Waverly novels in the box I had sent here. We shall have it tomorrow, or the next day at the latest. I was wondering whether he could read the Scotch as it ought to be read. I have never heard it spoken, and I don't know how to imagine it."

"We can try him," said Florimel. "It will be great fun anyhow. He is *such* a character! You will be *so* amused with the remarks he will make!"

"But can you venture to let him talk to you?"

"If you ask him to read, how will you prevent him? Unfortunately, he has his thoughts, and they *will* come out."

"Is there no danger of his being rude?"

"If speaking his mind about anything in the book be rudeness, he will most likely be rude. Any other kind of rudeness is as impossible to Malcolm as to any gentleman in the land."

"How can you be so sure of him?" said Clementina, a little anxious as to the way in which her friend regarded the young man.

"My father was—yes, I may say so—attached to him; so much so that he—I can't quite say what—but something like made him promise never to leave my service. And this I know for myself that not once, ever since that man came to us, has he done a selfish thing or one to be ashamed of. I could give you proof after proof of his devotion."

Florimel's warmth did not reassure Clementina. She was never quite so generous toward human beings as toward animals. "I would not have you place too much confidence in him, Florimel," she said. "There is something about him I cannot get at the bottom of. Depend upon it, a man who can be cruel would betray on the least provocation."

Florimel smiled, as she had good reason to, but Clementina did not understand the smile and therefore did not like it. She feared the young fellow had already gained too much influence over his mistress. "Florimel, my love," she said, "listen to me. Your experience is not so ripe as mine. That man is not what you think him. One day or other he will, I fear, make himself worse than disagreeable. How *can* a cruel man be unselfish?"

"I don't think him cruel at all. But then I haven't such a soft heart for animals as you. We should think it silly in Scotland. You wouldn't teach a dog manners at the expense of a howl. You would let him be a nuisance rather than give him a cut with a whip. What a nice mother of children you will make, Clementina! That's how the children of good people are so often a disgrace to them."

"You are like all the rest of the Scotch I ever knew," said Lady Clementina. "The Scotch are always preaching. I believe it is in their blood. You are a nation of parsons. Thank goodness my morals go no further than doing as I would be done by! I want to see creatures happy about me."

Malcolm was pulling up his mare some hundred yards off. Even now she was unwilling to stop, but it was at last only from pure objection to whatever was wanted of her. When she did stand she stood stock-still, breathing hard. "I have actually succeeded in taking a little out of her at last, my lady," said Malcolm as he dismounted. "Have you got a bit of sugar in your pocket, my lady? She would take it quite gently now."

Florimel had none, but Clementina had, for she always carried sugar for her horse. Malcolm held the demoness very watchfully, but she took the sugar from Florimel's palm as neatly as an elephant and let her stroke her nose over her wide red nostrils without showing the least of her usual inclination to punish a liberty with death. Then Malcolm rode her home, and she was at peace till evening, when he took her out again.

15 The Reading

And now followed a pleasant time. Wastbeach was the quietest of neighborhoods. It was the loveliest of spring-summer weather, and the variety of scenery on moor, in woodland and on the coast within easy reach of such good horsewomen was wonderful. The first day they rested the horses that would rest, but the next they were in the saddle immediately after an early breakfast. They took the forest way. In many directions were tolerably smooth rides. Malcolm, so far as human companionship went, found it dull, for Lady Clementina's groom regarded him with the contempt of superior age—the most contemptible contempt of all, since years are not the wisdom they ought to bring, and the first sign of that is modesty. Again and again his remarks tempted Malcolm to incite him to ride Kelpie. But conscience, the thought of the man's family, and the remembrance that Kelpie required all his youthful strength, schooled him to the endurance of middle-aged arrogance.

When his mistress mentioned the proposal of her friend with regard to the new novel, he at once expressed his willingness to attempt compliance, fearing only, he said, that his English would prove offensive and his Scotch unintelligible. The task was nowise alarming to him, for he had read aloud much to the schoolmaster, who had insisted that he should read aloud when alone, especially verse, in order that he might get all the good of its outside as well as inside—its sound as well as its thought. On the whole they were so much pleased with his first day's reading, which took place the very day the box arrived, that they concluded to have him read to them daily while they busied their fingers with their embroidery.

There was not much of a garden about the place, but there was a little lawn amongst the pines, in the midst of which stood a huge old patriarch with red stem and grotesquely contorted branches. Beneath it was a bench, and there, after their return from their two hours' ride, the ladies sat, while the sun was at its warmest, on the mornings of their first and second readings. Malcolm sat on a wheelbarrow. On the second day they resolved to send for their reader again as soon as they had tea. But when they sent, he was nowhere to be found, and they concluded on a stroll.

Anticipating no further requirement of his service that day, Malcolm had gone out. Drawn by the sea, he took his way through the dim, solemn, boughless wood, as if to keep a moonlight tryst with his early love. As dusk fell he wandered along the sand, far down the shore and back, and then began to sing an old Scotch ballad.

Ever as he halted for a word the moonlight and the low waves on the sand filled up the pauses. He looked up to the sky, at the moon and rose-diamond stars, his thought half dissolved in feeling and his feeling half crystallized to thought.

Out of the dim wood came two lovely forms into the moonlight and softly approached him—so softly that he knew nothing of their nearness until Florimel spoke. "Is that you, MacPhail?" she said.

"Yes, my lady," answered Malcolm.

"What were you singing?"

"You could hardly call it singing, my lady. We should call it crooning in Scotland."

"Croon it again, then."

"I couldn't, my lady. It's gone."

"You don't mean to pretend that you were extemporizing?"

"I was crooning what came like the birds, my lady. I couldn't have done it if I had thought anyone was near." Then, half ashamed, and anxious to turn the talk from the threshold of his secret chamber, he said, "Did you ever see a lovelier night, ladies?"

"Not often, certainly," answered Clementina.

She was not quite pleased and not altogether offended at his addressing them dually. A curious sense of impropriety in the state of things bewildered her—she and her friend talking thus in the moonlight on the seashore, doing nothing, with her groom—and such a groom!—she asking him to sing again and he addressing them both with a remark on the beauty of the night. Yet all the time she had a doubt whether this young man, whom it would certainly be improper to encourage by addressing from any level but one of lofty superiority, did not belong to a higher sphere than theirs; while certainly no man could be more unpresuming or less forward, even when opposing this opinion to theirs.

"This is just the sort of night," Malcolm resumed, "when I could almost persuade myself I was not quite sure I wasn't dreaming. It makes a kind of borderland between waking and sleeping, knowing and dreaming. In a night like this I fancy we feel something like the color of what God feels when He is making the lovely chaos of a new world—a new kind of world such as has never been before."

"I think we had better go in," said Clementina to Florimel and turned away.

Florimel made no objection, and they walked toward the wood.

"You really must get rid of him as soon as you can," said Clementina when again the moonless night of the pines had received them. "He is certainly more than half a lunatic. It is almost full moon now," she added, looking up. "I have never seen him so bad."

Florimel's clear laugh rang through the wood. "Don't be alarmed, Clementina," she said. "He has talked like that ever since I knew him; and if he is mad, at least he is no worse than he has always been. It is nothing but poetry—yeast on the brain, my father used to say. We should have a fish-poet of him—a new thing in the world, he said. He would never be cured till he broke out in a book of poetry. I should be afraid my father would break the catechism and not rest in his grave till the resurrection if I were to send Malcolm away."

For Malcolm, he was at first not a little amazed at the utter blankness of the wall against which his words had dashed themselves. Then he smiled queerly to himself and said, "I used to think every pretty lady was bound to be a poetess, for how else would she be pretty except for the harmony within her being? And what's that but the poetry of *the* Poet. But I know better than that now. For there go two of the prettiest I've ever seen, but there's more poetry in old man-faced Miss Horn than a dozen like them. Has anybody ever seen a sight so grand as my Lady Clementina? But to hear the nonsense that comes out of her. And all because she won't let her heart rest long enough to let it grow bigger but has always got to be setting things right before their time and before she's even fit for the job!"

Florimel succeeded so far in reassuring her friend as to the safety if not the sanity of her groom that she made no objection to yet another reading from the novel, upon which occasion an incident occurred that did far more to reassure her than all the attestations of his mistress.

Clementina, in consenting, had proposed it being a warm, sunny afternoon, that they should go down to the lake and sit with their work on the bank while Malcolm read. More than a mile in length, but quite narrow, it lay on the seashore—a lake of deep, fresh water, with nothing between it and the sea but a bank of sand. Clementina was describing to Florimel the peculiarities of the place: how there was no outlet to the lake, how the water went filtering through the sand into the sea, how in some parts it was very deep and what large pike there was in it. Malcolm sat a little aside, as usual, with his face toward the ladies and the book open in his hand, waiting a sign to begin. He was looking at the lake, which here was some fifty yards broad, reedy at the edge, dark and deep in the center.

All at once he sprang to his feet, dropped the book, ran down to the brink of the water undoing his buckled belt and pulling off his coast as he ran, threw himself over the bordering reeds into the pool, and disappeared with a great splash. Clementina gave a scream. She had no doubt that in the sudden ripeness of his insanity, he had committed suicide. But Florimel, though startled by her friend's cry, laughed and cried out assurances that Malcolm knew well enough what he was about. It was longer, however, than even she found pleasant before a black head appeared—yards away, for he had risen at great slope, swimming toward the other side. What *could* he be after? Near the middle he swam more softly and almost stopped. Then first they spied a small dark object on the surface. Almost at the same moment it rose into the air. They thought Malcolm had flung it up. Instantly they perceived that it was a bird, a swift. Somehow it had dropped into the water, but a lift from Malcolm's hand had restored it to the air of its bliss.

But instead of turning and swimming back, Malcolm held on and, getting out on the farther side, ran down the beach and rushed into the sea, rousing once more the apprehensions of Clementina. The shore slopped rapidly, and in a moment he was in deep water. He swam a few yards out, swam ashore again, ran round the end of the lake, found his coat and got from it his pocket handkerchief. Having therewith dried his hands and face, he wrung out the sleeves of his shirt a little, put on his coat, returned to his place, and said as he took up the book and sat down, "I beg your pardon, my ladies, but just as I heard my Lady Clementina say '*pikes*,' I saw the little swift in the water. There was no time to lose; Swiftie had but a poor chance." As he spoke he proceeded to find the place in the book.

"You don't imagine we are going to have you read in such a plight as that? cried Clementina.

"I will take good care, my lady. I have books of my own, and I handle them like babies."

"You foolish man! It is of you in your wet clothes, not of the book, I am thinking," said Clementina indignantly.

"I'm much obliged to you, my lady, but there's no fear of me. You saw me wash the fresh water out. Salt water never hurts.

"You must go and change, nevertheless," said Clementina.

Malcolm looked to his mistress. She gave him a sign to obey and he rose. He had taken three steps toward the house when Clementina recalled him. "One word, if you please," she said. "How is it that a man who risks his life for that of a little bird can be so heartless to a great noble creature like that horse of yours? I cannot understand it."

"My lady," returned Malcolm with a smile, "I was no more risking my life than you would be in taking a fly out of the milk jug. And for your question, if your ladyship will only think you cannot fail to see the difference. Indeed, I explained my treatment of Kelpie to your ladyship that first morning in the park, when you so kindly rebuked me for it, but I don't think your ladyship listened to a word I said."

Clementina's face flushed, and she turned to her friend with a "Well!" in her eyes. But Florimel kept her head bent over her embroidery, and Malcolm, no further notice being taken of him, walked away.

16   The Discussion

The next day the reading was resumed and for several days was regularly continued. Each day, as their interest grew, longer and longer time was devoted to it. A question of morals began to arise in Malcolm's mind and finally he paused a moment and said, "Do you think it was right, my ladies, for the hero here to lay down his wealth on behalf of the lady?"

"It was most generous of him," said Clementina.

"Splendidly generous," replied Malcolm, "but I so well remember when Mr. Graham first made me see that the question of duty does not always lie between a good thing and a bad thing. A man has very often to decide between one good thing and another."

"What are the two good things here to choose between?" asked Clementina.

"That is the right question and logically put, my lady," rejoined Malcolm. "The two things are—let me see—on one hand the protection of my lady, and on the other what he owed to his tenants and perhaps society in general. There is generosity on the one side and dry duty on the other." Naturally, by this point, Malcolm's personal interest in the story and discussion was excited—here were elements strangely correspondent with the circumstances of his present position.

"But," said Lady Clementina, "is not generosity something more than duty—something higher, something beyond it?"

"Yes," answered Malcolm, "so long as it does not go against duty, but keeps in the same direction—is in harmony with it. I imagine as we grow we shall come to see that generosity is but our duty. The man who chooses generosity at the expense of justice, even if he gives up everything of his own, is nothing beside the man who for the sake of right will even appear selfish in the eyes of men and may even, at times, go against his own heart. How two men may look—from the outside—is nothing."

Florimel made a neat little yawn over her work. Clementina's hands rested a moment in her lap, and she looked thoughtful. "Then you are taking the side of duty against generosity?" she said after a moment.

"Think, my lady," said Malcolm. "The essence of wrong is injustice. To help another by wrong is to do injustice to somebody else. What honest man could think of that twice?"

"Might not what he did be wrong in the abstract, without having reference to any person?"

"There is no wrong man can do but against the living Right. Surely you believe, my lady, that there is a living Power of right, who *will* have right done?"

"In plain language, I suppose you mean, do I believe in a God?"

"That is what I mean, if by a God you mean a being who cares about us and loves justice—that is, fair play—one whom, therefore, we wrong to the very heart when we do a thing that is not just."

"I would gladly believe in such a being if things were so that I could. As they are, I confess it seems to be the best thing to doubt it. How can I help doubting it when I see so much suffering, oppression, and cruelty in the world?"

"I used to find that a difficulty. Indeed, it troubled me sorely until Mr. Graham helped me see that ease and prosperity and comfort—indeed, the absence of those things you mentioned—are far from what God intends us to have. What if these things, or the lack of them, should be but the means of our gaining something in its very nature so much better that—"

"But why should a being have to suffer for that 'something better' you speak of? What kind of a God would make that 'the means' for our betterment? Your theory is so frightful!"

"But suppose He knows that the barest beginnings of the good He intends would reconcile us to those difficult means and even cause us to choose His will at any expense of suffering?"

Clementina said nothing for a moment. Religious people, she found, could think as boldly as she.

"I tell you, Lady Clementina," said Malcolm, rising and approaching her a step or two, "if I had not the hope of one day being good like God himself, if I thought there was no escape out of the wrong and badness I feel within me, not all the wealth and honors of the world could reconcile me to life."

"I have read of saints," said Clementina with yet a cool dissatisfaction in her tone, "uttering such sentiments, and I do not doubt such were imagined by them. But I fail to understand how, even supposing these things true, a young man like yourself should, in the midst of a busy world and with an occupation which, to say the least . . ."

Here she paused. After a moment Malcolm ventured to help her: "Is so far from an ideal one, would you say, my lady?"

"Something like that," answered Clementina and concluded, "I wonder how *you* can have arrived at such ideas."

"There is nothing so unusual about it, my lady," returned Malcolm. "Why should not a youth, a boy, a child desire with all his might that his heart and mind should be clean, his will strong, his thoughts just, his head clear, his soul dwelling in the place of life? Why should I not desire that my life should be a complete thing and an outgoing of life to my neighbor?"

"Still, how did you come to begin so much earlier than others?"

"All I know, my lady, is that I had the best man in the world to teach me."

"And why did not I have such a man to teach me? I could have learned of such, too."

"If you are able now, my lady, it does not follow that it would have been the best thing for you sooner. Some learn far better for not having begun early and will get on faster than others who have been at it for years. As you grow ready for it, somewhere or other you will find what is needful for you in a book or a friend, or best of all, in your own thoughts."

"But I still want you to explain to me how the God in whom you profess to believe can make use of such cruelties?"

"My lady," remonstrated Malcolm, "I never pretended to explain. All I say is that if I had reasons for hoping there was a God and I found from my observations of life that suffering often was able to lead to a valued good, then there would be nothing unreasonable about His using suffering for the highest, purest, and kindest of motives. If a man would lay claim to being a lover of truth, he ought to give the idea—the mere idea—of God fair play, lest there should be a good God after all and he all his life doing Him the injustice of refusing Him his trust and obedience."

"And how are we to give the mere idea of Him fair play?" asked Clementina, by this time fighting with her emotions, confused and troublesome.

"By looking at the heart of whatever claims to be a revelation of Him."

"It would take a lifetime to read the half of such."

All this time Florimel was working away at her embroidery, a little smile of satisfaction flickering on her face. She was pleased to hear her clever friend talking so with her strange vassal. As to what they were saying, she had no idea. Probably it was all right, but to her it was not interesting. She was mildly debating with herself whether she should tell her friend about Lenorme.

Clementina's work now lay on her lap and her hands on her work, while her eyes at one time gazed on the grass at her feet, at another searching Malcolm's face with a troubled look. The light of Malcolm's candle was beginning to penetrate into her dusky room, the power of his faith to tell upon the weakness of her unbelief. For there is no strength in unbelief.

But whatever the nature of Malcolm's influence upon Lady Clementina, she resented it. Something in her did not like him, or was it his confidence. She knew he did not approve of her, and she did not like being disapproved of. Neither did she approve of him. He was far too good for an honest and brave youth. Not that she could say she had seen dishonesty or cowardice in him, or that she could have told which vice she would prefer to season his goodness and thus bring him to the level of her ideal. And then, for all her theories of equality, he was a groom! Therefore, to a lady, he ought to be repulsive, at least when she found him intruding into the chamber of her thoughts!

For a time her eyes had been fixed on her work, and there had been silence in the little group.

"My lady," said Malcolm, and drew a step nearer to Clementina.

She looked up. How lovely she was with the trouble in her eyes! "If only she were what she might be!" he thought. "If the form were but filled with the Spirit, the body with life!"

"My lady," he repeated, a little embarrassed, "I fear you will never arrive at an understanding of God so long as you cannot bring yourself to see the good that often comes as a result of pain. For there is nothing, from the lowest, weakest tone of suffering to the loftiest acme of pain, to which God does not respond. There is nothing in all the universe which does not in some way vibrate within the heart of God. No creature suffers alone; He suffers with His creatures and through it is in the process of bringing His sons and daughters through the cleansing and glorifying fires, without which the created cannot be made the very children of God, partakers of the divine nature and peace."

"I cannot bring myself to see the right of it."

"Nor will you, my lady, so long as you cannot bring yourself to the good they get by it. My lady, when I was trying my best with poor Kelpie, you would not listen to me."

"You are ungenerous," said Clementina, flushing.

"My lady," persisted Malcolm, "you would not understand me.

120

You denied me a heart because of what seemed in your eyes cruelty. I knew I was saving her from death at the least, probably from a life of torture. There is but one way God cares to govern—the way of the Father-King. Poor parable though it be, my relation to Kelpie must somehow parallel God's dealing with us. The temporary suffering is for a greater good."

After a few moments of silence, Clementina took up her work. Malcolm walked slowly away.

After his departure, Clementina attempted to find what Florimel thought of the things her strange groom had been saying. But she had not thought about them nor had a single notion concerning the matter of their conversation. Seeking to interest her in it and failing, she found, however, that she had greatly deepened its impression upon herself.

Florimel had not yet quite made up her mind whether or not she should open her heart to Clementina, but she approached the door of it in requesting her opinion upon the matter of marriage between persons of social conditions widely parted. Now Clementina was a radical of her day, a reformer, one who complained bitterly that some should be so rich and some so poor. But it is one thing to have opinions and another to be called upon to show them beliefs. It is one thing to declare all men equal and another to tell the girl who looks up to you for advice that she ought to feel at perfect liberty to marry—say, a groom. And when Florimel proposed the general question, Clementina might well have hesitated, and indeed she did hesitate, but in vain she tried to persuade herself that it was solely for the sake of her young and inexperienced friend that she did so. Had Florimel been open with her and told her what sort of man was in her thoughts—had she told her that he was a gentleman, a man of genius, noble, and indeed better bred than any man she knew—the fact of his profession as an artist would only have clenched Lady Clementina's decision in his favor. But Florimel putting the question as she did, how should Clementina imagine anything other than that it referred to Malcolm? A strange confusion of feeling was the consequence. Her thoughts heaved in her like the half-shaped monsters of a spiritual chaos, and amongst them was one she could not at all identify. A direct answer she found impossible. She therefore declined giving an answer of any sort—was not prepared with one, she said. Much was to be considered; no two cases were just alike.

They were summoned to tea, after which she retired to her room, shut the door, and began to think—an operation which, seldom easy if worth anything, was in the present case peculiarly difficult, both because Clementina was not used to it and the subject of it was herself.

Lady Clementina's attempt was as honest as she dared make it. It went something after this fashion: "How is it possible I should counsel a young creature like that, with all her gifts and privileges, to marry a groom? Yes, I know how different he is from any other groom that ever rode behind a lady. But does she understand him? Is she capable of such a regard for him as could outlast a week of closer intimacy? At her age it is impossible she should know what she was doing in daring such a thing. And how could I advise her to do what I could not do myself? But, then, is she in love with him?"

She rose and paced the room, then threw herself on the couch, burying her face in the pillow. Presently, however, she rose again and walked up and down the room—almost swiftly now. I can but indicate the course of her thoughts: "If what he says be true, it opens another and higher life. What a man he is, and so young! Has he not convicted me of feebleness and folly and made me ashamed of myself? What better thing could man or woman do for another than give the chance of becoming such as she had but dreamed the shadow of? He is a gentleman—every inch! Hear him talk! Scotch, no doubt and, well, a *little* long-winded—a bad fault at his age! But see him ride! See him swim—and to save a bird! But then he is hard—severe at best! All religious people are so severe! They think they are safe themselves and so can afford to be hard on others! He would serve his wife the same as his mare if he thought she required it! And I *have* known women for whom it might be the best thing. I am a fool, a soft-hearted idiot! He told me I would give a baby a lighted candle if it cried for it. Or didn't he? I believe he never uttered a word of the sort; he only thought it."

She stood still in the middle of the room. For a minute she stood without definite thought in her brain. Then came something like this: "Then Florimel *does* love him and wants help to decide whether she should marry him or not. Poor, weak thing! But if I were in love with him, I would marry him. Would I? It is well, perhaps, that I am not! But she! He is ten times too good for her! But I am *her* counsel, not his. And what better could come to her than to have such a man for a husband instead of that contemptible Liftore, with his grand earldom ways and proud nose? But this groom is a man—all a man, grand from the center out, as the great God that made him! Yes, it must be a great God that made such a man as that—that is, if he *is* the same as he looks—the same all through. But am I bound to give her advice? Surely not, I may refuse. And rightly so! A woman that marries from advice instead of from a mighty love is wrong. I need not speak. I shall just tell her to consult her own heart and conscience and follow them. But gracious me! Am I then going to fall in love with the fellow—this stableman who pretends to know his Maker? Certainly not! There is *nothing* of the kind in my thoughts. Besides, how should I know what falling in love means? I was never in love in my life and don't mean to be. If I were so foolish as to imagine myself in any danger, would I be such a fool as be caught in it? I should think not, indeed!"

Here came a pause. Then she started once more walking up and down the room, now hurriedly. "I will *not* have it!" she cried aloud, and checked herself, alarmed at the sound of her own voice. But her soul went on loud enough for the thought-universe to hear: "There *can't* be a God, or He would never subject His women to what they don't choose. If a God had made them, He would have them be queens over themselves at least. A slave to things inside myself—thoughts and feelings I refuse, and which I *ought* to have control over! I don't want this in me, yet I can't drive it out! I *will* drive it out. It is not me. But it will not go!"

Again she threw herself on her couch, but only to rise again and yet once more pace the room: "Nonsense! it is *not* love. It is merely that nobody could help thinking about one who had been so much before her mind for so long—one, too, who had made her think. Ah, there, I do believe, lies the real secret of it all! There's the main cause of my trouble and nothing worse! I must not be foolhardy, though, and remain in danger, especially as, for anything I can tell, he may be in love with that foolish child. People, they say, like people that are not at all like themselves. Then I am sure he might like me! She *seems* to be in love with him! I know she cannot be half in real love with him; it's not in her."

She did not rejoin Florimel that evening; it was part of the understanding between the ladies that each should be at absolute liberty. She slept little during the night, started awake as often as she began to slumber, and before morning came was a good deal humbled. When she appeared at breakfast her countenance bore traces of her suffering, but a headache—real enough—gave answer to the not very sympathetic solicitude of Florimel. Happily, the day of their return was near at hand. She must put an end to the interaction she was compelled to admit was, at least, in danger of becoming dangerous. This much she had with certainty discovered concerning her own feelings, that her head grew hot and her heart cold at the thought of the young man belonging more to the mistress who could not understand him than to herself who imagined she could, and it wanted no experiences in love to see it was therefore time to be on guard against herself.

17 The Pictures

The next was the last day of the reading. They must finish the tale that morning and on the following set out to return home, traveling as they had come.

" 'It is the opinion of many that he has entered into a Moravian mission, for the use of which he had previously drawn considerable sums . . . ,' " read Malcolm, and paused with the book half closed.

"Is that all?" asked Florimel.

"Not quite, my lady," he answered. "There isn't much more, but I was just thinking whether we hadn't come upon something worth a little reflection—whether we haven't here a window into the mind of the author."

"And you think you can find him out?" said Clementina dryly.

"I believe he's just around a single corner. One thing I think I can say for certain—he believes in a God."

"How do you make that out?"

"Because the author makes his noble-hearted hero—whom he certainly had no intention of disgracing—turn Moravian. My conclusion from it is that, in his judgment, nobleness leads in the direction of religion, that he considers it natural for a noble mind to seek comfort there for its deepest sorrows."

"Well, it may be so. But what is religion without consistency in action?" said Clementina.

"Nothing," answered Malcolm.

"Then how can you, professing to believe as you do, cherish such feelings of anger as you confessed you sometimes had?"

"I don't cherish them, my lady. But I succeed in avoiding hate better than in suppressing contempt, which perhaps is the worse of the two."

Here he paused, for here was a chance that was not likely to recur. He might say before two ladies what he could not say before one. If he could but rouse Florimel's indignation! Clementina's eyes continued fixed upon him. At length he spoke: "I will try to make two pictures in your mind, my lady, if you will help me to paint them: a long seacoast, my lady, and a stormy night. On the margin of the sea a long dune or sandbank and on top of it, her head bare and her thin cotton dress nearly torn from her by the wind, a young woman, worn and white, with an old, faded tartan shawl tight about her shoulders, and the shape of a baby inside it upon her arm."

"Oh, she doesn't mind the cold," said Florimel. "When I was there I didn't mind it a bit."

"She does not mind the cold," answered Malcolm; "she is far too miserable for that."

"But she has no business to take the baby out on such a night," continued Florimel, carelessly critical. "You ought to have painted her by the fireside. They all have fires to sit at. I have seen them through the windows many a time."

"Shame had driven her from it," said Malcolm, "and there she was."

"Do you mean you saw her yourself wandering about?" asked Clementina.

"Twenty times, my lady."

Clementina was silent.

"Well, what comes next?" said Florimel.

"Next comes a young gentleman—but this is a picture in another frame, although of the same night—a young gentleman in evening dress, sipping his wine warm and comfortable, in the bland temper that should follow the best of dinners, his face beaming with satisfaction after some boast concerning himself, or with silent success in the concoction of one or two compliments to have at hand when he joins the ladies in the drawing room."

"Nobody can help such differences," said Florimel. "If there were nobody rich, who would there be to do anything for the poor? It's not the young gentleman's fault that he is better born and has more money than the poor girl."

"No," said Malcolm, "but what if the poor girl has the young gentleman's child to carry about from morning to night?"

"Oh, well, I suppose she's paid for it," said Florimel, whose innocence must have been supplemented by some stupidity born of her flippancy.

"Do be quiet, Florimel," said Clementina; "you don't know what you are talking about."

Her face was in a glow, and one glance at it set Florimel's in a flame. She rose without a word, but with a look of mingled confusion and offence, and walked away. Clementina gathered her work together. But ere she followed her she turned to Malcolm, looked him calmly in the face and said, "No one can blame you for being angry—even for hating—such a man."

"Indeed, my lady, but someone would—the only One for whose praise or blame we ought to care more than a straw for. He tells us we are neither to judge nor to hate. But—"

"I cannot stay and talk with you," said Clementina. "You must pardon me if I follow your mistress."

Another moment and he would have told her all, in the hope of her warning Florimel. But she was gone.

Florimel was offended with Malcolm; he had put her confidence in him to shame. But Clementina was not only older than Florimel, but in her loving endeavors had heard many a pitiful story and was now saddened by the tale rather than shocked at the teller. Indeed, Malcolm's mode of acquainting her with the grounds of the feeling she had challenged pleased both her heart and her sense of what was becoming; while as a partisan of women, finding a man also of their part, she was ready to offer him the gratitude of womankind. "What a rough diamond is here!" she thought. "Yet, what fault could the most fastidious find with his manners? True, he speaks as a servant. But where would be his manners if he did not? But in no way of thinking is he in the smallest degree servile. He is like a great pearl, clean out of the sea—bred, it is true, in the midst of strange surroundings, but pure as the moonlight; and if a man, so environed, yet has grown so grand, what might he not become with such privileges as—"

Good Clementina! what did she mean? Did she imagine that such mere gifts as she might give him could do for him more than the great sea, with the torment and conquest of its winds and tempests, more than his own ministrations of love and victories over passion and pride?

Not for a moment did she imagine him in love with her. Possibly she admired him too much to attribute to him such an intolerable and insolent presumption as that would have appeared to her own inferior self. In one resolve she was confident that her behavior toward him should be such as to keep him just where he was, affording him no smallest excuse for taking one step nearer, and they would soon be in London, where she would see nothing—or next to nothing—more of him. But should she ever cease to thank God—that is, if ever she came to find Him—that in this room He had shown her what He could do in the way of making a man? Heartily she wished she knew a nobleman or two like him. In the meantime, she meant to enjoy with carefulness the ride to

London, after which things should be as before they left.

The morning arrived; they finished breakfast; the horses came round, all but Kelpie. The ladies mounted. Ah, what a morning to leave the country and go back to London! The sun shone clear on the dark pine woods; the birds were radiant in song; all under the trees the ferns were unrolling each its mystery of ever-generating life.

They started without Malcolm, for he must always put his mistress up and then go back to the stable for Kelpie. In a moment they were in the wood, crossing its shadows. It was like swimming their horses through a sea of shadows. Then came a little stream and the horses splashed it about like children. Half a mile more and there was a sawmill with a mossy wheel, a pond behind dappled with sun and shade, a dark rush of water along a brown trough, and the air full of the sweet smell of sawn wood. Clementina had not once looked behind and did not know whether Malcolm had yet joined them or not. All at once the wild vitality of Kelpie filled the space beside her, and the voice of Malcolm was in her ears. She turned her head. He was looking very solemn. "Will you let me tell you, my lady, what this always makes me think of?" he said.

"What in particular do you mean?" returned Clementina coolly.

"This smell of new-sawn wood that fills the air, my lady."

She bowed her head in consent.

"It makes me think of Jesus in His father's workshop," said Malcolm—"how He must have smelled the same sweet scent of the trees of the world, broken for the uses of men; that is so sweet to me. Oh, my lady, it makes the earth very holy and very lovely to think that as we are in the world, so was He in the world. Oh, my lady, think! If God should be so nearly one with us that it was nothing strange to Him thus to visit His people, then He is so entirely our Father that He cares even to death that we should understand and love Him!"

He reined Kelpie back, and as she passed on his eyes caught a glimmer of emotion in Clementina's. He fell behind and all that day did not come near her again.

Florimel asked her what he had been saying, and she compelled herself to repeat a part of it.

"He is always saying such odd, out-of-the-way things," remarked Florimel. "I used to, like you, fancy him a little astray, but I soon found I was wrong. I wish you could have heard him tell a story he once told my father and me. It was one of the wildest you ever heard. I can't tell to this day whether or not he himself believed it. He told it quite as if he did."

"Could you not make him tell it again as we ride along? It would shorten the way."

"Do you want the way shortened? I don't. But indeed it would not do to tell it here. It ought to be heard just where I heard it. You must come and see me at Lossie House in autumn, and then he shall tell it to you. Besides, it ought to be told in Scotch, and there you will soon learn enough to follow it. Half the charm depends on that."

Although Malcolm did not again approach Clementina that day, he watched almost her every motion as she rode. Her lithe, graceful back and shoulders, the noble poise of her head, and the motions of her arms, easy yet decided, were ever present to him, though sometimes he could not have told whether to his sight or his mind—now in the radiance of the sun, now in the shadow of the wood, now against the green of the meadow, now against the blue of the sky, and now in the faint moonlight.

Day glided after day. Soft and lovely as a dream the morning dawned, the noon flowed past, the evening came. Through it all, daydream and nightly trance, before him glowed the shape of Clementina, its every motion a charm. After that shape he could have been content—oh, how content—to ride on and on. Occasionally his mistress would call him to her, and then he would have one glance at the dayside of the wondrous world he had been following. Little he thought that all the time she was thinking more of him than of her surroundings. That he was the object of her thoughts, not a suspicion crossed the mind of the simple youth. How could he imagine a lady like her taking a fancy to what, for all his marquisate, he still was in his own eyes—a raw young fisherman, only just learning how to behave himself? Even the intellectual phantom, nay, even the very phrase, of being in love with her, had never risen upon the dimmest verge of his consciousness; and that although her being had now become to him of all but absorbing interest. Malcolm's main thought was: what a grand thing it would be to rouse a woman like Clementina to lift her head into the higher regions into which a knowledge of God would bring her! All the journey Malcolm was thinking how to urge the beautiful lady into finding for herself whether she had a Father in heaven or no.

On the second day of the journey he rode up to his mistress and told her, taking care that Lady Clementina should hear, that Mr. Graham was now preaching in London, adding that for his part he had never before heard anything fit to call preaching. Florimel did not show much interest, but asked where, and Malcolm fancied he could see Lady Clementina make a mental note of the place.

"If only," he thought, "she would let the power of that man's faith have a chance of influencing her."

The ladies talked a good deal, but Florimel was not in earnest about anything. Besides, Clementina's thoughts could not have passed into Florimel and become her thoughts. Their hearts, their natures, would have to come nearer first. Advise Florimel to disregard rank and marry the man she loved! As well counsel the child to give away the cake he would cry for with intensified selfishness the moment he had parted with it! Still, there was that in her feeling for Malcolm which rendered her doubtful in Florimel's presence.

Between the grooms little passed. Griffith's contempt for Malcom found its least offensive expression in silence, its most offensive in the shape of his countenance. He could not make him the simplest reply without a sneer. Malcolm was driven to keep mostly behind. If by any chance he got in front of his fellow groom, Griffith would instantly cross his direction and ride between him and the ladies. His look seemed to say he had to protect them.

18 The Return

The latter part of the journey was not so pleasant; it rained. It was not cold, however, and the ladies did not mind it much. It accorded with Clementina's mood; and as to Florimel, but for the thought of meeting Caley, her fine spirits would have laughed the weather to scorn. Malcolm was merry. Griffith was the only miserable one of the party. He was tired, and did not relish the thought of the work to be done before getting home. They entered London in a wet fog, streaked with rain and dyed with smoke. Florimel went with Clementina for the night, and Malcolm carried a note from her to Lady Bellair, after which, having made Kelpie comfortable, he went to his lodgings.

When he entered the curiosity shop below his room, the woman received him with evident surprise, and when he would have passed through to the stairs, stopped him with the unwelcome information that, finding he did not return and knowing nothing about himself or his occupation, she had, as soon as the week for which he had paid in advance was out, let the room to an old lady from the country.

"It's no great matter to me," said Malcolm; "only I am sorry you could not trust me a little."

"It's all you know, young man," she returned. "People as lives in London must take care of themselves, not wait for other people to do it. I took your things and laid them all together, and the sooner you find another place for them the better.

In ten minutes he had gathered his belongings in his carpetbag and a paper parcel; then carrying them he reentered the shop. "Would you oblige me by allowing these to stay here till I can come for them?"

The woman was silent for a moment. "I'd rather see the last of them," she answered. "You'll find plenty who'll take you in. No, I can't do it. Take 'em with you."

Malcolm turned and, with his bag in one hand and the parcel under the other, stepped from the shop into the dreary night. There he stood in the drizzle. He concluded after a moment to leave the things with Merton while he went to find a lodging.

Merton was a decent sort of fellow, and Malcolm found him quite as sympathetic as the small occasion demanded. "It ain't no sort of night," he said, "to go lookin' for a bed. Let's go speak to my old woman."

He lived over the stable and they had but to go up the stairs. Mrs. Merton sat by the fire. A cradle with a baby was in front of it. On the other side sat Caley whose exultation she suppressed as they entered—for here came what she had been waiting for—the firstfruits of certain arrangements between her and Mrs. Catanach. She greeted Malcolm distantly, but not spitefully. "I didn't know you lodged with Mrs. Merton, MacPhail," she said with a look at the luggage he had placed on the floor.

"Lawks, miss!" cried the woman, "wherever should we put him?"

"You'll have to find that out, Mother," said Merton. "Surely you've enough room for him someplace, with a truss of straw to help. You'll manage somehow, I'll be bound." And with that he told of Malcolm's condition.

"Well, I suppose we must manage somehow," answered his wife, "but I'm afraid we couldn't make him over-comfortable."

"I don't know, but I suppose we *could* take him at the house," said Caley reflectively. "There is a small room empty in the garret, I know. It ain't much more than a closet, to be sure, but if he could put up with it for a night or two, just till he found better. I could run across and see what they say."

Malcolm wondered at the change in her, but could not hesitate. The least chance of getting settled into the house was not to be thrown away. He thanked her heartily. She rose and went, and they sat and talked till her return. She had been delayed, she said, by the housekeeper—"the cross old patch" had objected to taking in anyone from the stables.

"I'm sure," she went on, "there ain't a ghost of a reason why you shouldn't have the room. Nobody else wants it, or is likely to.

But it's all right now, and if you'll come across in about an hour, you'll find it ready for you. One of the girls in the kitchen—I forget her name—offered to make it tidy for you. Only take care—I give you warning. She's a great admirer of you, Mr. MacPhail."

Therewith she took her departure, and at the appointed time Malcolm followed her. The door was opened to him by one of the maids whom he knew by sight and she led him to that part of the house he liked best, immediately under the roof. The room was indeed little more than a closet in the slope of the roof, with only a skylight. But just outside the door was a storm window from which he had a glimpse of the mews-yard. The place smelt rather badly of mice, but in other respects looked clean, and his education had not tended to fastidiousness. He took a book from his bag and read a good while, then went to bed and fell fast asleep.

In the morning he woke early as was his habit, sprung at once on the floor, dressed, and went quietly down. The household was yet motionless. He had begun to descend the last stair when all at once he turned deadly sick and had to sit down, grasping the balusters. In a few minutes he recovered and made the best speed he could to the stable where Kelpie was now beginning to demand her breakfast.

Malcolm had never in his life felt a sickness like that, and it seemed awful to him. He found himself trembling. Just as he reached the stable, where he heard Kelpie clamoring with hoofs and teeth in her usual manner when she judged herself neglected, the sickness returned and with it such a fear of the animal he heard thundering and clashing on the other side of the door as amounted to nothing less than horror. She was a man-eating horse, and was now crying out for her groom, that she might devour him! He gathered, with agonizing effort, every power within him: "How can I quail in the face of such a creature?" he said to himself. "Doesn't God demand of me action according to what I *know*, not what I may chance to *feel*? Well, God is my strength, and I will lay hold of my strength—Kelpie, here I am!"

Therewith the sickness abated so far that he was able to open the stable door. Having brought himself at once into the presence of his terror, his will arose and lorded it over his shrinking, quivering nerves and like slaves they obeyed him. Malcolm tottered to the cornbin, staggered up to Kelpie, fell against her hindquarters as they dropped from a great kick, but got into the stall beside her. She turned eagerly, darted at her food, swallowed it greedily, and was quiet as a lamb while he dressed her.

Meantime, things were going rather badly at Portlossie and Scaurnose, and the factor was the cause of it. Some said he had indeed come under the influence of the devil; others said he took more counsel with his bottle than was good for him. Almost all the fishers found him surly, and upon some he broke out in violent rage, while to certain whom he regarded as Malcolm's special friends he carried himself with even more cruel oppression. Ever since Malcolm's departure to London, Mr. Crathie's bitterness had grown extreme, not only toward him but against Blue Peter for his hand in the affair.

The notice to leave at midsummer clouded the destiny of Joseph Mair and his family, and every householder in the two villages believed that to take them in would be to call down the same fate upon himself. But Meg Partan at least was not to be intimidated. Let the factor rage as he would, Meg was absolute in her determination that if the cruel sentence were carried out—which she hardly expected—her house would be shelter for the Mairs. That would leave her own family and theirs three months more to look for another abode. Certain of Blue Peter's friends ventured a visit of intercession to the factor, and were received with composure until their object appeared, and his wrath burst forth once more.

Only the day before he had learned from Miss Horn that Malcolm was still in the service of the marchioness and in constant attendance upon her when she rode. It almost maddened him. He had, for some time, taken to drinking more toddy after his dinner, and it was fast ruining his temper. To complete the troubles of the fisher-folk the harbor at the Seaton had, by a severe storm, been so filled with sand as to be now inaccessible at lower than half tide, nobody as yet having made it his business to see it attended to.

But in the midst of his anxieties about Florimel, Malcolm had not been forgetting his people. As soon as he was a little settled in London, he had written to Mr. Soutar, and to architects and contractors, on the subject of a harbor at Scaurnose. But there were difficulties, and the matter had been making slow progress. Malcolm, however, insisted, and in consequence of his determination to have the possibilities of the thing thoroughly understood, three men appeared one morning on the rocks at the bottom of the cliff on the west side of the Nose. The children of the village discovered them and carried their news. The men being all out in the bay, the women left their work and went to see what the strangers were about. Since they could make nothing of their proceedings, they naturally became suspicious. To whom the fancy first occurred nobody ever knew, but such was the unhealthiness of the moral atmosphere of the place caused by the injustice of Mr. Crathie that it quickly became universally received that they were sent by the factor, and for some purpose only too consistent with the treatment Scaurnose had invariably received ever since it was first the dwelling of fishers. For what rents they had to pay! And how poor was the shelter for which they paid so much—without a foot of land to grow a potato in! To crown all, the factor was now about to drive them in a body from the place—Blue Peter first, one of the best and most considerate men among them. His notice to quit was but the beginning of a clearance.

It was, therefore, easy to see what these villains were about on the precious rock which was their only friend, that did its best to give them the sole shadow of a harbor they had cutting off the wind from the northeast a little. What could they be about but marking the spots where to bore the holes for the blasting powder that should scatter it to the winds and allow the wild sea howling in upon Scaurnose. It would be seen what their husbands and fathers would say to it when they came home! In the meantime, they must themselves do what they could. What were they men's wives for if not to act for their husbands when they happened to be away?

The result was a shower of stones upon the unsuspecting surveyors, who immediately fled and carried the report of their reception to Mr. Soutar at Duff Harbor. He wrote to Mr. Crathie who, till then, had heard nothing of the business, and the news increased both his discontent with his superiors and his wrath with those whom he had come to regard as his rebellious subjects.

19   The Attack

Though unable to eat any breakfast, Malcolm persuaded himself that he felt nearly as well as usual when he went to receive his mistress' orders. Florimel would not ride today, so he saddled Kelpie and rode the Chelsea to look in on the progress of the boat once more. To get rid of the mare, he rang the stable bell at Mr. Lenorme's and the gardener let him in. As he was putting her up, the man told him that the housekeeper had heard from his master. Malcolm went to the house to learn what he might and found, to his surprise, that if Lenorme had gone to the Continent, he was there no longer. That the letter, which contained only directions concerning some of his pictures, was dated from Newcastle and bore the Durham postmark of a week ago. Malcom remembered he had heard Lenorme speak of Durham cathedral, and in the hope that he might be spending some time there, begged the housekeeper to allow him to go to the study to write to her master. When he entered, however, he saw something that made him change his plan, and, having written, instead of sending the letter as he had intended to the postmaster at Durham, he left it upon an easel. It contained merely an earnest entreaty to be made and kept acquainted with his movements, that he might at once let him know if anything should occur that he ought to be informed of.

He found all on board the yacht in shipshape, only Davy was absent. Travers explained that he sent him on shore for a few hours every day. He was a sharp boy, he said, and the more he saw the more useful he would be.

"When do you expect him?" asked Malcolm.

"At one o'clock," answered Travers.

"It is one now," said Malcolm.

A shrill whistle came from the Chelsea shore.

"And there's Davy," said Travers.

Malcolm got into the dinghy and rowed ashore.

"Davy," he said, "I don't want you to be all day on board, but I can't have you be longer away than an hour at a time. Now listen well."

"Ay, ay, sir," said Davy.

"Do you know Lady Lossie's house?"

"No, sir; but I know what she looks like."

"How is that?"

"I've seen her two or three times, riding with yourself to the house over there."

"Would you know her again?"

"I would."

"It's a good way to see a lady across the Thames and know her again."

"Ow! but I used the spyglass," answered Davy.

"You are sure of her, then?"

"I am that, sir."

"Then come with me and I will show you where she lives. I will not ride faster than you can run. But mind you don't look as if you belonged to me."

"Okay, sir, but there's someone taking notice of me already."

"What do you mean?" asked Malcolm.

"There's a wee laddie been after myself several times."

"Did you do anything?"

"He wasn't big enough to lick."

To see what the boy could do, Malcolm let Kelpie go at a good trot. Davy kept up without effort, now shooting ahead, now falling behind, now stopping to look in at a window, and now to cast a glance at a game of pitch-and-toss. No mere passerby could have suspected that the sailor boy belonged to the horseman. He dropped him not far from Portland Place, telling him to go and look at the number but not stare at the house.

All the time he had had no return of the sickness, but, although thus occupied, he had felt greatly depressed. Having some business in the afternoon at the other end of Regent's Park, he was returning through the park on foot when, sunk in thought and suspecting no evil, he was struck down from behind and lost his consciousness. When he came to himself he was lying in a nearby public house, with his head bound up, and a doctor standing over him who asked him if he had been robbed. He searched his pockets and found that his old watch was gone, but his money left.

One of the men standing about said he would see him home. He half thought he had seen him before and did not like the look of him, but accepted the offer, hoping to get on the track of something thereby. As soon as they entered the comparative solitude of the park once more, he begged his companion, who had scarcely spoken all the way, to give him his arm and leaned upon it as if still suffering, but watched him closely.

About the middle of the park, where not a creature was in sight, he felt him begin to fumble in his coat pocket and draw something from it. But when Malcom snatched away his other arm, his fist followed it and the man fell. He made no resistance while Malcolm took from him a short stick, loaded with lead, and his own watch, which he found in his waistcoat pocket. Then the fellow rose with apparent difficulty, but the moment he was on his legs, ran like a hare, and Malcolm let him go, for he felt unable to follow.

As soon as he reached home he went to bed for the rest of the day, for his head ached severely! Before he came to himself, Malcolm had a dream, which, although very confused, was in parts more vivid than any he had ever had. His surroundings in it were those in which he actually lay, and he was ill, but he thought it the one illness he had had just recently. His head ached, and he could rest in no position he tried. Suddenly he heard a step he knew better than any other approaching the door of his chamber. It opened, and his grandfather in great agitation entered, not following his hands, however, in the fashion usual to blindness, but carrying himself like any man. He went straight to the washstand, took up the water bottle and, with a look of mingled wrath and horror, dashed it on the floor. That same instant a cold shiver ran through the dreamer, and his dream vanished. But instead of waking in his bed, he found himself standing in the middle of the floor, his feet wet, the bottle in shivers about them, and the neck of the bottle in his hand. He lay down, grew delirious, and tossed about.

It was evening, and someone was near his bed. He saw the glitter of two great black eyes watching him and recognized the young woman who had admitted him to the house the night of his return and whom he had since met once or twice as he came and went. It was his secret admirer, the scullery maid, who, the moment she perceived he was aware of her presence, threw herself on her knees at his bedside, hid her face, and began to weep. The sympathy of his nature rendered yet more sensitive by weakness and suffering, Malcolm laid his hand on her head and sought to comfort her.

"Don't be alarmed about me," he said, "I shall soon be all right again."

"I can't bear it," she sobbed. "I can't bear to see you like that and all my fault."

"Your fault! What can you mean?" said Malcolm.

"But I did go for the doctor, for all it may be the hanging of me," she sobbed. "Miss Caley said I wasn't to, but I would and I did. They can't say I meant it—can they?"

"I don't understand," said Malcolm feebly.

"The doctor says somebody's been poisoning you," said the girl, with a cry that sounded like a mingled sob and howl; "and he's been apokin' all sort of things down your poor throat."

And again she cried aloud in her agony.

"Well, never mind. I'm not dead you see, and I'll take better care of myself after this. Thank you for being so good to me; you've saved my life."

"Oh, you won't be so kind to me when you know all, Mr. MacPhail," sobbed the girl. "It was me that gave you the horrid stuff, but God knows I didn't mean to do you no harm no more than your own mother."

"What made you do it, then?" asked Malcolm.

"The witch-woman told me to. She said that if I gave it to you, you would—you would—"

She buried her face in the bed and so stifled a fresh howl of pain and shame.

"And it was all lies—lies!" she resumed, lifting her face again which now flashed with rage, "for I know you'll hate me worse than ever now."

"My poor girl, I never hated you," said Malcolm.

"No, but you did as bad; you never looked at me. And now you'll hate me out and out. And the doctor says if you die, he'll have it all searched into, and Miss Caley looks at me as if she suspects me of a hand in it. They won't let alone till they've got me hanged for it, and it's all of love for you."

"Well, you see I'm not going to die just yet," he said, "and if I find myself going, I shall take care the blame falls on the right person. What was the witch-woman like? Sit down on the chair there and tell me about her."

She obeyed with a sigh and gave him such a description as he could not mistake. He asked where she lived, but the girl had never met her anywhere but in the street, she said.

Questioning her very carefully as to Caley's behavior to her, Malcolm was convinced that she had a hand in the affair. Indeed, she had happily more to do with it than even Mrs. Catanach knew, for she had traversed her treatment to the advantage of Malcolm. The midwife had meant the potion to work slowly, but the lady's maid had added to the pretended philtre a certain ingredient, and the combination, while it wrought more rapidly, had yet apparently set up a counteraction favorable to the efforts of his struggling vitality.

But Malcolm's strength was now exhausted. He turned faint, and the girl had the sense to run to the kitchen and get him some soup. As he took it, her demeanor made him uncomfortable. It is to any true man a hateful thing to repel a woman's affections—it is such a reflection upon her.

"I've told you everything, Mr. MacPhail, and it's gospel truth I've told you," said the girl, after a long pause. It was a relief when she first spoke, but the comfort vanished as she went on and with slow, perhaps unconscious movements approached him. "I would have died for you, and here that devil of a woman has been making me kill you! Oh, how I hate her! Now you will never love me a bit—not one tiny little bit forever!"

There was a tone of despairing entreaty in her words that touched Malcolm deeply.

"I am more indebted to you than I can speak or you imagine," he said. "You have saved me from my worst enemy. Do not tell any other what you have told me, or let anyone know that we have talked together. The day will come when I shall be able to show my gratitude."

Something in his tone struck her, even through the folds of her passion. She looked at him a little amazed and for a moment the tide ebbed. Then came a rush that overmastered her. She flung her hands above her head and cried, "That means you will do anything but love me!"

"I cannot love you as you mean," said Malcolm. "I promise to be your friend, but more is out of my power."

A fierce light came into the girl's eyes. But that instant a terrible cry such as Malcolm had never heard, but which he knew must be Kelpie's, rang through the air, followed by shouts of men, the tones of fierce execration, and the clash and clang of hoofs. In Malcolm's absence for most of the afternoon and evening, Kelpie had become so wildly uproarious that Merton could hardly manage the other horses. Forgetting everything else, Malcolm sprang from the bed and ran to the window outside his door.

The light of their lanterns dimly showed a confused crowd in the yard of the mews, and amidst the hellish uproar of their coarse voices, he could hear Kelpie plunging and kicking. Again she uttered the same ringing scream. He threw the window door open and cried to her that he was coming, but the noise was far too great for his enfeebled voice. Hurriedly he added a garment or two to his half dress, rushed to the stairs, hardly seeing his new friend who watched anxiously at the head of it, and shot from the house.

When he reached the yard the uproar had not abated. But when he cried out to Kelpie, through it all came a whinny of appeal, instantly followed by a scream. When he got up to the lanterns, he found a group of wrathful men with stable forks surrounding the poor animal, from whom the blood was streaming before and behind. Fierce as she was she dared not move, but stood trembling, with the sweat of terror pouring from her. Yet her eye showed that not even terror had cowed her. She was but biding her time.

Her master's first impulse was to scatter the men right and left, but on second thought, of which he was even then capable, he saw that they might have been driven to apparent brutality in defence of their lives, and besides he could not tell what Kelpie might do if suddenly released. So he caught her by the broken halter and told them to fall back. They did so carefully—it seemed unwillingly. But the mare had eyes and ears only for her master. What she had never done before, she nosed him over face and shoulders, trembling all the time. Suddenly one of her tormentors darted forward and gave her a terrible prod in the off hindquarter. But he paid dearly for it. Before he could draw back, she lashed out, and shot him half across the yard with his knee joint broken. The whole set of them rushed at her.

"Leaver her alone!" shouted Malcolm, "or I will take her part. Between us we'll do for a dozen of you."

"The devil's in her," said one of them.

"You'll find more of him in that rascal groaning yonder. You had better see to him. He'll never do such a thing again, I fancy. Where is Merton?"

They drew off and went to help their comrade, who lay senseless. When Malcolm led Kelpie in, she stopped suddenly at the stable door and started back shuddering, as if the memory of what she had endured there overcame her. Every fibre of her trembled. He saw that she must have been pitifully used before she broke loose and got out. But she yielded to his coaxing, and he led her to the stall without difficulty.

Kelpie had many enemies amongst the men of the mews. Merton had gone out for the evening, and they had taken the opportunity of getting into her stable and tormenting her. At length she broke her fastenings; they fled, and she rushed out after them.

Malcolm washed and dried his poor animal, handling her as gently as possible, for she was in a sad plight. It was plain he must not have her here any longer; worse to her, at least, was sure to follow. He went up, trembling himself now, to Mrs. Merton. She told him she was just running to fetch him when he arrived; she had no idea how ill he was. But he felt all the better for the excitement, and after he had taken a cup of strong tea, wrote to Mr. Soutar to provide men on whom he could depend, if possible the same who had taken her there before, to await Kelpie's arrival at Aberdeen. There he must also find suitable housing and attention for her at any expense until further direction, or until, more probably, he should claim her himself. He added many instructions to be given as to her treatment.

Until Merton returned he kept watch, then went back to the chamber of his torture which, like Kelpie, he shuddered to enter. The cook let him in and gave him his candle, but hardly had he closed his door when a tap came on it and there stood Rose, his preserver. He could not help feeling embarrassed when he saw her.

"I see you don't trust me," she said.

"I do trust you," he answered. "Will you bring me some water. I dare not drink anything that has been standing."

She looked at him with inquiring eyes, nodded her head, and went. When she returned, he drank the water.

"There! you see I trust you," he said with a laugh. "But there are people about who, for certain reasons, want to get rid of me. Will you be on my side?"

"That I will," she answered eagerly.

"I have not got my plans laid yet, but will you meet me somewhere near this time tomorrow night? I shall not be home, perhaps, all day."

She stared at him with great eyes, but agreed at once, and they appointed time and place. He then bade her good-night, and the moment she left him he lay down on the bed to think. But he did not trouble himself yet to unravel the plot against him, or to determine whether the violence he had suffered had the same origin with the poisoning. Nor was the question merely how to continue to serve his sister without danger to his life; for he had just learned what rendered it absolutely imperative that she should be removed from her present position. Mrs. Merton had told him that Lady

Lossie was about to accompany Lady Bellair and Lord Liftore to the Continent. That must not be, whatever means might be necessary to prevent it. Before he went to sleep, things had cleared themselves up considerably.

20 The Abduction

Malcolm awoke much better and rose at his usual hour. His head felt clear, his body refreshed, and his determination as strong as ever. Kelpie rejoiced him by affording little other sign of the cruelty she had suffered than the angry twitching of her skin when hand or brush approached a wound. Having urgently committed her to Merton's care, he mounted Honor and rode to Aberdeen wharf. There to his relief, for time was growing precious, he learned that a smack was due to sail the next morning for Aberdeen. He arranged at once for Kelpie's passage and, before he left, saw to every contrivance he could think of for her safety and comfort. He then rode to the Chelsea Reach.

At his whistle Davy tumbled into the dinghy and was rowing for the shore almost before his whistle had ceased ringing in Malcolm's own ears. He left him with his horse, went on board, and gave various directions to Travers. Then he took Davy with him and bought many things at different shops, which he ordered to be delivered to Davy when he should call for them. Having next instructed him to get everything on board as soon as possible and appointed to meet him at the same place and hour he had arranged with Rose, he went home.

A little anxious lest Florimel might have wanted him, for it was now past the hour at which he usually waited her orders, he learned to his relief that she had gone shopping with Lady Bellair. Malcolm set out for the hospital where they had carried the man Kelpie had so terribly mauled. He went, not merely led by sympathy, but urged by a suspicion also which he desired to verify or remove. On the plea of identification, he was permitted to look at him for a moment but not to speak to him. It was enough. He recognized him at once as the same whose second attack he had foiled in Regent's Park. He remembered having seen him about the stable, but had never spoken to him. Returning, he gave Merton a hint to keep his eye on the man and some money to spend for him as he judged best. He then took Kelpie for an airing. To his surprise she fatigued him so much that when he had put her up again, he was glad to go and lie down.

When it came near the time of meeting Rose and Davy, he got his things together in the old carpetbag, which held all he cared for, and carried it with him. As he drew near the spot, he saw Davy already there, keeping a sharp lookout on all sides. Presently Rose appeared, but drew back when she saw Davy. Malcolm went to her.

"Rose," he said, "I am going to ask you to do me a great favor. But you cannot except you are able to trust me."

"I do trust you," she answered.

"All I can tell you now is that you must go with that boy tomorrow. Before night you shall know more. Will you do it?"

"I will."

"Be at this very spot, then, tomorrow morning at six o'clock. Come here, Davy. This boy will take you where I shall tell him."

She looked from the one to the other.

"I'll risk it," she said.

"Put on a clean frock, and take a change of linen with you and your dressing things. No harm shall come to you."

"I'm not afraid," she answered, but looked as if she would cry.

"Of course you will not tell anyone."

"I will not, Mr. MacPhail."

"You are trusting me a great deal, Rose; but I am trusting you too—more than you think. Be off with that bag, Davy, and be here at six tomorrow morning to carry this young woman's for her." Davy vanished.

"Now, Rose," continued Malcolm, "you had better go and make your preparations."

"Is that all, sir?" she said.

"Yes. I shall see you tomorrow. Be brave."

Something in Malcolm's tone and manner seemed to work strangely on the girl. She gazed up at him half frightened, but submissive, and went at once, looking, however, somewhat disappointed.

Malcolm rose early the next morning and, having fed and dressed Kelpie, strapped her blanket behind her saddle and rode her to the wharf. He had no great difficulty with her on the way, though it was rather nervous work at times. But of late her submission to her master had been decidedly growing. When he reached the wharf, he rode her straight along the gangway onto the deck of the smack, as the easiest if not perhaps the safest way of getting her on board. As soon as she was properly secured, and he had satisfied himself as to the provision they had made for her, impressed upon them the necessity of being bountiful to her and brought a loaf of sugar on board for her use, he left her with a lighter heart than he had had ever since he fetched her from a similar deck.

It was a long way to walk home, but he felt much better and thought nothing of it. And all the way, to his delight, the wind met him in the face; a steady westerly breeze was blowing. He reached Portland Place in time to present himself for orders at the usual hour. On these occasions his mistress not infrequently saw him herself, but to make sure, he sent up the request that she would speak with him.

"I am sorry to hear you have been ill, Malcolm," she said kindly, as he entered the room where he happily found her home.

"I am quite well now, thank you, my lady," he returned. "I thought your ladyship would like to hear something I happened to come to the knowledge of the other day."

"Yes, what was that?"

"I called at Mr. Lenorme's to learn what news there might be of him. The housekeeper let me go up to his painting room, and what should I see there, my lady, but the portrait of my lord marquis more beautiful than ever, the brown smear all gone and the likeness, to my mind, greater than before."

"Then Mr. Lenorme is come home!" cried Florimel, scarce

attempting to conceal the pleasure his report gave her.

"That I cannot say," said Malcolm. "His housekeeper had a letter from him a few days ago from Newcastle. If he is come back, I do not think she knows it. It seems strange, for who should touch one of his pictures but himself except, indeed, he got some friend to set it to right for your ladyship? Anyhow, I thought you would like to see it again."

"I will go at once," Florimel said, rising hastily. "Get the horses, Malcolm, as fast as you can."

"If my lord Liftore should come before we start?" he suggested.

"Make haste," returned his mistress impatiently.

Malcolm did make haste and so did Florimel. What precisely was in her thoughts who shall say, when she could not have told herself? But doubtless the chance of seeing Lenorme urged her more than the desire to see her father's portrait. Within twenty minutes they were riding down Grosvenor Place and happily heard no following hoofbeats.

When they came near the river, Malcolm rode up to her and said, "Would your ladyship allow me to put up the horses in Mr. Lenorme's stable? I think I could show your ladyship a point or two about the portrait that may have escaped you."

Florimel thought for a moment and concluded it would be less awkward, would indeed tend rather to her advantage with Lenorme, should he really be there, to have Malcolm with her.

"Very well," she answered. "I see no objection. I will ride round with you to the stable, and we can go in the back way."

They did so. The gardener took the horses, and they went up to the study. Lenorme was not there, and everything was just as when Malcolm was last in the room. Florimel was much disappointed, but Malcolm talked to her about the portrait and did all he could to bring back vivid the memory of her father. At length with a little sigh she made a movement to go.

"Has your ladyship ever seen the river from the next room?" said Malcolm, and as he spoke, threw open the door near which they stood.

Florimel, who was always ready to see, walked straight into

the drawing room and went to the window.

"There is that yacht lying there still," remarked Malcolm. "Does she not remind you of the *Psyche*, my lady?"

"Every boat does that," answered his mistress. "I dream about her. But I couldn't tell her from many another."

"People used to boats learn to know them like the faces of their friends, my lady. What a day for a sail!"

"Do you suppose there is one for hire?" said Florimel.

"We can ask," replied Malcolm, and with that went to another window, raised the sash, put his head out, and whistled. Over tumbled Davy into the dinghy at *Psyche*'s stern and was rowing for the shore ere the minute was out.

"Why, they're answering your whistle already!" said Florimel.

"A whistle goes farther and perhaps is more imperative than any other call," returned Malcolm evasively. "Will your ladyship come down and hear what they say?"

A wave from her girlhood came washing over her, and Florimel flew merrily down the stairs and across the hall and garden and road to the riverbank, where was a little wooden landing, with a few steps, at which the dinghy was landing.

"Will you take us on board and show us your boat?" asked Malcolm.

"Ay, ay, sir," answered Davy.

Without a moment's hesitation, Florimel took Malcolm's offered hand and stepped into the boat. Malcolm took the oars and shot the little tub across the river. When they got alongside the cutter, Travers reached down both his hands for hers, and Malcolm held one of his for her foot, and Florimel sprang on deck.

"Young woman on board, Davy?" whispered Malcolm.

"Ay, sir—down below," answered Davy, and Malcolm jumped up and stood by his mistress.

"She is like the *Psyche*," said Florimel, turning to him, "only the mast is not so tall."

"Her topmast is struck, you see, my lady—to make sure of her passing clear under the bridges."

"Ask them if we couldn't go down the river a little way," said Florimel. "I should so like to see the houses from it."

Malcolm conferred a moment with Travers and returned.

"They are quite willing, my lady," he said.

"What fun!" cried Florimel, her girlish spirit all at the surface. "How I should like to run away from horrid London altogether and never hear of it again! Dear old Lossie House and the boats and the fishermen!" she added meditatively.

The anchor was already up and the yacht drifting with the falling tide. A moment more and she spread a low treble-reefed mainsail behind, a little jib before and the western breeze filled and swelled and made them alive. With wind and tide she went swiftly down the smooth stream. Florimel clapped her hands with delight. The shores and all their houses fled up the river. They slid past rowboats and great heavy barges loaded to the lip, with huge red sails and yellow, glowing and gleaming in the sun.

"This is the life!" cried Florimel, as the river bore them nearer and nearer to the vortex—deeper and deeper into the tumult of London. They darted through under Westminster Bridge, and boats and barges more and more numerous covered the stream. Waterloo Bridge, Blackfriar's Bridge they passed; Southwark Bridge—and only London Bridge lay between them and the open river, still widening as it flowed to the ocean. London and the parks looked unendurable from this more varied life, more plentiful air and, above all, more abundant space. The very spirit of freedom seemed to wave his wings about the yacht, fanning full her sails. Florimel breathed as if she never could have enough of the sweet wind. For minutes she would be silent, her parted lips revealing her absorbed delight; then she would break out in a volley of questions, now addressing Malcolm, now Travers. She tried Davy too, but Davy knew nothing except his duty there. Not indeed until Gravesend appeared did it occur to Florimel that perhaps it might be well to think by-and-by of returning. But she trusted everything to Malcolm, who, of course, would see that everything was as it ought to be.

Her excitement began to flag a little. She was getting tired. The bottle had been strained by the ferment of the wine. She turned to Malcolm. "Had we not better be putting about?" she said. "I should like to go on forever, but we must come another day, better provided. We shall hardly be in time for lunch." It was nearly four o'clock, but she rarely looked at her watch and indeed wound it up only now and then.

"Will you not go below and have some lunch, my lady?" said Malcolm.

"There can't be anything on board!" she answered.

"Come and see, my lady," rejoined Malcolm, and led the way. When she saw the little cabin, she gave a cry of delight.

"Why, it is just like our own cabin in the *Psyche*," she said, "only smaller, isn't it, Malcolm?"

"It is smaller, my lady," returned Malcolm, "but then there is a little stateroom beyond."

On the table was a nice meal—cold, but not the less agreeable in the summer weather. Everything looked charming. There were flowers; the linen was snowy, and the bread was the very sort Florimel liked best.

"It is a perfect fairy tale!" she cried. "And I declare, here is our crest on the forks and spoons! What does it all mean, Malcolm?"

But Malcolm had slipped away and gone on deck again, leaving her to food and conjecture, while he went to bring Rose up from the forecabin for a little air. Finding her fast asleep, however, he left her undisturbed.

Florimel finished her meal and set about examining the cabin more closely. The result was bewilderment. How could a yacht, fitted with such completeness, such luxury, be lying for hire in the Thames? As for the crest on the plate, that was a curious coincidence; many people had the same crest. But both materials and colors were like those of the *Psyche*! Then the pretty bindings on the bookshelves attracted her. Every book was either one she knew or one of which Malcolm had spoken to her! He must have had a hand in the business! Next she opened the door of the stateroom. But when she saw the lovely little white berth and the indications of every comfort belonging to a lady's chamber, she could keep her pleasure to herself no longer. She hastened to the companionway, and called Malcolm.

150

"What does it all mean?" she said, her eyes and cheeks glowing with delight.

"It means, my lady, that you are on board your own yacht, the *Psyche*. I brought her with me from Portlossie and have had her fitted up according to the wish you once expressed to my lord, your father, that you could sleep on board. Now you might make a voyage of many days in her."

"Oh, Malcolm!" was all Florimel could answer. She was too pleased to think as yet of any of the thousand questions that might naturally have followed.

"Why, you've got the *Arabian Nights* and all my favorite books there!" she said at length. "How long shall we have before we get among the ships again?"

She fancied she had given orders to return and that the boat had been put about.

"A good many hours, my lady," answered Malcolm.

"Ah, of course!" she returned; "it takes much longer against the wind and tide. But my time is my own," she added, rather in the manner of one asserting a freedom she did not feel, "and I don't see why I should trouble myself. It will make some to-do, I daresay, if I don't appear at dinner; but it won't do anybody any harm. They wouldn't break their hearts if they never saw me again."

"Not one of them, my lady," said Malcolm.

She lifted her head sharply, but took no further notice of his remark.

"I won't be plagued anymore," she said, holding counsel with herself, but intending Malcolm to hear. "I will break with them rather. Why shouldn't I be free?"

"Why indeed?" said Malcolm. A pause followed, during which Florimel stood apparently thinking, but in reality growing sleepy.

"I will lie down a little," she said, "with one of these lovely books."

The excitement, the air, and the pleasure generally had wearied her. Nothing could have suited Malcolm better. He left her. She went to her berth and fell fast asleep.

21   The Disclosure

When Florimel awoke, it was some time before she could think where she was. A strange, ghostly light was about her, in which she could see nothing plain; but the motion helped her to understand. She rose and crept to the companion ladder and up on deck. Wonder upon wonder! A clear, full moon reigned high in the heavens, and below there was nothing but water, rushing past the boat. Here and there a vessel, a snow cloud of sails, would glide between them and the moon and turn black. The mast of the *Psyche* had shot up to its full height; the reef points of the mainsail were loose, and the gaff was crowned with its topsail; foresail and jib were full, and she was flying as if her soul thirsted within her after infinite spaces. Yet what more could she want? All around her was wave rushing upon wave and above her blue heaven and regnant moon. Florimel gave a great sigh of delight.

But what did it mean? What was Malcolm about? Where was he taking her? What would London say to such an extraordinary escapade? Lady Bellair would be the first to believe she had run away with her groom—she knew so many instances of that sort of thing—and Lord Liftore would be the next. It was too bad of Malcolm! But she did not feel very angry with him, notwithstanding, for had he not done it to give her pleasure? And assuredly he had not failed. He knew better than anyone how to please her—better even than Lenorme.

She looked around her. No one was to be seen but Davy, who was steering. The mainsail hid the men, and Rose, having been on deck for two or three hours, was again below. Florimel turned to Davy, but the boy had been schooled and only answered, "I mustn't talk so long's I'm steering, mem."

She called Malcolm. He was beside her in a moment. The boy's reply had irritated her and, coming upon this sudden and utter change in her circumstances, made her feel as one no longer lady of herself and her people, but a prisoner.

"Once more, what does this mean, Malcolm?" she said, in high displeasure. "You have deceived me shamefully! You led me to believe we were on our way back to London, and here we are out to sea! Am I no longer your mistress? Am I a child, to be taken where you please? And what, pray, is to become of the horses you left at Mr. Lenorme's?"

Malcolm was glad of a question he was prepared to answer.

"They are in their own stalls by this time, my lady. I took care of that."

"Then it was all a trick to carry me off against my will!" she cried, with growing indignation.

"Hardly against your will, my lady," said Malcolm, embarrassed and thoughtful, in a tone apologetic.

"Utterly against my will!" insisted Florimel. "Could I ever have consented to go to sea with a boatful of men and not a woman on board? You have disgraced me, Malcolm."

Between anger and annoyance she was on the point of crying.

"It's not so bad as that, my lady. Here, Rose!"

At his word Rose appeared.

"I've brought one of Lady Bellair's maids for your service, my lady," Malcolm went on. "She will do the best she can to wait on you."

Florimel gave her a look. "I don't remember you," she said.

"No, my lady. I was in the kitchen."

"Then you can't be of much use to me."

"A willing heart goes a long way, my lady," said Rose prettily.

"That is true," returned Florimel, rather pleased. "Can you get me some tea?"

"Yes, my lady."

Florimel turned and, much to Malcolm's content, vouchsafing him not a word more, went below.

Presently a little silver lamp appeared in the roof of the cabin, and in a few minutes Davy came, carrying the tea tray and followed by Rose with the teapot. As soon as they were alone, Florimel began to question Rose; but the girl soon satisfied her that she knew little or nothing. When Florimel pressed her how she could go she knew not where at the desire of a fellow servant, she gave such confused and apparently contradictory answers that Florimel began to think ill of both her and Malcolm and to feel more uncomfortable and indignant. The more she dwelt upon Malcolm's presumption and speculated as to his possible design in it, the angrier she grew.

She went again on deck. By this time she was in a passion, little mollified by the sense of her helplessness.

"MacPhail," she said, laying the restraint of dignified utterance upon her word, "I desire you to give me a good reason for your most unaccountable behavior. Where are you taking me?"

"To Lossie House, my lady."

"Indeed!" she returned with scornful and contemptuous surprise. "Then I order you to change your course at once and return to London!"

"I cannot, my lady."

"Cannot! Whose orders but mine are you under, pray?"

"Your father's, my lady."

"I have heard more than enough of that unfortunate statement and the measureless assumptions founded upon it. I shall heed it no longer!"

"I am only doing my best to take care of you, my lady, as I promised him. You will know it one day if you will but trust me."

"I have trusted you ten times too much and have gained nothing in return but reasons for repenting it. Like all other servants made too much of, you have grown insolent. But I shall put a stop to it. I cannot possibly keep you in my service after this. Am I to pay a master where I want a servant?"

Malcolm was silent.

"You must have some reason for this strange conduct," she went on. "How can your supposed duty to my father justify you in treating me with such disrespect? Let me know your reasons. I have a right to know them."

"I will answer you, my lady," said Malcolm. "Davy, go forward; I will take the helm. Rose, bring my lady a fur cloak you will find in the cabin.—Now, my lady, if you will speak low that neither Davy nor Rose shall hear us—Travers is nearly deaf—I will answer you."

"I ask you," said Florimel, "why you have dared to bring me away like this. Nothing but some danger threatening me could justify it."

"There you say it, my lady."

"And what is the danger, pray?"

"You were going on the Continent with Lady Bellair and Lord Liftore and without me to do as I had promised."

"You insult me!" cried Florimel. "Are my movements to be subject to the approbation of my groom? Is it possible my father could give his henchman such authority over his daughter? I ask you again, where was the danger?"

"In your company, my lady."

"So!" exclaimed Florimel, attempting to rise in sarcasm as she rose in wrath, lest she should fall into undignified rage. "And what may be your objection to my companions?"

"That Lady Bellair is not respected in any circle where her history is known and that her nephew is a scoundrel."

"It but adds to the wrong you heap on me that you compel me to hear such wicked abuse of my father's friends," said Florimel, struggling with tears of anger. But for regard to her dignity she would have broken out in fierce and voluble rage.

"If your father knew Lord Liftore as I do, he would be the last man my lord marquis would see in your company."

"Because he gave you a beating, you have no right to slander him," said Florimel spitefully.

Malcolm laughed.

"May I ask how your ladyship came to hear of that?"

"He told me himself," she answered.

"Then, my lady, he is a liar, as well as worse. It was I who gave him the drubbing he deserved for his insolence to my—mistress. I am sorry to mention the disagreeable fact, but it is absolutely necessary you should know what sort of man he is."

"And if there be a lie, which of the two is more likely to tell it?"

"That question is for you, my lady, to answer."

"I never knew a servant who would not tell a lie," said Florimel.

"I was brought up a fisherman," said Malcolm.

"And," Florimel went on, "I have heard my father say no gentleman ever told a lie."

"The Lord Liftore is no gentleman," said Malcolm. "But I am not going to plead my own cause even to you, my lady. If you can doubt me, do. I will let his lordship's character and actions speak for themselves."

"And what, pray tell, am I to take that to mean?"

"Just this, my lady, that there is even now a poor fisher-girl at Portlossie who knows more as to his true nature than you do yourself."

"What am I to care for some girl I don't even know?"

"If you would be a marchioness, she would be your subject, and it would therefore be your duty to care. And for her child as well, brought into this world through the evil and selfish whim of a man not worthy to marry a single poor fisher-girl in the whole village."

"How dare you drag me into such talk! Even you ought to know there are things a lady cannot hear. You affront me so, after I made the mistake of thinking you had good breeding! Can I not escape your low talk?"

"My lady, I am sorrier than you think; but which is worse, that you should hear such a thing spoken of, or make a friend of the man who did it—Lord Liftore."

Florimel turned away, and gave her seeming attention to the moonlit waters, sweeping past the swift-sailing cutter. Malcolm's heart ached for her; he thought she was deeply troubled. But she was not half so shocked as he imagined. Infinitely worse would have been the shock to him could he have seen how little the charge against Liftore had touched her. Alas! evil communications had already in no small degree corrupted her good manners. But had she spoken out what was in her thoughts as she looked over the great wallowing water, she would merely have said that for all that, Liftore was no worse than other men. They were all the same. It was very unpleasant, but how could a lady help it? What need Lady Lossie care about the fisher-girl, or any other concerned with his past, so long as he behaved like a gentleman to her? Malcolm was a foolish, meddling fellow, whose interference was the more troublesome than it was honest.

She stood thus gazing on the waters that heaved and swept astern, but without knowing that she saw them, her mind full. And still and even the waters rolled and tossed away behind in the moonlight.

"Oh, my lady!" exclaimed Malcolm at last, "what it would be to have a soul as big and clean as all this—the water, the sky, the stars!"

She made no reply, did not turn her head or acknowledge that she heard him. A few minutes more she stood, then went below in silence, and Malcolm saw no more of her that night.

22 The Preacher

It was on the Sunday during which Malcolm lay at the point of death from the poisoning that while he was at the worst, Florimel was talking to Clementina, who had called to see whether she would not go and hear the preacher of whom he had spoken with such fervor.

Florimel laughed. "You seem to take everything for gospel Malcolm says, Clementina."

"Certainly not," returned Clementina, rather annoyed. "But I do heed what Malcolm says and intend to find out, if I *can*, whether there is any reality in it. I thought you had a high opinion of your groom."

"I would take his word for anything a man's word can be taken for," said Florimel.

"But you don't set much store by his judgment?"

"Oh, I daresay he's right. But I don't care for the things you like so much to talk to him about. He's a sort of poet, anyhow, and poets must be absurd. They are always either dreaming or talking about their dreams; they care nothing for the realities of life. No, if you want advice you must go to your lawyer or clergyman, or some man of common sense, neither groom nor poet."

"Then, Florimel, it comes to this—that this groom of yours is one of the truest of men and one who possessed your father's confidence, but you are so much his superior that you are incapable of judging him and justified in despising his judgment."

"Only in practical matters, Clementina."

"A duty toward God is with you such a practical matter that you cannot listen to anything he has got to say about it?"

Florimel shrugged her shoulders.

"For my part, I would give all I have to know there was a God worth believing in."

"Clementina!"

"What?"

"Of course there's a God. It is very horrible to deny it."

"Which is worse—to deny *it* or to deny *Him*? Now, I confess to doubting *it*—that is, the very fact of a God. But you seem to me to deny God himself, for you admit there is a God—think it very wicked to deny that—and yet you don't take interest enough in Him to wish to learn anything about Him. You won't *think*, Florimel. I don't fancy you every really *think*."

Florimel again laughed. "I am glad," she said, "that you don't judge me *incapable* of that high art. But it is not so very long since Malcolm used to hint something much the same about yourself, my lady."

"Then he was quite right," returned Clementina. "I am only just beginning to think, and if I can find a teacher, here am I, his pupil."

"Well, I suppose I can spare my groom quite enough to teach you all he knows," Florimel said.

Clementina reddened. "I was thinking of his friend Mr. Graham, not himself," she said.

"You cannot tell whether he has got anything to teach you."

"Your groom's testimony gives likelihood enough to make it my duty to go and see. I intend to find the place this evening."

"It must be some little ranting Methodist conventicle. He

would not be allowed to preach in a church, you know, removed from the parish on charges of heresy."

"Of course not. The Church of England is like the apostle that forbade the man casting out devils and got forbid himself for it. She is the most arrant respecter of persons I know, and her Christianity is worse than a farce. It was that first of all that drove me to doubt."

Once more Flormiel laughed aloud. "Another revolution, Clementina, and we shall have you heading the riffraff to destroy Westminster Abbey."

"I would follow any leader to destroy falsehood," said Clementina.

"Really, Clementina," said Florimel, "my groom is quite an aristocrat beside you!"

"Well, will you or will you not go with me to hear this schoolmaster?"

"I will go with you anywhere if only it were to be seen with such a beauty," said Florimel, and the thing was settled.

Later that day, when they arrived at Hope Chapel, the ladies were ushered in and Clementina sat waiting her hoped-for instructor. When Mr. Graham rose to read the psalm, great was Clementina's disappointment. He looked altogether, as she thought, of a sort with the place—dreary—and she did not believe it could be the man of whom Malcolm had spoken.

But she soon began to alter her involuntary judgment of him when she found herself listening to an utterance beside which her most voluble indignation would have been but as the babble of a child. Sweeping, incisive denunciation, logic and poetry combining in one torrent of genuine eloquence, poured confusion and dismay upon head and heart of all those who set themselves up for pillars of the Church without practicing the first principles of the doctrine of Christ. Clementina listened with her very soul. All doubt as to whether this was Malcolm's friend vanished within two minutes of his commencement. If she rejoiced a little more in finding that such a man thought as she thought, she gained this good notwithstanding—the presence and power of a man who believed the doctrine he taught. She saw that if what this man said was true, then the gospel was represented by men who knew nothing of its real nature, and by such she had been led into a false judgment.

During the week that followed, Clementina reflected with growing delight on what she had heard and looked forward to hearing more of a kind correspondent on the approaching Sunday. Nor did the shock of the disappearance of Florimel with Malcolm abate her desire to be taught by Malcolm's friend.

Lady Bellair was astounded, mortified, enraged. Liftore turned gray with passion, then livid with mortification at the news. Not one of all their circle, as Florimel had herself foreseen, doubted for a moment that she had run away with that groom of hers. Indeed, upon examination it became evident that the scheme had gone for some time in hand. The yacht they had been on board had been lying there for months, and although she was her own mistress and might marry whom she pleased, it was no wonder she had run away. For how could she have held her face to it, or up, after it?

The latter part of that week was the sorest time Clementina had ever passed. But, like a true woman, she fought her own misery and sense of loss, as well as her annoyance and anxiety, constantly saying to herself that, be the thing as it might, she could never cease to be glad that she had known Malcolm MacPhail.

Whatever may have been the influence of the schoolmaster upon the congregation gathered in Hope Chapel, there were those whose foundations were seriously undermined by his forthrightness. He shortly thereafter received a cool letter of thanks for his services, written by the ironmonger in the name of the deacons, enclosing a check in acknowledgment of them. The check Mr. Graham returned saying that, as he was not a preacher by profession, he had no right to take fees.

When the end of her troubled week came, Clementina walked across the Regent's Park to Hope Chapel but found no Mr. Graham in the pulpit. A strange sense of loneliness and desolation seized her, yet she lingered on the porch. Now that Malcolm was gone, how was she to learn when Mr. Graham would be preaching?

"If you please, ma'am," said a humble and dejected voice.

She turned and saw the tired and smoky face of the pew-opener, who had been watching her from the lobby and had crept out after her. She dropped a curtsey and went on. But he spoke up, detaining her: "Oh, ma'am, we shan't see *him* no more. Our people here—they're good people, but they don't like to be told the truth. It seems to me as if they knowed it so well, they thought as how there was no need for them to mind it."

"You don't mean that Mr. Graham has given up preaching here?"

"They've given up astin' of 'im to preach, lady. But if ever there was a good man in that pulpit, Mr. Graham he do be that man."

"Do you know where he lives?"

"Yes, ma'am, but it would be hard to direct you."

"I should be greatly obliged to you," said Clementina; "only I am sorry to cause you the trouble."

"To tell the truth, I'm only too glad to get away," he returned, "for the place do look like a cemetery, now *he's* out of it."

It was a good half-hour's walk, and during it Clementina held what conversation she might with her companion. When they reached the place, the Sunday-sealed door of the stationer's shop—for there was no private entrance to the house—was opened by a sad-faced woman. She led her through the counter into his dingy little room above, looking out on a yard but a few feet square. There sat the schoolmaster in conversation with a lady, one of the leaders in the church, trying in vain to set some of Mr. Graham's dangerous ideas straight in his mind.

"I hope you will pardon me," said Clementina, "for venturing to call upon you and, as I have had the misfortune to find you occupied, allow me to call another day."

"Stay now if you will, madam," returned the schoolmaster with an old-fashioned bow of courtesy. "This lady has done laying her commands upon me, I believe."

"As you think proper to call them commands, Mr. Graham, I conclude you intend to obey them," said Mrs. Marshall with a forced smile and an attempt at pleasantry.

"Not for the world, madam," he answered.

The lady made no answer beyond a facial flush as she turned to Clementina, "Good evening, ma'am," she said, and walked out.

"I beg your pardon," said the schoolmaster when she was gone. "But indeed the poor woman can hardly help her rudeness, for she is very worldly and believes herself very pious. It is the old story—hard for the rich."

Clementina was struck. "I, too, am rich and worldly," she said. "But I know that I am not pious, and if you would but satisfy me that religion is common sense, I would try to be religious with all my heart and soul."

"I willingly undertake the task. But let us know each other a little first. And lest I should afterward seem to have taken an advantage of you, I hope you have no wish to be nameless to me, for my friend Malcolm MacPhail had so described you that I recognized your ladyship at once."

"Indeed, it is because of what Malcolm said of you that I ventured to come to you."

"Have you seen Malcolm lately?" he asked, his brow clouding a little. "It is more than a week since he has been to me."

Thereupon, with embarrassment such as she would never have felt except in the presence of pure simplicity, she told of his disappearance with his mistress.

"And you think they have run away together?" said the schoolmaster, his face beaming with what, to Clementina's surprise, looked almost like merriment.

"Yes, I think so," she answered. "Why not, if they choose?"

"I will say this for my friend Malcolm," returned Mr. Graham composedly, "that whatever he did I should expect to find not only all right in intention but prudent and well devised also. The present may well seem a rash, ill-considered affair for both of them, but—"

"I see no necessity either for explanation or excuse," said Clementina, too eager to mark that she interrupted Mr. Graham. "In making up her mind to marry him Lady Lossie has shown greater wisdom and courage that, I confess, I had given her credit for."

"And Malcolm?" rejoined the schoolmaster softly. "Should you say of him that he showed equal wisdom?"

"I decline to give an opinion upon the gentleman's part in the business," answered Clementina laughing, but glad there was so little light in the room, for she was painfully conscious of the burning of her cheeks. "Besides, I have no measure to apply to Malcolm," she went on a little hurriedly. "He is like no one I have ever talked with, and I confess there is something about him I cannot understand. Indeed, he is beyond me altogether."

"Perhaps, having known him from infancy, I might be able to explain him," returned Mr. Graham in a tone that invited questioning.

"Perhaps, then," said Clementina, "I may be permitted, in jealousy for the teaching I have received of him, to confess my bewilderment that one so young should be capable of dealing with such things as he delights in. The youth of the prophet makes me doubt his prophecy."

"At least," rejoined Mr. Graham, "the phenomenon coincides with what the Master of these things said of them—that they were revealed to babes and not to the wise and prudent. As to Malcolm's wonderful facility in giving them form and utterance, that depends so immediately on the clear sight of them that, granted a little of the poetic gift developed through reading and talk, we need not wonder much at it."

"You consider your friend a genius?" asked Clementina.

"I consider him possessed of a kind of heavenly common sense. A thing not understood lies in his mind like a fretting foreign body. But there is a far more important factor concerned than this exceptional degree of insight. Understanding is the reward of obedience. Obedience is the key to every door. I am perplexed at the stupidity of the ordinary religious being. In the most practical of all matters he will talk and speculate and try to feel, but he will not set himself to *do*. It is different with Malcolm. From the first he has been trying to obey. Nor do I see why it should be strange that even a child should understand these things. If a man may not understand the things of God whence he came, what shall he understand?"

"How, then, is it that so few understand?"

"Because where they know, so few obey. This boy, I say, did. If you had seen, as I have, the almost superhuman struggles of his will to master the fierce temper his ancestors gave him, you would marvel less at what he has so early become. I have seen him, white with passion, cast himself on his face on the shore and cling with his hands to the earth as if in a paroxysm of bodily suffering, then after a few moments rise and do a service to the man who had wronged him. Is it any wonder that the light should so soon spring forth in a soul like that? When I was a younger man, I used to go out with the fishing boats now and then, drawn chiefly by my love for the boy who earned his own bread that way before he was in his teens. One night we were caught in a terrible storm and had to stand out to sea in the pitch dark. He was not then fourteen. 'Can you let a boy like that steer?' I said to the captain. 'Yes, a boy like that's just the right kind,' he answered. 'Malcolm'll steer as straight as a porpoise because there's no fear of the sea in him.' When the boy was relieved, he crept over to where I sat. 'You're not afraid, Malcolm?' I asked. 'Afraid?' he rejoined with some surprise. 'I wouldn't want to hear the Lord say, *"O you of little faith!"*' 'But,' I persisted, 'God may mean to drown you.' 'And why not?' he returned. 'If you were to tell me I might be drowned without His meaning it, then I should be frightened enough.' Believe me, my lady, the right way is simple to find, though only they that seek it can find it. But I have allowed myself," concluded the schoolmaster, "to be carried adrift in my laudation of Malcolm. You did not come to hear praises of him, my lady."

"I owe him much," said Clementina. "But tell me, Mr. Graham, how is it that you know there is a God and one fit to be trusted as you trust Him?"

"In no way that I can bring to bear on the reason of another so as to produce conviction."

"Then what is to become of me?"

"I can do for you what is far better. I can persuade you to look for yourself to see whether or not there lies a gate, a pathway, into belief right before you. Entering by that gate, walking on that path, you shall yourself arrive at the conviction which no man could give you. The man who seeks the truth in any other manner will never find it. Listen to me a moment, my lady. I loved that boy's mother. Because she could not love me, I was very unhappy. Then I sought comfort from the unknown Source of my life. He gave me to understand His Son, and so I understood himself, came to know Him, and was comforted."

"But how do you know it was not all a delusion, the product of your own fervid imagination? Do not mistake me; I want to find it true."

"It is a right and honest question, my lady. I will tell you. First of all, I have found all my difficulties and confusions clearing themselves up ever since I set out to walk in that way. Not life's difficulties, but difficulties of belief. My consciousness of life is threefold what it was: my perception of what is lovely around me, and my delight in it; my power of understanding things and of ordering my way; the same with my hope and courage, my love to my kind, my power of forgiveness. In short, I cannot but believe that my whole being and its whole world are in the process of rectification for me. And if I thus find my whole being enlightened and redeemed and know, therefore, that I fare according to the word of the Man of whom the old story tells; if I find that His word and the resulting action founded on that word correspond and agree and open a heaven in and beyond me; if the Lord of the ancient tale, I say, has thus held word with me, am I likely to doubt much or long whether there be such a Lord or no?"

"What, then, is the way that lies before me for my own door? Help me to see it."

"It is just the old way—that of obedience. If you have ever seen the Lord, if only from afar—if you have any vaguest suspicion that the Jew Jesus, who professed to have come from God, was a better man, a different man, than other men—one of your first duties must be to open your ears to His words and see whether they seem to you to be true. Then, if they do, to obey them with your whole strength and might. This is the way of life, which will lead a man out of its miseries into life indeed."

There followed a little pause and then a long talk about what the schoolmaster had called the old story, in which he spoke with such fervid delight of this and that point in the tale, removing this and that stumbling block by giving the true reading or right interpretation, showing the what and why and how, that, for the first time in her life, Clementina began to feel as if such a man must really have lived, that His feet must really have walked over the acres of Palestine, that His human heart must indeed have thought and felt, worshiped and borne, with complete humanity. Even in the presence of her new teacher and with his words in her ears, she began to desire her own chamber that she might sit down with the neglected story and read her herself.

23   The Crisis

When Mr. Crathie heard of the outrage the people of Scaurnose had committed upon the surveyors, he vowed he would empty every house in the place. His wife warned him that such a wholesale proceeding would put him in the wrong in the eyes of the whole country since they could not *all* have been guilty. He replied that it would be impossible—the rascals hung together so—to find out the ringleaders. She returned that even if his discrimination was not altogether correct, he should nevertheless make a difference. The factor was persuaded and made out a list of those who were to leave, in which he took care to include all the principal men of the place.

Scaurnose, on the receipt of the papers all at the same time, was like a hive about to swarm. Endless and complicated were the comings and goings between the houses the dialogues and consultations. In the middle of it, in front of the little public house, stood all that day and the next a group of men and women, never the same in its composition for five minutes at a time, but like a cloud ever dissolving and continuously reforming. The result was a conclusion to make common cause with the first victim of the factor's tyranny—namely, Blue Peter, whose expulsion would arrive three months before theirs.

Three of them, therefore, repaired to Joseph's house, commissioned with the following proposal and condition—that Joseph should defy the notice given him to quit, they pledging themselves that he should not be expelled. Whether he agreed or not, they were equally determined, they said, when their turn came, to defend the village. But if he would cast his lot with them, they would, in defending him, gain the advantage of having the question settled three months sooner for themselves. Blue Peter sought to dissuade them, specially insisted on the danger of bloodshed. They had anticipated the objection, but being of the youngest and roughest in the place, the idea of a scrimmage was not at all repulsive to them. They answered that a little bloodletting would do nobody any harm, neither would there be much of that, for they scorned the use of any weapon sharper than their fists. Nobody would be killed but every meddlesome authority taught to let Scaurnose and the fishers alone.

It was a lovely summer evening a few days later, and the sun going down just beyond the point of the Scaurnose shone straight upon the Partan's door. That it was closed in such weather had a significance. Doors were oftener closed in the Seaton now. The spiritual atmosphere of the place was less clear and open than before. The behavior of the factor and the troubles of their neighbors had brought a cloud over the feelings and prospects of its inhabitants.

A shadow darkened the door of the Findlay's cottage. An aged man in highland dress stood and knocked. The many-colored ribbons adorning the bagpipes which hung at his sides somehow enhanced the look of desolation in his appearance. He was bent over his staff. His knock was tentative and doubtful, as if unsure of a welcoming response. He was broken and sad.

A moment passed. The door was unlatched and within stood the Partaness, wiping her hands in her apron. "Preserve us all! You're a sight for sore eyes, Master MacPhail," she cried, holding out her hand which the blind man took as if he saw as well as she. And so he was, for Duncan looked older and feebler and certainly shabbier than before in his worn-out dress. "Well, come into the house—you're as welcome as ever!"

"Thanks to yourself, Mistress Partan," said Duncan as he followed her in, "and my heart thanks you for ta coot welcome. It will pe a long time since I saw you."

Meg stopped in the middle of the kitchen to get a chair for the old man. "Sit ye down there by the fire till I make ye a cup of tea. Or maybe you would prefer a bowl of porridge and milk. It's not that much I have to offer you, but you couldn't be more welcome!"

The old man sat down with a grateful, placid look, and while the tea was steeping, Mrs. Findlay, by judicious questions, gathered from him the history of his recent adventures.

Unable to rise above the terrible schism in his being occasioned by the conflict between horror at the Campbell blood and affection for the youth in whose veins it ran, he had concluded to rid himself of all the associations of place and people and event now grown so painful to him and to make his way back to his native Glencoe—there to endure his humiliation as best he might. But he had not gone many day's journey before a farmer found him on the road insensible and took him home. As he recovered he found his longing for his boy Malcolm growing. He had been a good boy, he said to himself; there was not a least fault to find in him. He was as brave as he was kind, as sincere as clever, as strong as he was gentle, and he could play on the bagpipes. But his mother was a Campbell, and for that there was no help. He had lived as a man of honor, and he would have to die a man of honor as well, hating the Campbells to their last generation. Hard fate for him! How bitter to actually love a Campbell! Mrs. Catanach had indeed won her revenge. But though he could not tear the youth from his heart, at least he could go farther and farther from him.

As soon as he was able, he resumed his journey westward and southward, and at length reached his native glen, the wildest spot for miles. There he found the call of the winds unchanged, yet when his soul cried out in its agonies, they held no soothing response for the heart of the suffering man. Days passed before he came upon a creature who remembered him; for more than twenty years were gone and a new generation had come up since he left the glen. Worst of all, the clan spirit was dying out. The hour of the Celt was gone. There was not even a cottage where he could hide his head. The one he had forsaken had fallen to ruins, and now there was nothing left but its foundations. The people of the inn at the mouth of the valley did their best for him, but he learned by accident that they had had Campbell connections, and rising that instant, he left it forever.

He wandered about for a time, playing his pipes, and everywhere was hospitably treated. But at length his heart could endure its hunger no more; he *must* see his boy, or die. He gathered himself, therefore, to return from whence he had come and walked as straight as possible, for one in his condition, to the cottage of his quarrelsome but true friend Meg Partan—to learn that his benefactor, the marquis, was dead and Malcolm gone.

But here alone could he hope ever to see him again, and so that same night he sought his cottage on the grounds of Lossie House, never doubting his right to reoccupy it. But the door was locked and he could find no entrance. He went to the House and there was referred to the factor. But when he knocked at his door and requested the key of the cottage, Mr. Crathie came raging out of his dining room, cursed him for an old highland goat, and heaped insults on him and his grandson. It was well for him he kept his distance from the old man, for thenceforth the door of the factor's cottage carried in it the marks of every weapon that Duncan bore.

He returned to Mistress Partan white and trembling in a mountainous rage with "ta low-pred hount of a factor!" Her sympathy was enthusiastic, for they shared a common wrath. Then she divulged to him the tale of the factor's cruelty to the fishers, his hatred of Malcolm, and his general wildness of behavior.

Duncan remained where he was, and the general heart of the Seaton was a little revived by the return of one whose presence reminded them of a better time. The factor was foolish enough to attempt to induce Meg to send her guest away.

"We want no such knaves, old or young, about Lossie," he said. "If the place is not kept decent, we'll never get the young marchioness to come near it again."

"Indeed, factor," returned Meg, enhancing the force of her statement by a marvelously rare composure, "the first thing that'll make the place as decent as it's been for the last ten years would be to send factors back where they came from."

"And where might that be?" asked Mr. Crathie.

"That's more than I can rightly say," answered Mrs. Findlay, "but wise old folk say it's somewhere within the swing of Satan's tail."

The reply on the factor's lips as he left the house tended to justify the rude sarcasm.

24   The Truth

There came a breath of something in the east. It was neither wind nor warmth. It was light before it is light to the eyes of men. Slowly and slowly it grew until, like the dawning soul in the face on one who lies in faint, the life of light came back to the world. Florimel woke, rose, went on deck, and for a moment was fresh born. The sun peered up like a mother waking and looking out on her frolicking children. Black shadows fell from sail to sail, slipping and shifting, and one long shadow of the *Psyche* herself shot over the world to the very gates of the west. The joy of bare life swelled in Florimel's bosom. She looked up, she looked around, she breathed deep. She turned and saw Malcolm at the tiller, and the cloudy wrath sprang upon her. He stood composed and clear and cool as the morning, now glancing at the sunny sails, where swayed across and back the dark shadows of the rigging, as the cutter leaned and rose, like a child running and staggering over the multitudinous and unstable hillocks. She turned from him.

"Good morning, my lady! What a morning it is!"

Florimel cast on him a scornful look. For he had the impertinence to speak as if he had done nothing amiss, and she had no ground for being offended with him. She made him no answer. A cloud came over Malcolm's face, and until she went again below, he gave his attention to his steering.

In the meantime, Rose, who happily had turned out as good a sailor as her new mistress, had tidied the little cabin; and Florimel found, if not quite such a sumptuous breakfast laid as at Portland Place, yet a far better appetite than usual to meet what there was. When she had finished, her temper was better, and she was inclined to think less indignantly of Malcolm's share in causing her so great a pleasure. At this moment she could have imagined no better thing than thus to go tearing through the water to her home. For although she had spent little of her life at Lossie House, she could not but prefer it unspeakably to the schools in which she had passed almost the whole of the preceding portion of it. There was little in the affair she could have wished otherwise except its origin. She was mischievous enough to enjoy even the thought of the consternation it would cause at Portland Place. She did not realize all its awkwardness. A letter to Lady Bellair when she reached home, she said to herself, would set everything right; and if Malcolm had now repented and put about, she would instantly have ordered him to hold on for Lossie. But is was mortifying that she should have come at the will of Malcolm and not by her own—worse than mortifying that perhaps she would have to say so. If she were going to say so, she must turn him away as soon as she arrived. She dared not keep him after that in the face of society. But she might take flight as altogether her own madcap idea. Her thoughts went floundering until she was tired.

The dawning out of the dreamland of her past appeared the image of Lenorme. Her behavior to him had not yet roused in her shame or sorrow or sense of wrong. She had driven him from her; she was ashamed of her relation to him; she had caused him bitter suffering; she had all but promised to marry another man. Yet, she had not the slightest wish for that man's company there and then; with no one of her acquaintance but Lenorme could she have shared this conscious splendor of life. "Would to God he had been born a gentleman instead of a painter!" she said to herself.

The day passed on. Florimel grew tired and went to sleep, woke and had her dinner, took a volume of the *Arabian Nights* and read herself again to sleep; woke again, went on deck, saw the sun growing weary in the west. And still the unwearied wind blew, and still the *Psyche* danced on as unwearied as the wind.

Not a word all day had been uttered between Malcolm and his mistress. When the moon appeared, with the waves sweeping up against her face, he approached Florimel where she sat in the stern. Davy was steering.

"Will your ladyship come forward and see how the *Psyche* goes?" he said. "At the stern you can see only the passive part of her motion. It is quite another thing to see the will of her at work in the bows."

At first she was going to refuse, but changed her mind. She said nothing, but rose and permitted Malcolm to help her forward.

It was the moon's turn now to be level with the water, and as Florimel stood on the starboard side, leaning over and gazing down, she saw her shine through the little feather of spray the cutwater sent curling up before it and turn it into pearls and semiopals.

"My lady," said Malcolm breaking the silence, "I can't bear to have you angry with me."

"Then you ought not to have deserved it," returned Florimel.

"My lady, if you knew all, you would not say I deserved it."

"Tell me all, then, and let me judge."

"I cannot tell you all yet, but I tell you something which may perhaps incline you to feel merciful. Did your ladyship ever think what could make me so much attached to your father?"

"No, indeed. I never saw anything peculiar in it. Even nowadays there are servants to be found who love their masters. It seems to me natural enough. Besides, he was very kind to you."

"It was natural indeed, my lady—more natural than you think. Kind to me he was, and that was natural too."

"Natural to him, no doubt, for he was kind to everybody."

"My grandfather told you something of my early history, did he not, my lady?"

"Yes—at least I think I remember his doing so."

"Will you recall it, and see whether it suggests something?"

But Florimel could remember nothing in particular, she said. She had, in truth, forgotten almost everything of the story, as much as she was interested at the time.

"I cannot think what you mean," she added. "If you are going to be mysterious, I shall resume my place by the tiller."

"My lady," said Malcolm, "your father knew my mother and persuaded her that he loved her."

Florimel drew herself up and would have looked him to ashes if wrath could burn. Malcolm saw he must come to the point at once or the parley would cease.

"My lady," he said, "your father was my father too. I am the son of the marquis of Lossie and your brother—your ladyship's half brother, that is."

She looked a little stunned. The gleam died out of her eyes and the glow out of her cheek. She turned and leaned over the bulwark. He said no more, but stood watching her.

She raised herself suddenly, looked at him and said, "Do I understand you?"

"I am your brother," Malcolm repeated.

She made a step forward and held out her hand. He tenderly took the little thing in his great gasp. Her lip trembled. She gazed at him for an instant, full in the face, with a womanly, believing expression.

"My poor Malcolm," she said, "I am sorry for you."

For a moment her heart was softened and it almost seemed as though some wrong had been done. Why should one be a marchioness and the other but a groom? Yet it also explained so much—every peculiarity of the young man, every gift of mind and body, his strength and courage and nobleness.

As usual her thoughts were confused. The one moment the poor fellow seemed to exist only on sufferance, the next she thought how immeasurably he was indebted to the family of Colonsays. Then arose the remembrance of his arrogance and presumption in assuming on such low ground her guardianship—absolute tyranny over her. Was she to be dictated to by a low-born, low-bred fellow like that? Especially when he presumed to have a right to such power? Such a right ought to exclude him forever from her presence! She turned to him again.

"How long have you known this—painful you must find it—

this awkward and embarrassing fact? I presume you do know it?" she said coldly and searchingly.

"My father confessed it on his deathbed."

"Confessed!" echoed Florimel's pride, but she restrained her tongue. "It explains much," she continued. "There has been a great change in you since then. Mind you, I only say explains. It could never justify such behavior as yours—no, not if you had been my true brother. There is some excuse, I daresay, to be made for your ignorance and inexperience. No doubt the discovery turned your head. Still I am at loss to understand how you could imagine that sort of—that sort of thing gave you any right over me."

"Love has its rights, my lady," said Malcolm.

Again her eyes flashed and her cheek flushed. "I cannot permit you to talk so to me. You must not flatter yourself that you can be allowed to cherish the same feelings toward me as if you were really my brother. I am sorry for you, Malcolm, as I said already; but you have altogether missed your mark if you think this can alter facts, or shelter you from the consequences of presumption."

Again she turned away. Malcolm's heart was sore for her. How grievously she had sunk from the Lady Florimel of the old days! Had he been able to see such a rapid declension, he would have taken her away long ago and let come of her feelings what might. He had been too careful over them.

"Indeed," Florimel resumed, but this time without turning toward him, "I do not see how things can possibly, after what you have told me, remain as they are. I should not feel at all comfortable in having one about me who would be constantly supposing he had rights. It is very awkward indeed, Malcolm, very awkward! But it is your own fault you are so changed, and I must say I should not have expected it. I should have thought you had more good sense. If I kept you and tried to tell people why I wanted to have you about me, they would tell me to get rid of you. And if I said nothing, there would always be something coming up that required explanation. Besides, you would forever be trying to convert me to one or another of your foolish notions. I hardly know what to do. If you had been my real brother, it would have been different."

"I am your real brother, my lady, and have tried to behave like one since I knew it."

"Yes, you have been troublesome. But if you had been a real brother, of course, I should have treated you differently."

"I don't doubt it, my lady, for everything would have been different then. I should have been the marquis of Lossie, and you would have been Lady Florimel Colonsay. But it would have made little difference in one thing—I could not have loved you better than I do now."

The emotion in Malcolm's voice seemed to touch her a little.

"I believe it, my poor Malcolm. But then you are so rude! Take things into your own hands and do things for me I don't want done. Don't you see the absurdity of it all? It would be very awkward indeed for me to keep you now, forever having to explain about you. Perhaps when I am married it might be arranged, I don't know. Possibly a gamekeeper's place—how would that suit you? That is a half-gentlemanly kind of post. I will speak to the factor and see what can be done. But now, on the whole, Malcolm, I think it would be better for you to go. I am very sorry. I wish you had not told me."

"What will you do with Kelpie, my lady?" asked Malcolm quietly.

"There it is, you see!" she returned. "So awkward! If you had not told me, things could have gone on as before, and for your sake I could have pretended I came on this voyage of my own will and pleasure. Now, I don't know what I can do—except, indeed, you—let me see—I don't know, but you might be able to stay till you got her so far trained that another man could manage her. I might even be able to ride her myself. Will you promise?"

"I will promise not to let the fact come out so long as I am in your service, my lady."

"After all that has passed, I think you might promise me a little more! But I will not press it."

"May I ask what that might be, my lady?"

"I am not going to press it, for I do not choose to make a favor of it. Still, I do not see that it would be such a mighty favor to ask—of one who owes respect at least to the House of Lossie. But

I will not ask. I will only suggest, Malcolm, that you should leave this part of the country—say this country altogether—and go to America, or South Wales, or the Cape of Good Hope. If you will take the hint and promise never to speak a word of this unfortunate—yes, I must be honest and allow there is a sort of relationship between us—but if you will keep it secret, I will take care that something is done for you, something more than you could have any right to expect. And mind, I am not asking you to conceal anything that could reflect honor upon you or dishonor upon us."

"I cannot, my lady."

"I scarcely thought you would. Only you hold such grand ideas about God and self-denial that I thought it might be agreeable to you to have an opportunity of exercising the virtue at a small expense and a great advantage."

Malcolm was miserable. Who could have dreamed to find her such a woman of the world! He must break off the hopeless interview.

"Then, my lady," he said, "I suppose I am to give my chief attention to Kelpie, and things are to be as they have been?"

"For the present. And as to this last piece of presumption—concerning this voyage—I will so far forgive you as to take the proceeding on myself—mainly because it would have been my very choice had you submitted it to me. There is nothing I should have preferred to a sea voyage and returning to Lossie House at this time of the year. But you also must be silent on your insufferable share in the business. And for the other matter, the least arrogance or assumption I shall consider to absolve me at once from all obligation toward you of any sort. Such relationships are never acknowledged."

"Thank you—sister," said Malcolm—a last forlorn experiment. And as he said the word he looked lovingly in her eyes.

"If I once hear that word on your lips again as between you and me, Malcolm, I shall that very moment discharge you from my service! You have no claim upon me, and the world will not blame me."

"Certainly not, my lady. I beg your pardon. But there is one perhaps who will blame you a little."

"I know what you mean, but I don't pretend to any of your religious motives. When I do, then you may bring them to bear upon me."

"I was not so foolish as you think me, my lady. I merely imagined you might be as far on as a Chinaman," said Malcolm, with a poor attempt at a smile.

"What insolence do you intend now?"

"The Chinese, my lady, pay highest respect to their departed parents. When I said there was one who would blame you a little, I meant your father."

He touched his cap and withdrew.

"Send Rose to me," Florimel called after him and presently, with her, went down to the cabin.

And still the *Psyche* flew.

During the voyage no further allusion was made by either to what had passed. By the next morning Florimel had yet again recovered her temper, and, nothing fresh occurring to irritate her, kept it and was kind.

By the time their flight was over, Florimel almost felt as if it had indeed been undertaken at her own desire and notion and was quite prepared to assert that such was in fact the case.

25 The Piper

It was two days after the longest day of the year, when there is no night in those regions, only a long twilight. There had been a week of variable weather, with sudden changes of wind to east and north and round again by south to west, and then there had been a calm for several days. All Portlossie, more or less, the Seaton especially, was in a state of excitement, and its little neighbor Scaurnose was more excited still. There the man most threatened, and with the greatest injustice, was the only one calm amongst the men, and amongst the women his wife was the only one that was calmer than he. Blue Peter was resolved to abide the stroke of wrong and not resist the powers of the factor. He had a dim perception that it was better that one should suffer than that order should be destroyed and law defied. Suffering, he might still in patience possess his soul and all be well with him. But what would become of the country if everyone wronged were to take the law into his own hands? He had not found a new home. Indeed, he had not heartily set about searching for one; in part because he was buoyed up by the hope he read so clearly in the face of his more trusting wife—that Malcolm would come to deliver them.

Miss Horn was growing more and more uncomfortable concerning events and dissatisfied with Malcolm for allowing them to progress unimpeded. She had not for some time heard from him, and here was his most important duty unattended to—she would not yet say neglected—the well-being of his tenantry, left in the hands of an unsympathetic, self-important underling, who was fast losing all the good sense he had once possessed! Was the life and history of all these brave fishermen and their wives and children to be postponed to the pampered feelings of one girl? said Miss Horn to herself. She had written to him within the last month a very hot letter indeed, which had afforded no end of amusement to Mrs. Catanach, as she sat in his old lodging over the curiosity shop, but, I need hardly say, had not reached Malcolm.

The blind piper had been restless all day. Questioned again and again by Meg Partan as to what was amiss with him, he always returned her odd and evasive answers. Every few minutes he got up from cleaning her lamp to go to the shore. He had but to cross the threshold and take a few steps through the yard to reach the road that ran along the seafront of the village. On the one side were the cottages; on the other, the shore and ocean wide outstretched. He would walk straight across this road until he felt the sand under his feet and there stand for a few moments facing the sea and, with nostrils distended, breathing deep breaths of the air from the northeast, then turn and walk back to Meg Partan's kitchen to resume his ministration of light.

Thus it went on the whole day, and as the evening approached he grew still more agitated. The sun went down and the twilight began and, as the twilight deepened, still his excitement grew. Straightaway it seemed as if the whole Seaton had come to share in it. Men and women were all out-of-doors; and, late as it was when the sun set, there could hardly have been one older that a baby yet in bed. The men with their hands in their trouser pockets were lazily smoking pigtail in short clay pipes, and some of the women, in short blue petticoats, doing the same. Some stood in their doors talking with neighbors, but these were mostly the elder women; the younger ones—all but Lizza Findlay—were out in the road. One man half leaned on the windowsill of Duncan's former abode, and round him were two or three more and some women, talking about Scaurnose and the factor and what the lads would do tomorrow, while the hush of the sea on the pebbles mingled with their talk.

Once more there was Duncan, standing as if looking out to sea and shading his brows with his hand as if to protect his eyes from the glare of the sun and thus enable his sight.

"There's the old piper again!" said one of the group, a young woman. "He looks foolish enough standing there like that, as if he couldn't see for the sun in his eyes."

"Hold your tongue, lass," rejoined an elderly woman beside her. "There's more things than you know, as the Book says. There's eyes that can see and there's eyes that can't and some eyes—"

"Ta poat! Ta poat of my chief!" cried the seer suddenly. "She is coming like a dream in ta night, put one tat will not pe cone with ta morning!"

He spoke as one suppressing a wild joy.

"What'll that be, Grandfather?" the woman who had last spoke, respectfully inquired, while those within hearing hushed each other and stood in silence.

"And who will it pe put my own son?" answered the piper. "Who should it pe put my own Malcolm! I see his poat coming rount ta Tead Head. She flits over ta water like a pale ghost over Morven. Put it's ta young and ta strong she is pringing home to Tuncan."

Involuntarily all eyes turned toward the point called Death's Head, which bounded the bay on the east.

"It's too dark to see anything," said the man on the windowsill. "There's a bit of a fog come up."

"Yes," said Duncan, "it'll pe too tark for you who have no eyes put to speak of. Put you'll wait a few, and you'll pe seeing as well as me. Oh, my poy! My poy! Ta Lord pe praised! I'll die in peace, for he'll pe only the one half of him a Cawmill, and he'll pe safe at last, as sure as tere's a heaven to come to and a hell to come from. For the half tat's not a Cawmill must pe ta strong half, and it will trag ta other half into heaven—where it will not pe welcome, howefer."

As if to get rid of the unpleasant thought that his Malcolm could not enter heaven without taking half a Campbell with him, he turned from the sea and hurried into the house but to catch up his pipes and hasten out again, filling the bag as he went. Arriving once more on the verge of the sand, he stood facing the northeast, and began blowing a pilbroch loud and clear.

Meantime Meg Partan had joined the same group.

"Hech, sirs!" she cried, "if the old man's right, it'll be the marchioness herself that's heard of the ill doings of her factor and now's coming to see after her fold. And it'll be Malcolm's doing. But the fine lad won't know the state of the harbor and he'll be making for the mouth of it and he'll run that bonny boat aground between the two piers. And that'll not be a proper homecoming for the lady of the land. And what's more, Malcolm'll get the blame. So some of you must get down to the pierhead to look out and give him warning!"

Her own husband was the first to start, proud of the foresight of his wife.

"Faith, Meg!" he cried, "you're just as good at seeing in the distance as the piper himself!"

By the time the Partan and his companions reached the pierhead, something was dawning in the vague of sea and sky that might be a sloop standing for the harbor. In a moment they were in a boat and making for the open bay.

The wind had now fallen to the softest breath, and the little vessel came on slowly. The men rowed hard, shouting and waving a white shirt, and soon they heard a hail which none could mistake for other than Malcolm's. In a few minutes they were on board, greeting their old friend with jubilation. Briefly the Partan communicated the state of the harbor and recommended running the Fisky ashore about opposite the brass swivel.

"All the men and women in the Seaton," he said, "will be there to haul her up."

Malcolm took the helm, gave his orders, and steered further westward. By this time the people on shore had caught sight of the cutter. They saw her come stealing out of the thick dark and go gliding along the shore like a sea ghost over the dusky water— faint, uncertain, noiseless, glimmering. It could be no other than the Fisky! Both their lady and their friend Malcolm must be on board. They were certain, for how could the one of them come without the other? And doubtless the marchioness, whom they all remembered as a good-humored, handsome young lady, never shy of speaking to anybody, had come to deliver them from the hateful red-nosed ogre, her factor! Out at once they all set along the shore to greet her arrival, each running regardless of the rest, so that from the Seaton to the middle of the Boar's Tail dune there was a long, straggling broken string of hurrying fisher-folk, men and women, old and young, followed by all the children. The piper, too asthmatic to run, but not too asthmatic to walk and play his bagpipes, delighted the heart of Malcolm, who could not mistake the style, believed he brought up the rear, but he was wrong. The very last came Mrs. Findlay and Lizza, carrying between them their little deal kitchen table for her ladyship to step out of the boat upon, and Lizza's child fast asleep on the top of it.

The foremost ran and ran until they saw that the Fisky had chosen her couch and was turning her head to the shore, when they stopped and stood ready with greased planks and ropes to draw her up. In a few moments the whole population was gathered in the June midnight, darkening the yellow sands between tide and dune. The *Psyche* was well manned now with a crew of six. On she came under full sail till within a few yards of the beach, when in one and the same moment every sheet was let go, and she swept softly up like a summer wave and lay still on the shore. The butterfly was asleep. But before she came to rest, the instant indeed that her canvas went fluttering away, thirty strong men had rushed into the water and laid hold of the now broken-winged thing. In a few minutes she was high and dry.

Malcolm leaped on the sand just as the Partaness came bustling up with her kitchen table between her two hands like a tray. She set it down and across it shook hands with him violently, then caught it up and deposited it firmly on its legs beneath the cutter's waist.

"Now, my lady," said Meg, looking up at the marchioness, "set your little foot on my table and we'll think of it ever after when we eat our dinner from it."

Florimel thanked her, stepped lightly upon it, and sprang to the sand, where she was received with words of welcome from many and shouts which rendered them inaudible from the rest. The men, their hats in their hands, and the women, curtseying, made a lane for her to pass through.

Followed by Malcolm, she led the way over the dune, nor would she accept any help in climbing it, straight for the tunnel. Malcolm had never laid aside the key to the private doors his father had given him while he was yet a servant. They crossed by the embrasure of the brass swivel. That implement had now long been silent, but they had not gone many paces from the bottom of the dune when it went off with a roar. The shouts of the people drowned out the startled cry with which Florimel, involuntarily mindful of old and, for her, better times, turned toward Malcolm. For a brief moment the spirit of her girlhood came back. She had not looked for such a reception and was both flattered and touched by it. Possibly, had she then understood her position and her duty toward them.

Malcolm unlocked the door of the tunnel, and she entered, followed by Rose, who felt as if she were walking in a dream. As he stepped in after them, he was seized from behind and clasped in an embrace he knew at once.

"Daddy, Daddy!" he said, and turning, threw his arms round the piper.

"My poy, my poy! My own son Malcolm!" cried the old man in a whisper of intense satisfaction and suppression. "You must pe forgifing me for coming pack to you. Put I cannot help lofing you, and you must forget that you are a Cawmill."

Malcolm kissed his cheek and said, also in a whisper, "My own daddy! I've a heap to tell you, but I must see my lady home first!"

"Co! Co!" cried the old man, pushing him away. "Do your duties to my ladyship first, and then come to your old daddy."

"I'll be with you in half an hour or less."

"Coot poy! Coot poy! Come to Mistress Partan's."

"Ay, ay, Daddy!" said Malcolm, and hurried through the tunnel.

As Florimel approached the ancient dwelling of her race, now her own to do with as she would, her pleasure grew. Whether it was the time that had passed or the twilight, everything looked strange—the grounds wider, the trees larger, the house grander and more anciently venerable. And all the way the birds sang in the hollow. The spirit of her father seemed to hover about the place and, while the thought that her father's voice would not greet her when she entered the hall cast a solemn, funereal state over her simple return, her heart yet swelled with satisfaction and pride. All this was hers to work her pleasure with, to confer as she pleased! No thought of her tenants, fishers, or farmers, who did their strong part in supporting the ancient dignity of her house, had even an associated share in the bliss of the moment. She had forgotten her reception already, or regarded it only as the natural homage to such a position and power as hers.

The drawing room and hall were lighted. Mrs. Courthope was at the door, as if she expected her, and greeted her warmly, but Florimel was careful to take everything as a matter of course.

"When will your ladyship please to want me?" asked Malcolm.

"At the usual hour, Malcolm," she answered.

He turned and ran to the Seaton.

His first business was the accommodation of Travers and Davy, but he found them already housed at the Salmon Inn, with Jamie Ladle teaching Travers to drink toddy. They had left the *Psyche* snug: she was high above the highwater mark, and there were no tramps about. They had furled her sails, locked the companion door, and left her.

Mrs. Findlay rejoiced over Malcolm as if he had been her own son from a far country; but the poor piper between politeness and gratitude on the one hand and the urging of his heart on the other was sorely tried by her talkativeness. He could hardly get in a word. Malcolm perceived his suffering and, as soon as seemed prudent, proposed that he should walk with him to Miss Horn's, where he was going to sleep, he said, that night.

As soon as they were out of the house, Malcolm assured Duncan, to the old man's great satisfaction, that had he not found him there, he would within another month have set out to roam Scotland in search of him.

Miss Horn had heard of their arrival and was wandering about the house, unable even to sit down until she saw the marquis. To herself she always called him the marquis; to his face he was always Malcolm. If he had not come, she declared, she could not have gone to bed—yet she received him with an edge to her welcome. He had to answer for his behavior. They sat down, and Duncan told a long, sad story; which finished with the toddy that had sustained him during the telling. The old man thought it better, for fear of annoying his Mistress Partan, to go home. As it was past one o'clock, they both agreed.

And then, at last, Malcolm poured forth his whole story, and his heart with it, to Miss Horn, who heard and received it with understanding and a sympathy which grew ever as she listened. At length she declared herself perfectly satisfied, for not only had he done his best, but she did not see what else he could have done. She hoped, however, that now he would contrive to get this part over as quickly as possible, for which, in the morning, she said she would show him good reasons.

26 The Homecoming

Malcolm had not yet, after all the health-giving of the voyage, entirely recovered from the effects of the ill-compounded potion. Indeed, sometimes the fear crossed his mind that never would he be the same man again. Hence, it came that he was weary and overslept himself the next day—but it was no great matter; he had yet time enough. He swallowed his breakfast as a working man alone can and set out for Duff Harbor. At Leith, where they had put in for provisions, he had posted a letter to Mr. Soutar, directing him to have Kelpie brought on to his own town, whence he would fetch her himself. The distance was several miles, the hour nine, and he was a good enough walker. It was the loveliest of mornings to be abroad.

When he reached the Duff Arms, he walked straight into the yard where the first thing he saw was a stableboy in the air, hanging on to a twitch on the nose of the rearing Kelpie. In another instant he would have been killed or maimed for life and Kelpie loose, scouring the streets of Duff Harbor. When she heard Malcolm's voice and the sound of his running feet, she stopped as if to listen. He flung the boy aside and caught her halter. Once or twice more she reared, in the vain hope of so ridding herself of the pain that clung to her lip and nose, nor did she, through the mist of her anger and suffering, quite recognize her master in his yacht uniform. But the torture decreasing, she grew able to scent his presence, welcomed him with her usual glad whinny and allowed him to do with her as he would.

Having fed her, found Mr. Soutar and arranged several matters with him, he set out for him.

That was a ride! Kelpie was mad with life! He jumped her into every available field, and she tore its element of space at least to shreds with her spurning hoofs. He would have entered at the grand gate, but found no one at the lodge, for the factor, to save

185

a little, had dismissed the old keeper. He had, therefore, to go through the town, where, to the awestricken eyes of the population peeping from doors and windows, it seemed as if the terrible horse would carry him right over the roofs of the fisher-cottages below and out to sea. "Eh, but he's a terrible creature that Malcolm MacPhail!" said the old wives to each other, for they felt there must be something wicked in him to ride like that. But he turned her aside from the steep hill and passed along the street that led to the town gate of the House.

Whom should he see, as he turned into it, but Mrs. Catanach, standing on her own doorstep, shading her eyes with her hand and looking far out over the water through the green smoke of the village below. As long as he could remember her, it had been her wont to gaze thus; though what she could at such times be looking for, except it were the devil in person, he found it hard to conjecture.

The keeper of the town gate greeted Malcolm, as he let him in, with a pleased old face and words of welcome; but added instantly, as if it were no time for the indulgence of friendship, that it was a terrible business going on at the Nose.

"What is it?" asked Malcolm, in alarm.

"You've been so long away," answered the man, "that I doubt you'll even know the factor—But the Lord save me! If he knew I had said such a thing, he would turn me out of my house in a minute."

"But you've said nothing yet," rejoined Malcolm.

"I said factor and that's almost enough, for he's like a roaring lion and raging bear among the people ever since you left."

"But you haven't told me what is the matter at Scaurnose!" said Malcolm impatiently.

"Oh, just this—that on this same midsummer's day, Blue Peter, honest fellow, is to quit his house. He's been under notice for three months. You see—"

"To quit!" exclaimed Malcolm. "What for? Such a thing's never been heard of."

"Faith, it's heard of now," returned the gatekeeper. "Quitting's as plentiful as crabgrass. Indeed, there's nothing else heard of around here *but* quitting, for the full half of Scaurnose is under the same notice for Michaelmas, and the Lord knows when it will all end."

"But what's it for? Blue Peter's not the man to misbehave himself."

"Well, you know more yourself than anyone else as to what it's all about; for they say—that is, *some* say, that it's all your fault, Malcolm."

"What do you mean, man? Speak out," said Malcolm.

"They say it's all because of your abducting the marquis' boat and because you and Peter went off together."

"That'll hardly hold, seeing the marchioness herself came home in her last night."

"Ay, but you see the decree's already gone out, and what the factor says is like the laws of the Medes and the Persians, that they says is not to be altered. I don't know myself."

"Oh, well, if that be all, I'll see to it with the marchioness."

"Ay, but you see there's a lot of lads there, I'm told, that has vowed that neither the factor, or factor's man, shall ever set foot in Scaurnose from this day on. Go down to the Seaton yourself and see how many of your old friends you'll find there. Man, they're all over at Scaurnose to see what's going to happen. The factor's there I know and some constables with him—to see that his order's carried out. And the lads, they've been fortifying the place—as they call it—for the last time. They've dug a trench, they tell me, that no one but a hunter on his horse could jump over, and they're posted along the town side of it with sticks and stones and boat oars and guns and pistols. And if there's not a man or two killed already—"

Before he finished his sentence Kelpie was levelling herself for the sea gate.

Johnny Bykes was locking it on the other side, in haste to secure his eye-share of what was going on, when he caught sight of Malcolm tearing up. Mindful of the old grudge, also that there was no marquis now to favor his foe, he finished the arrested act of turning the key, drew it from the lock, and to Malcolm's orders, threats, and appeals, returned for all answer that he had no time to attend to him, and so left him looking through the bars. Malcolm dashed across the turn and round the base of the hill, dismounted, unlocked the door in the wall, got Kelpie through, and was in the saddle again before Johnny was halfway from the gate. When he saw him, he trembled, turned, and ran for its shelter again in terror and did not perceive until he reached it that the insulted groom had gone off like the wind in the opposite direction.

Malcolm soon left the high road and cut across the fields over which the wind bore cries and shouts, mingled with laughter and the animal sounds of coarse jeering. When he came nigh the cart-road which led into the village, he saw at the entrance of the street a crowd and rising from it the well-known shape of the factor on his horse. Nearer the sea, where was another entrance through the backyards of some cottages, was a smaller crowd. Both were now pretty silent, for the attention of all was fixed on Malcolm's approach. As he drew Kelpie up, foaming and prancing, and the group made way for her, he saw a deep, wide ditch across the road, on whose opposite side was ranged irregularly the flower of Scaurnose's younger manhood, calmly, even merrily prepared to defend their entrenchment. They had been chafing the factor and loudly challenging the constables to come on, when they recognized Malcolm in the distance, and expectancy stayed the rush of their bruising wit. For they regarded him as beyond a doubt come from the marchioness with messages of goodwill. When he rode up, therefore, they raised a great shout, everyone welcoming him by name. But the factor, who, to judge by appearances had had his forenoon dram ere he left home, burning with wrath, moved his horse in between Malcolm and the assembled Scaurnoseans on the other side of the ditch. He had self-command enough left, however, to make an attempt at the lofty superior. "Pray, what is your business?" he said, as if he had never seen Malcolm in his life before. "I presume you come with a message?"

"I come to beg you, sir, not to go further with this business. Surely the punishment is already enough!" said Malcolm respectfully.

"Who sends me this message?" asked the factor, his teeth clenched, and his eyes flaming.

"One," answered Malcolm, "who has some influence for justice and will use it, upon whichever side the justice may lie."

The factor cursed, losing utterly his slender self-command and raising his whip.

Malcolm took no heed of the gesture, for he was at the moment beyond his reach.

"Mr. Crathie," he said calmly, "you are banishing the best man in the place."

"No doubt! No doubt, seeing he's a crony of yours," laughed the factor in mighty scorn. "A canting, prayer-meeting rascal!" he added.

"Is that any worse than a drunken elder of the church?" cried Dubs from the other side of the ditch, raising a roar of laughter.

The very purple forsook the factor's face and left it a corpse-like gray in the fire of his fury.

"Come, come, my men! that's going too far!" said Malcolm.

"And who are you for a truant fisherman to be giving counsel without our asking for it?" shouted Dubs, altogether disappointed in the poor part Malcolm seemed to be taking. "Give the factor there your counsel."

"Out of my way," said Mr. Crathie, still speaking through clenched teeth. He came straight upon Malcolm. "Home with you! or-r-r—"

Again he raised his whip, this time plainly with intent.

"For heaven's sake, factor, mind the mare!" cried Malcolm. "Ribs and legs and bones will start breaking all round if you anger her with your whip."

As he spoke, he drew a little aside that the factor might pass if he pleased. A noise arose in the smaller crowd, and Malcolm turned to see what it meant. Off his guard, he received a stinging cut over the head from the factor's whip. Simultaneously Kelpie stood up on end, and Malcolm tore the weapon from the treacherous hand.

"If I gave you what you deserve, Mr. Crathie, I should knock you and your horse together into that ditch. A touch of the spur would do it. I am not quite sure that I oughtn't to. A nature like yours takes forbearance for fear."

While he spoke, his mare was ramping and kicking, making a clean sweep all around her. Mr. Crathie's horse turned restive from sympathy, and it was all his rider could do to keep his seat. As soon as he got Kelpie a little quieter, Malcolm drew near and returned him his whip. He snatched it from his outstretched hand and essayed a second cut at him, which Malcolm rendered powerless by pushing Kelpie close up to him. Then suddenly wheeling, he left him.

On the other side of the trench the fellows were shouting and roaring with laughter.

"Men!" cried Malcolm, "you have no right to stop up this road. I want to go and see Blue Peter."

"Come on, then!" cried one of the young men, emulous of Dubs' humor, and spread out his arms as if to receive Kelpie to his bosom.

"Stand out of the way," said Malcolm, "I am coming." As he spoke he took Kelpie a little around, keeping out of the way of the factor who sat trembling with rage on his still excited animal, and sent her at the trench. The men scampered right and left and Malcolm, rather disgusted, took no notice of them, flew over the trench, and sent Kelpie at a full gallop toward Blue Peter's.

A cart, loaded with their little all, the horse in the shafts, was standing at Peter's door, but nobody was near it. Hardly was Malcolm well into the yard, however, when out rushed Annie and, heedless of Kelpie's demonstrative repellance, reached up her hands like a child, caught him by the arm while he was busied with his troublesome charge, drew him toward her, and held him till, in spite of Kelpie, she had kissed him again and again.

"Oh, Malcolm! Oh, my lord!' she said, "you have saved my faith. I knew you would come!"

"Hold your tongue, Annie. I mustn't be known," said Malcolm.

Out next came Blue Peter, his youngest child in his arms.

"Eh, Peter! I'm happy to see you!" cried Malcolm. "Give me a grip of your honest hand!"

The two friends shook hands heartily.

"Peter," said Malcolm, "you were right not to resist the factor. But I'm glad they wouldn't let you go."

"I would have been halfway to Port Gordon by now," said Peter.

"But you'll not be going to Port Gordon by now," said Malcolm. "Just go to the Salmon Inn for a few days till we see how things turn out."

"I'll do anything you like, Malcolm," said Peter and went into the house to get his hat.

In the street arose the cry of a woman, and into the yard rushed one of the fisher-wives, followed by the factor. He had found a place on the eastern side of the village, where, jumping a low earth wall, he got into a little backyard. When the woman to whose cottage it belonged caught sight of him through the window, she ran out and fell to abusing him in no measured language. He rode at her in his rage, and she fled shrieking her vituperation. Beside himself with the rage of murdered dignity, he rode up and struck at her over the corner of the cart, whereupon, from the top of it, Annie Mair ventured to expostulate.

"Hoot, sir! Have you forgotten yourself altogether to hit at a woman like that!"

He turned upon her and gave her a cut on the arm and hand, so stinging that she cried out and nearly fell from the cart. Out rushed Peter and flew at the factor, who from his seat of vantage began to ply his whip about his head. But Malcolm, who, when the factor appeared, had moved aside to keep Kelpie out of mischief and saw only the second of the two assaults, came forward with a scramble and a bound.

"Stand back, Peter," he cried. "This belongs to me. I gave him back his whip so I'm accountable.—Mr. Crathie!" and as he spoke he edged his mare up to the panting factor, "the man who strikes a woman must be taught that he is a scoundrel, and that job I take. I would do the same if you were the lord of Lossie instead of his factor."

Mr. Crathie, knowing himself now in the wrong, was a little frightened at the speech and began to bluster and stammer, but the swift descent of Malcolm's heavy riding whip on his shoulders and back made him voluble in curses. Then began a battle that could not last long with such odds on the side of justice. In less than a minute the factor turned to flee and, spurring out of the court, galloped up the street at full stretch.

While Malcolm was thus occupied, his sister was writing to Lady Bellair. She told her that having gone out for a sail in her yacht, which she had sent for from Scotland, the desire to see her home had overpowered her to such a degree that of the intended sail she had made a voyage, and here she was, longing just as much now to see Lady Bellair; and if she thought proper to bring a gentleman to take care of her, he also should be welcomed for her sake. It was a long way for her to come, she said, and Lady Bellair knew what sort of place it was; but there was nobody in London now, and if she had nothing more enticing on her schedule, etc. She ended with begging her, if she was mercifully inclined to make her happy with her presence, to bring her Caley and her hound Demon. She had hardly finished when Malcolm presented himself.

She received him very coldly and declined to listen to anything about the fishers. She insisted that, being one of their party, he was prejudiced in their favor; and that, of course, a man of Mr. Crathie's experience must know better than he what ought to be done with such people, in view of protecting her rights and keeping them in order. She declared that she was not going to disturb the old way of things to please him, and said that he had now done her all the mischief he could, except, indeed, he were to head the fishers and sack Lossie House. Malcolm found that by making himself known to her as her brother, he had but given her confidence in speaking her mind when she desired to humiliate him. She was still, however, so far afraid of her brother that she sat in some dread lest he might chance to see the address of the letter she had been writing.

I may mention here that Lady Bellair accepted the invitation with pleasure for herself and Liftore, promised to bring Caley, but utterly declined to take charge of the dog. Thereupon, Florimel, who was fond of the animal, wrote to Clementina, urging her to visit her and begging her, if she could find it within herself to comply, to allow the deerhound to accompany her. Clementina was the only one of her friends, she said, for whom the animal had shown a preference.

Malcolm retired from his sister's presence much depressed,

saw Mrs. Courthope, who was kind as ever, and betook himself to his own room, next to that in which his strange history began. There he sat down and wrote urgently to Lenorme, stating that he had an important communication to make and begging him to start for the north the moment he received the letter. A messenger from Duff Harbor well mounted, he said, would insure his presence within a couple of hours.

He found the behavior of his old acquaintances and friends in the Seaton much what he had expected: the few were as cordial as ever, while the many still resented, with a mingling of the jealousy of affection, his forsaking of the old life for a calling they regarded as unworthy of one bred, at least, if not born a fisherman. The women were all cordial.

27 The Preparation

The heroes of Scaurnose expected a renewal of the attack, and in greater force, the next day. They made their preparations accordingly, strengthening every weak point around the village. They were put in great heart by Malcolm's espousal of their cause, as they considered his punishment of the factor. But when he prevailed upon them to allow Blue Peter to depart, arguing that they had less right to prevent than the factor had to compel him, they once more turned upon him. What right had he to dictate to them? He did not belong to Scaurnose! He reasoned with them that the factor, although he had not justice, had the law on his side and could turn out whom he pleased. They said, "Let him try!" He told them that they had given great provocation, for he knew that the men they had assaulted came surveying for a harbor, and that they ought at least to make some apology for having mistreated them. It was all useless. That was the women's doing, they said; besides, they did not believe him. If what he said was true, what was the thing to them, seeing they were all under notice to leave? Malcolm said that perhaps an apology would be accepted. They told him if he did not take himself off, they would serve him as he had served the factor. Finding expostulation a failure, therefore, he begged Joseph and Annie to settle themselves again as comfortably as they could and left them.

Contrary to the expectation of all, however, and considerably to the disappointment of the party of hotheads, the next day was as peaceful as if Scaurnose had been a halcyon nest floating on the summer waves; and it was soon reported that, in consequence of the punishment he had received from Malcolm, the factor was far too ill to be troublesome to any but his wife. This was true, but, severe as his chastisement was, it was not severe enough to have had any such consequences but for his late growing habit of drinking whiskey. Malcolm, on his part, was greatly concerned to hear the result of his severity. He refrained, however, from calling to inquire, knowing it would be interpreted as an insult, not accepted as a sign of sympathy. He went to the doctor instead, who, to his consternation, looked very serious at first. But when he learned all about the affair, he changed his view considerably and condescended to give good hopes of his coming through, even adding that it would lengthen his life by twenty years if it broke him of his habits of whiskey drinking and rage.

And now Malcolm had a little time of leisure, which he put to the best possible use in strengthening his relations with the fishers. He had nothing to do about the House except look after Kelpie; and Florimel, as if determined to make him feel that he was less to her than before, much as she used to enjoy seeing him sit his mare, never took him out with her—always Stoat. He resolved, therefore, seeing he must yet delay action a while in the hope of the appearance of Lenorme, to go out as in the old days after the herring, both for the sake of splicing, if possible, what strands had been broken between him and the fishers and of renewing for himself the delights of elemental conflict. With these views, he hired himself to the Partan, whose boat's crew was shorthanded. And now, night after night, he revelled in the old pleasure, enhanced by so many months of deprivation. Joy itself seemed embodied in the wind blowing on him. When it came on to blow hard, instead of making him feel small and weak in the midst of the storming forces, it gave him a glorious sense of power and unconquerable life.

It answered also all his hopes in regard to his companions and the fisher-folk generally. Those who had really known him found the same old Malcolm, and those who had doubted him soon began to see that at least he had lost nothing in courage or skill or good-will. Before long he was even a greater favorite than before.

Duncan's former dwelling happened to be then occupied by a lonely woman. Malcolm made arrangements with her to take them both in; so that in relation to his grandfather, too, something very much like the old life returned for a time.

The factor continued very ill. He had sunk into a low state, in which his former indulgence was greatly against him. Every night the fever returned, and at length his wife was worn out with watching and waiting upon him.

And every morning Lizza Findlay, without fail, called to inquire how Mr. Crathie spent the night. To the last, while quarreling with every one of her neighbors with whom she had anything to do, he had continued kind to her, and she was more grateful than one in other trouble than hers could have understood. But she did not know that an element in the origination of his kindness was the belief that it was by Malcolm she had been wronged and forsaken.

Again and again she had offered, in the humblest manner, to ease his wife's burden by sitting with him at night; and at last, finding she could hold up no longer, Mrs. Crathie consented. But even after a week she found herself still unable to resume the watching. So, night after night, resting at home during a part of the day, Lizza sat by the sleeping factor, and when he woke ministered to him like a daughter. Nor did even her mother object, for sickness is a wondrous reconciler. Little did the factor suspect, however, that it was partly for Malcolm's sake she nursed him, anxious to shield the youth from any possible consequences of his righteous vengeance.

"I'm a poor creature, Lizzy," he said, turning his heavy face one midnight toward the girl, as she sat half dozing, ready to start awake.

"God comfort ye, sir!" said the girl.

"He'll take good care of that!" returned the factor. "What did I ever do to deserve it? There's that MacPhail, now—to think of him! Didn't I do what man could for him? Didn't I keep him about the place when all the rest were dismissed? Didn't I give him the key of the library that he might read and improve his mind? And look what comes of it!"

"Ya mean, sir," said Lizza, quite innocently, "that that's the way you've done toward God, so He won't heed you?"

The factor had meant nothing in the least like it. He had merely been talking as the imps of suggestion tossed up. His logic was as sick and helpless as himself. So that he held his peace—stung in his pride, at least, perhaps in his conscience too—only he was not prepared to be rebuked by a girl like her, who had—well, he must let it pass. How much better was he himself?

But Lizza was loyal. She could not hear him speak so of Malcolm and hold her peace as if she agreed in his condemnation.

"You'll know Malcolm better some day, sir," she said.

"Well, Lizzy," returned the sick man, in a tone that but for feebleness would have been indignant, "I have heard a good deal of the way women will stand up for men that have treated them cruelly, but for you to stand up for *him*, well that passes—"

"He's the best friend I ever had," said Lizza.

"Girl! How can you sit there and tell me so to my face?" cried the factor, his voice strengthened by the righteousness of the reproof it bore. "If it were not the dead of the night—"

"I tell you nothing but the truth, sir," said Lizza, as the threat died away. "But you must lie still or I will go for your wife. If you are worse in the morning, it will be my fault, because I couldn't stand to hear such things said about Malcolm."

"Do you mean to tell me," persisted her charge, heedless of her expostulation, "that the fellow who brought you to disgrace and left you with a child you could ill provide for—and I well know never sent you a penny all the time he was away, whatever he may have done now—is the best friend you ever had!"

"Now, God forgive you, Mr. Crathie, for thinking such a thing!" cried Lizza, rising as if she would leave him. "Malcolm MacPhail is as innocent of any sin like mine as my little child itself."

"You mean to tell me he's not the father?"

"No, nor never will be the father of any child whose mother isn't his wife!" said Lizza, with burning cheeks and resolute voice.

The factor, who had risen on his elbow to look her in the face, fell back in silence. Neither of them spoke for what seemed to the watcher a long time, and when she ventured to look at him, he was asleep.

He lay in one of those troubled slumbers into which weakness and exhaustion will sometimes pass very suddenly. When he awoke, there was Lizza looking down on him anxiously.

"What are you looking like that for?" he asked crossly.

She did not like to tell him that she had been alarmed by his dropping asleep. In her confusion she fell back on the last subject.

"There must be some mistake, Mr. Crathie," she said. "I wish you would tell me what makes you hate Malcolm MacPhail as you do."

The factor, although he seemed to himself to know well enough, was yet a little puzzled how to reply. Therewith, a process began that presently turned into something with which never in his life before had his inward parts been acquainted—a sort of self-examination. He said to himself, partly in the desire to justify his present dislike—he would not call it "hate," as Lizza did—that he used to get on with the lad well enough and had never taken offense at his freedoms, making no doubt his manner came of his blood, and he could not help it, being a chip off the old block. But when he ran away with the marquis' boat and went to the marchioness and told her lies against him, then what could he do but dislike him?

Arriving at this point, he opened his mouth and gave the substance of what preceded it for answer to Lizza's question. But she replied at once, "Nobody'll ever make me believe that Malcolm MacPhail ever told a lie against you or anybody. I don't believe he ever told a lie in his life. And about the boat, sir, you know that he was the master of it. It was under his charge, and besides, you yourself don't know that much about boats or sailing."

"But it was me that engaged him again after all the servants at the House had been dismissed. He was *my* servant!"

"That does make it look a little bad, no doubt," allowed Lizza, with something almost of cunning. "How was it, then, that he came to do it at all?"

"I discharged him."

"And what for, if I may be so bold as to ask?" she went on.

"For insolence!"

"Would you tell me how he answered you? Don't think me meddling, sir. But I'm sure there's been some mistake. You couldn't be so good to me and so mean to him without there being some misunderstanding."

It was consoling to the conscience of the factor, in regard of his behavior to the two women, to hear his own praise for kindness from a woman's lips. He took no offense, therefore, at her persistent questioning, but told her as well and as truly as he could remember, with no more than the all-but-unavoidable exaggeration with which feeling will color fact, the whole passage between Malcolm and himself concerning the sale of Kelpie. He closed with an appeal to the judgment of his listener, in which he confidently anticipated her verdict.

"A most ridiculous thing, as you can see yourself as well as anybody, Lizzy! To call an honest man like myself a hypocrite. There's not a child alive that doesn't know that the seller of a horse is bound to extol him and the buyer to take care of himself. I'm not saying it allowable to tell a downright lie, but you may come nearer it in horse-dealing without sinning than in any other kind of business. It's like love and war, in both of which it's well known that all things are fair. The law should read, 'Love and war and horse-dealing'—don't you see, Lizzy?"

But Lizza did not answer. The factor, hearing a stifled sob, lifted himself to his elbow.

"Lie still, sir," said Lizza. "It's nothing. I was only just thinking that that would be the way the father of my child reasoned with himself when he lied to me."

The astonished factor opened his mouth as if to speak, but then held his peace and settled back down on his bed, trying to think.

Now Lizza, for the last few months, had been going to school, the same school with Malcolm, open to all comers—the only school where one is sure to be led in the direction of wisdom. There she had been learning to some purpose—as plainly appeared before she had done with the factor.

"Which church are you an elder in, Mr. Crathie?" she asked presently.

"Why, the Church of Scotland, of course!" answered the patient in some surprise at her ignorance.

"Yes, I know," returned Lizza, "but whose property is it?"

"Whose but the Redeemer's."

"And do you think, Mr. Crathie, that if Jesus Christ had had a horse to sell that He would have hidden from the buyer one hair of a fault the beast had? Would He not have done to his neighbor as He would have his neighbor do to him?"

"Lassie, lassie! You can't compare the likes of Him to such as us. What would He have had to do with horseflesh anyway?"

Lizza held her peace. Here was no room for argument. He had flung the door of his conscience in the face of her who woke it. But it was too late, for the word was already in. God never gave man a thing to do concerning which it were irreverent to ponder how the Son of God would have done it.

The factor fell to thinking, and thinking more honestly than he had thought for many a day. Presently it was revealed to him, that, if he were in the horse market wanting to buy, and a man there who had to sell said to him—"He wouldn't do for you, sir; you would be tired of him in a week," he would never remark, "What a fool the fellow is!" but—"Well now, I call that neighborly!" He did not get quite so far, just then, as to see that every man to whom he might want to sell a horse was as much his neighbor as his own brother. But at least the warped glass of a bad maxim had been cracked in his window.

Days and days passed and still Malcolm had no word from Lenorme. He was getting hopeless in respect of that quarter of possible aid. But so long as Florimel could content herself with the quiet of Lossie House, there was time to wait, he said to himself. She was not idle, and that was promising. Every day she rode out with Stoat. Now and then she would make a call in the neighborhood and, apparently to trouble Malcolm, took care to let him know that on one of these occasions her call had been upon Mrs. Stewart. One thing he did feel was that she had made no renewal of her friendship with his grandfather. She had, alas, outgrown the girlish fancy. Poor Duncan took it much to heart. Though Malcolm knew not of it, Florimel was expecting the arrival of Lady Bellair and Lord Liftore with the utmost impatience. They, for their part, were making the journey by the easiest possible stages, tacking and veering and visiting everyone of their friends that lay between London and Lossie. They thought to give Florimel the little lesson that, though they accepted her invitation, they had plenty of friends in the world besides her ladyship and were not dying to see her.

One evening Malcolm, as he left the grounds of Mr. Morrison on whom he had been calling, saw a traveling carriage pass toward Portlossie. Something like fear laid hold of his heart, more than he had ever felt except when Florimel and he, on the night of the storm, took her father for Lord Gernon the wizard. As soon as he reached certain available fields, he sent Kelpie tearing across them, dodged through a firwood, and came out on the road half a mile in front of the carriage. As again it passed him, he saw that his fears were facts, for in it sat the bold-faced countess and the mean-hearted lord. Something must be done at last, and until it was done good, watch must be kept.

I must here note that, during this time of hoping and waiting, Malcolm had attended to another matter of importance. Over every element influencing his life, his family, his dependents, his property, he desired to possess a lawful, honest command. Where he had to render account, he would be head. Therefore, through Mr. Soutar's London agent, to whom he sent Davy and who he brought acquainted with Merton, and his former landlady at the curiosity shop, he had discovered a good deal about Mrs. Catanach from her London associates, among them the herb doctor and his little boy who had watched Davy. He had now almost completed an outline of evidence, which, grounded on that of Rose, might be used against Mrs. Catanach at any moment. He had also set inquiries on foot in the track of Caley's antecedents and had discovered more than the acquaintance between her and Mrs. Catanach. He was determined to crush the evil powers which had been ravaging his little world.

28 The Visit

Clementina was always ready to accord any reasonable request Florimel could make of her, but her letter lifted such a weight from her heart and life that she would now have done whatever she desired, reasonable or unreasonable. She had no difficulty in accepting Florimel's explanation that her sudden disappearance was but a breaking of the social jail, the flight of the weary bird from its foreign cage back to the country of its nest. That same morning she called upon Demon. The hound, feared and neglected, was rejoiced to see her and there was no ground for dreading his company. It was a long journey, but if it had been across a desert instead of through her own country, the hope that lay at the end of it would have made it more than pleasant.

The letter would have found her at Wastbeach instead of London had not the society and instructions of the schoolmaster detained her a willing prisoner to its heat and glare and dust. Him only in all London she must see to bid good-bye. To Camden Town therefore she went that same evening, when his work would be over for the day. As usual she was shown into his room, and as usual she found him poring over his Greek New Testament.

"Ah!" he said, and rose as she entered, "this, then, is the angel of my deliverance! You see," he went on, "old man as I am and peaceful, the summer does lay hold upon me and sets me longing after the green fields and living air."

"I wish I could be more a comfort to you," answered Clementina, "but I have come to tell you I am going to leave you, though for a little while only, I trust."

"You do not take me by surprise, my lady. I have, of course, been looking forward for some time to my loss and your gain. The world is full of little deaths—deaths of all sorts and sizes, rather let me say. For this one I was prepared. The good summer land calls you to its bosom, and you must go."

"Come with me!" cried Clementina.

"A man must not leave his work—however irksome—for the most peaceful pleasure," answered the schoolmaster.

"But you do not know where I want you to come."

"What difference can that make, my lady. I must be with the children whom I have been engaged to teach, and whose parents pay me for my labor—not with those who can do well without me."

"But I cannot do without you—not for long at least."

"What! Not with Malcolm to supply my place?"

Clementina blushed. "Ah! do not be unkind, master," she said.

"Unkind!" he repeated. "You could not yet imagine the half of what I hope for and from you."

"I *am* going to see Malcolm," she said with a little sigh. "That is, I am going to visit Lady Lossie at her place in Scotland—your old home, where so many must love you. Can't you come? I shall be traveling alone, except my servants."

A shadow came over the schoolmaster's face: "I never do anything of myself. I go not where I wish, but where I seem to be called or sent. I used to build many castles, not without a certain beauty of their own—that is, when I was less understanding. Now I leave them to God to build for me: He does it better and they last longer. But I do not think He will keep me here for long, for I find I cannot do much for these children. This ministration I take to be more for my good than theirs—a little trail of faith and patience for me. True, I *might* be happier where I could hear the larks, but I do not know anywhere that I have been more peaceful than in this little room."

"It is not at all a fit place for *you*," said Clementina.

"Gently, my lady. It is a greater than thou that sets the bounds of my habitation. Perhaps He may give me a palace one day. But the Father has decreed for His children that they shall know the thing that is neither their ideal nor His. All in His time, my lady. He has much to teach us. When do you go?"

"Tomorrow morning."

"Then God be with you. He *is* with you; only my prayer is that you may know it."

"Tell me one thing before I go," said Clementina. "Are we not commanded to bear each other's burdens and so fulfill the law of Christ? I read it today."

"Then why ask me?"

"For another question: does not that involve the command to those who have burdens that they should allow others to bear them?"

"Surely, my lady. But I have no burden to let you bear."

"Why should I have so much and you so little?"

"My lady, I have millions more than you. I have been gathering the crumbs under my Master's table for thirty years."

"I believe you are just as poor as the apostle Paul when he sat down to make a tent or as our Lord himself after He gave up carpentry."

"You are wrong there, my lady. I am not so poor as they must often have been."

"But I don't know how long I may be away, and you may fall ill, or—or—see—some book you may want very much."

"I have my Testament, my Plato, my Shakespeare, and one or two besides whose wisdom I have not yet quite exhausted."

"I can't bear it!" cried Clementina almost on the point of weeping. "Let me be your servant." As she spoke she rose, and walking softly up to him where he sat, knelt at his knees and held out suppliantly a little bag of silk. "Take it—Father," she said, hesitating and with effort, "take your daughter's offering—a poor thing to show her love, but something to ease her heart."

He took it, and weighted it up and down in his hand with an amused smile, but his eyes full of tears. It was heavy. He opened it and emptied it on a chair within his reach and laughed with delight as its contents came tumbling out. "I never saw so much gold in my life if it were all taken together," he said. "What beautiful stuff it is! But I don't want it, my dear. It would but trouble me. Besides, you will want it for your journey."

"That is a mere nothing. I am afraid I am very rich. It is such a shame! But I can't well help it. You must teach me how to become poor."

Clementina had been struggling with herself; now she burst into tears.

"Because I won't take a bagful of gold from you when I don't want it," he said, "do you think I should let myself starve without coming to you? I promise you I will let you know—come to you if I can—the moment I get too hungry to do my work well and have no money left. My sole reason for refusing it now is that I do not need it."

But for all his loving words and assurances, Clementina could not stay her tears.

"See then, for your tears are hard to bear, my daughter," he said, "I will take one of these golden ministers, and if it has flown from me before you return, I will ask for another."

A moment of silence followed, broken only by Clementina's failures in quieting herself.

He opened the bag and slowly, reverentially, drew from it one of the new sovereigns with which it was filled. She took his hand, pressed it to her lips, and walked slowly from the room.

He took the bag of gold from the chair and followed her down the stairs. Her carriage was awaiting her at the door. He handed her in, and laid the bag on the little seat in front.

The coachman took the queer, shabby, un-London-like man for a fortune-teller his lady was in the habit of consulting and paid homage to his power with the handle of his whip as he drove away. The schoolmaster returned to his room—not to his Plato or Shakespeare, not even to Saul of Tarsus, but to the Lord himself.

29   The Awakening

When Malcolm took Kelpie to her stall the night of the arrival of Lady Bellair and her nephew, he was rushed upon by Demon. The hound had arrived a couple of hours before, while Malcolm was out. He wondered he had not seen him with the carriage he had passed, never suspecting he had had another conductress.

I have not said much concerning Malcolm's feelings with regard to Lady Clementina, but all this time the sense of her existence had been like an atmosphere pervading his thoughts. He saw in her the promise of all he could desire to see in a woman. His love was not of the blind little-boy sort, but of a deeper, more exciting, keen-eyed kind, that sees faults where even a true mother will not, so jealous is it of the perfection of the beloved.

If I say, then, that Malcolm was always thinking about Lady Clementina when he was not thinking about something he *had* to think about, have I not said nearly enough? Should I ever dream of attempting to set forth what love is in such a man for such a woman? There are comparatively few that have more than the glimmer of a notion of what love means. God only knows how grandly, how passionately, yet how calmly the man and the woman He has made might love each other. Malcolm's lowly idea of himself did not at all interfere with his loving Clementina, for at first his love was entirely dissociated from any thought of hers. When the idea, the mere idea, of her loving him presented itself, he turned from it. The thought was in its own nature too unfit. From a social point of view there was, of course, little presumption in it. The marquis of Lossie bore a name that might pair itself with any in the land, but Malcolm did not yet feel that the title made much difference to the fisherman. He was what he was, and that was something very lowly indeed.

Yet the thought would at times dawn up from somewhere in the infinite matrix of thought that perhaps if he went to college and graduated and dressed like a gentleman and did everything as gentlemen do—in short, claimed his rank and lived as a marquis should—then was it not, might it not be, within the bounds of possibility—just within them—that the great-hearted, generous, liberty-loving Lady Clementina might not be disgusted if he dared feel toward her as he had never felt and never could feel toward any other? At length, such thoughts rising again and again—gradually more frequently—and ever accompanied by such reflections, he felt as if he must run to her, calling aloud that he was the marquis of Lossie, and throw himself at her feet.

But feeling thus, where was his faith in her principles? How, now, was he treating the truth of her nature? Where, now, were his convictions of the genuineness of her profession? Where were those principles, that truth, those professions if after all she would listen to a marquis and would not listen to a groom? To herald his suit with his rank would be to insult her. And would he not deprive her of the chance to prove her truth if, as he approached her, he called on the marquis to supplement the man!

But what, then, was the man, fisherman or marquis, to dare to such a glory as the Lady Clementina! And in the end he knew that he could not condescend to be accepted as Malcolm, marquis of Lossie, knowing he would have been rejected as Malcolm MacPhail, fisherman and groom. Accepted as marquis, he would forever be haunted with the question whether she would have accepted him as groom. No, he would choose the greater risk of losing her for the chance of winning her the greater.

So far Malcolm got with his theories; but the moment he began to think in the least practically, he recoiled altogether from the presumption. Under no circumstances could he ever have the courage to approach Lady Clementina with a thought of himself in his mind. She had never shown him personal favor. He could not tell whether she had listened to what he had tried to lay before her. He did not know that she had gone to hear his master. His surprise would have equaled his delight at the news that she had already become as a daughter to the schoolmaster.

And what had been Clementina's thoughts since learning that Florimel had not run away with her groom? Her first feeling was an utterly inarticulate, undefined pleasure that Malcolm was free to be thought about. The second was something like relief that the truest man she had ever met, except his master, was not going to marry such an unreality as Florimel. Clementina, with all her generosity, could not help being doubtful of a woman who could make a companion of such a man as Liftore.

Then she began to grow more and more curious about Malcolm. She had already gathered much real knowledge of him, both from himself and Mr. Graham. And she was curious as to whether he might not already be engaged to some young woman in his own station of life. In the lower ranks of society, men married younger. And yet, on the other hand, was it possible that in a fishing village there would be any choice of girls who could understand him when he talked about Plato and the New Testament? But of course, what did she know about the fishers, men and women? There were none at Wastbeach. For anything she knew to the contrary, they might all be philosophers, and a fitting match for Malcolm might be far easier to find amongst them than in the society to which she herself belonged, where in truth the philosophical element was rare enough.

Then arose in her mind the half-pictorial vision of a whole family of brave, believing, daring, saving fisher-folk sacrificing to the rest and all devoted to their neighbors. Their very toils and dangers were but additional means to press their souls together. Why had she been born an earl's daughter, never to look a danger in the face, never to have the chance of a true life—that is, a grand, simple, and noble one?

But had she no power to order her own steps, to determine her own being? Was she nailed to her rank? Was she not a free woman, without even a guardian to trouble her? She had no excuse to act ignobly. Would it then be—would it be a *very* unmaidenly thing if ... The rest of the sentence did not even take the shape of words. But she answered it nevertheless, "Not so unmaidenly as presumptuous." And besides, there was little hope that *he* would ever presume to.... He was such a modest youth, with all his directness and fearlessness. If he had no respect for rank—and that was—yes, she would say the word, *hopeful*—he had, on the other hand, the profoundest respect for the human, and she could not tell how that might come to bear in this case.

Then she fell to thinking of the difference between Malcolm and any other servant she had ever known. She knew that most servants, while they spoke with the appearance of respect in presence, altered their tone entirely when beyond the circle of the eye: theirs was eye-service. But here was a man who touched no imaginary hat while he stood in the presence of his mistress, neither swore at her in the stable yard. He looked her straight in the face and would upon occasion speak, not his mind, but the truth to her. The conviction was clear that if one dared in his presence but utter the name of his mistress lightly, whoever he were, he would have to answer to him for it. What a lovely thing was true service!

Ah, but for her to take the initiative would provoke the conclusion, as revolting to her as unavoidable to him, that she judged herself his superior—so much so as to be absolved from the necessity of behaving to him on the ordinary footing of man and woman. What a ground to start from with a husband! Especially since he was so immeasurably her superior that the poor little advantage of rank on her side vanished like a candle in the sunlight. No, she would have to let it all go—let him go, rather. For if she did approach him, what if he should be tempted by rank and wealth and accept her? That would be worse still—far worse—for then he would be shorn of his glory and prove to be of the ordinary human type after all. No, he could be nothing to her nearer than a bright star blazing unreachable above her.

Thus went the thoughts to and fro in the minds of each. Neither could see the way. Both feared the risk of loss; neither could hope greatly for gain.

30   The Petition

Having put Kelpie up and fed and bedded her, Malcolm took his way to the Seaton, full of busily anxious thought. Things had taken a bad turn. The enemy was in the House with his sister, and he had no longer any chance of judging how matters were going, as now he never rode with her. But at least he could haunt the House. He would run, therefore, to his grandfather and tell him that he was going to occupy his old quarters at the House that night.

Returning directly and passing through the kitchen to ascend the small corkscrew stairs the servants generally used, he encountered Mrs. Courthope, who told him that her ladyship had given orders that her maid, who had come with Lady Bellair, should have his room. He was at once convinced that Florimel had done so with the intention of banishing him from the House, for there were dozens of rooms vacant and many of them more suitable.

It was a hard blow! How he wished for Mr. Graham to consult! And yet Mr. Graham was not of much use where any sort of plotting was wanted. He asked Mrs. Courthope to let him have another room, but she looked so doubtful that he withdrew his request and went back to his grandfather. It was Saturday and not many of the boats would go fishing. But he could not rest and would go line fishing with the *Psyche*'s dinghy.

In an hour the sun was down, the moon was up, and he had caught more fish than he wanted. The fountain of his anxious thoughts was flowing more rapidly once again. He must go ashore. He must go up to the House. Who could tell what might be going on there? He drew in his line, purposing to take the best of the fist to Miss Horn and some to Mrs. Courthope, as in the old days.

The *Psyche* still lay on the sands, and he was rowing the dinghy toward her, when, looking shoreward, he thought he caught a glimpse of someone seated on the slope of the dune. Yes, there was someone there, sure enough. The old times rushed back on his memory. Could it be Florimel? Alas, it was not likely she would now be wandering about alone. But if it were! Then for one attempt more to rouse her slumbering conscience to break with Liftore!

He rowed swiftly to the *Psyche*, beached, and drew up the dinghy, and climbed the dune. Plainly enough, it was a lady who sat there. It might be one from the upper town enjoying the lovely night. It might be Florimel, but how could she have gotten away, or wished to get away, from her newly arrived guests? There was no other figure to be seen all along the sands. He drew nearer. The lady did not move. If it were Florimel, would she not know him as he came, and would she wait for him?

He drew nearer still. His heart gave a great throb. Could it be, or was the moon weaving some hallucination in his troubled brain? If it was a phantom, it was that of Lady Clementina. His spirit seemed to soar aloft and hang hovering over her while his body stood rooted to the spot. She sat motionless, gazing at the sea. Malcolm thought that she could not know him in his fisher-clothes and would take him for some rude fisherman staring at her. He must address her at once. He came forward and said, "My lady!"

She did not start; neither did she speak. She did not even turn her face. She rose first, then turned and held out her hand. Three steps more and he had it in his, and his eyes looked straight into hers. Neither spoke. The moon shone full on Clementina's face. A moment she stood, then slowly sank again upon the sand and drew her skirts about her with a silent show of invitation. The place where she sat was a little terraced hollow in the slope, forming a convenient seat. Malcolm saw, but could not believe she actually made room for him to sit beside her—alone with her in the universe. It was too much; he dared not believe it. Again she made a movement. This time he could not doubt her invitation. It was as if her soul made room in her unseen world for him to enter and sit beside her. But who could enter heaven in his workday garments?

Seeing his hesitation, she said, at last, "Won't you sit by me, Malcolm?"

"I have been catching fish, my lady," he answered, "and my clothes must be unpleasant. I will sit here."

He went a little lower on the slope and laid himself down, leaning on his elbow.

"Do freshwater fishes smell the same as sea fishes, Malcolm?" she asked.

"Indeed, I am not certain, my lady. Why?"

"Because if they do, do you remember what you said to me as we passed the sawmill in the wood?"

It was by silence Malcolm showed he did remember.

"Does not this night remind you of that one at Wastbeach when we came upon you singing?" said Clementina.

"It *is* like it, my lady—now. But, a little ago, before I saw you, I was thinking of that night and thinking how different this was."

Again a moon-filled silence fell, and once more it was the lady who broke it. "Do you know who is at the House?" she asked.

"I do, my lady," he replied.

"I had not been there more than an hour or two," she went on, "when they arrived. I suppose Florimel—Lady Lossie—thought I would not come if she told me she expected them."

"And would you have come, my lady?"

"I cannot endure the earl."

"Neither can I. But then I know more about him than your ladyship does, and I am miserable for my mistress."

It stung Clementina as if her heart had taken a beat backward. But her voice was steadier than it had yet been as she returned. "Why should you be miserable for Lady Lossie?"

"I would die rather than see her marry that man," he answered.

Again her blood stung her in the left side. "You do not want her to marry, then?" she said.

"I do," answered Malcolm, emphatically, "but not that fellow."

"Whom, then, if I may ask?" ventured Clementina trembling.

But Malcolm was silent. He did not feel it right to say.

Clementina turned sick at heart. "I have heard there is something dangerous about the moonlight," she said. "I think it does not suit me tonight. I will go home."

Malcolm sprang to his feet and offered his hand. She did not take it, but rose more lightly, though more slowly, than he. "How did you come from the park on the House grounds, my lady?" he asked.

"By a gate over there," she answered, pointing. "I wandered out after dinner and the sea drew me."

"If your ladyship will allow me, I will take you a much nearer way back," he said.

"Do then," she returned.

He thought she spoke a little sadly and set it down to her having to go back to her fellow guests. What if she should leave tomorrow morning? he thought. Could he ever be sure she had been with him this night? Or would he think it a dream?

They walked across the grassy sand toward the tunnel in silence, he pondering what he could say that might keep her from going so soon.

"My lady never takes me out with her now," he said at length. He was going to add that, if she liked, he and Kelpie could show her the country. But then he saw that if she were not with Florimel, his sister would be riding everywhere alone with Liftore. Therefore he stopped short.

"And you feel forsaken—deserted?" returned Clementina, sadly still.

"Rather, my lady."

They had reached the tunnel. It looked very black when he opened the door, but there was just a glimmer through the trees at the other end.

"Do I walk straight through?" she asked.

"Yes, my lady. You will soon come out in the light again," he said.

"Are there no steps to fall down?"

"None, my lady. But I will go first if you wish."

"No, that would but cut off the little light I have," she said. "Come beside me."

They passed through in silence, except for the rustle of her dress and the dull echo that haunted their steps. In a few moments they came out among the trees, but both continued silent. The still, thoughtful moonlight seemed to press them close together, but neither knew that the other felt the same.

They reached a point in the road where another step would bring them in sight of the House.

"You cannot go wrong now, my lady," said Malcolm. "If you please, I will go no farther."

"Do you not live in the House?" she asked.

"I used to do as I like, and could be there or with my grandfather. I did mean to be at the House tonight, but my lady has given my room to her maid."

"What! That woman Caley?"

"I suppose so, my lady. I must sleep tonight in the village. If you could, my lady—" he added, after a pause and faltering, hesitating. "If you could—if you would not be displeased at my asking you," he resumed—"if you *could* keep my lady from going farther with that—I shall call him names if I go on."

"It is a strange request," Clementina replied after a moment's reflection. "I hardly know, as the guest of Lady Lossie, what answer I ought to make to it. One thing I will say, however, though you may know more of the man than I, you can hardly dislike him more. Whether I can interfere is another matter. Honestly, I do not think it would be of any use. But I do not say I will not. Goodnight."

She hurried away and did not again offer her hand.

Malcolm walked back through the tunnel, his heart singing and making melody. Oh, how lovely—how more than lovely, how divinely beautiful she was! And so kind and friendly! But something seemed to trouble her too, he said to himself. He little thought that he, and no one else, had spoiled the moonlight for her. He went home to glorious dreams—she to a troubled, half-wakeful night. Not until she had made up her mind to do her utmost to rescue Florimel from Liftore, even if it gave her to Malcolm, did she find a moment's quiet. It was morning then, but she fell fast asleep, slept late and woke refreshed.

31   The Reconciliation

Mr. Crathie was slowly recovering, but still very weak. He did not, after having turned the corner, get well as fast as the doctor judged he ought, and the reason was plain to Lizza, dimly perceptible to his wife—he was ill at ease.

A man may have more on his mind and a more sensitive conscience than his neighbors give him credit for. They may know and understand him up to a certain point in his life, but then a crisis, by them unperceived, arrives after which the man, to all eternity, could never be the same as they had known him. The fact that a man has never up to any point yet been aware of anything outside himself cannot shut Him out who is beyond and who is able to sting even the most inactive of consciences.

The sources of restlessness deep in the soul of hard, commonplace, business-worshiping Hector Crathie were now two: the first, that he had lifted his hand to a woman; the second, the old ground of his quarrel with Malcolm brought up by Lizza.

All his life, Mr. Crathie had prided himself on his honesty in business and was therefore in one of the most dangerous moral positions a man can occupy. Asleep in the mud, he dreamed himself awake on a pedestal. The honesty in which a man can pride himself must be a small one, for mere honesty will never think of itself at all. The limited honesty of the factor clung to the interests of his employers, and he let the rights of those he encountered take care of themselves. Those he dealt with were to him rather as enemies than friends—not enemies to be prayed for, but to be spoiled. Malcolm's doctrine of honesty in horse-dealing was to him ludicrously new. His notion of honesty in that kind was to cheat the buyer for his master if he could, proud to write in his book a large sum against the name of the animal. He would have scorned the idea of making a farthing by it himself through any business quirk whatever, but he would not have been the least ashamed if, having sold

Kelpie, he had heard—say, after a week of her possession—that she had dashed out her purchaser's brains. He would have been a little shocked, a little sorry perhaps, but not at all ashamed. "By this time," he would have said, "the man ought to have been up to her and either taken care of himself or sold her again." —to dash out another man's brains instead!

That Malcolm or the fallen fisher-girl should judge differently in no way troubled him. What could they know about the rights and wrongs of business? The fact, which Lizza brought to bear upon him, that our Lord would not have done such a thing was to him no argument at all. He said to himself that no one could be expected to do like Him, that He was divine and didn't have to fight for a living and was only intended to show us what sinners we were, not to be imitated. After all, religion was one thing, but business was another. And a very proper thing too, with customs and, indeed, laws of its own far more definite than those of religion. To mingle the one with the other was not merely absurd; it was irreverent and wrong, certainly never intended in the Bible. It was always "the Bible" with him—never the will of Christ.

But though he could dispose of the questions thus satisfactorily, yet as he lay ill, without any distractions, the thing haunted him. A night came during which he was troubled and feverish. He had a dream in which he saw the face of Jesus looking at him, full of sorrowful displeasure. And in his heart he knew it was because of a certain transaction in horse-dealing for which he had lauded his own cunning—adroitness, he considered it—and success. One word only he heard from the Man in the dream: "Worker of iniquity!" and he woke with a great start.

From that moment truths began to be facts to him. The beginning of the change was indeed very small. Every beginning is small, but every beginning is a creation. His dull and unimaginative nature had received a gift in a dream, and the seed began to sprout. Henceforth, the claims of his neighbor began to reveal themselves and his mind to breed conscientious doubts and scruples with which, struggle as he might against it, a certain respect for Malcolm would keep coming and mingling.

Lizza's nightly ministrations had not been resumed, but she

called often and was a good deal with him; for Mrs. Crathie had learned to like the humble, helpful girl. One day, when Malcolm was seated, mending a net among the thin grass and great red daisies of the links by the banks of the stream where it crossed the sands from the Lossie grounds to the sea, Lizza came up to him and said, "The factor would like to see you, Malcolm, as soon as you could go to him." She waited for no reply. Malcolm rose and went.

At the factor's, the door was opened by Mrs. Crathie herself who led him into the dining room where she plunged at once into business, doing her best to keep down all manifestation of the profound resentment she had against him. "You see, Malcolm," she said, as if persuing instead of beginning a conversation, "he's pretty sore over the little fracas between you and him. Just make your apologies to him and tell him you're sorry for misbehaving to him. Tell him that, Malcolm, and here's a half crown for you."

"But, mem," said Malcolm, taking no notice for either the coin or the words that accompanied the offer, "I can't lie. I wasn't drunk and I'm not sorry."

"Hoot!" returned Mrs. Crathie, "I'll warrant you can lie well enough if you had the occasion. Take your money and do what I tell you!"

"If Mr. Crathie wishes to see me, mem," rejoined Malcolm, "I am ready. If not, please allow me to go."

The same moment the bell whose rope was at the head of the factor's bed rang. "Come this way," she said and, turning, led him up the stairs to the room where her husband lay.

Entering, Malcolm stood astonished at the change he saw upon the strong man, and his heart was filled with compassion. The factor was sitting up in bed, looking very white and worn and troubled. Even his nose had grown thin and white. He held out his hand to him and said to his wife, "Take the door to you, Mistress Crathie," indicating which side he wished it closed from.

"You were some hard on me, Malcolm," he went on grasping the youth's hand.

"I doubt it was too hard," said Malcolm who could hardly speak for the lump in this throat.

"Well, I deserved it. But eh, Malcolm. I can't believe it was me; it had to have been the drink."

"It *was* the drink," rejoined Malcolm, "so before you rise from that bed, sir, why don't you swear to our great God that you'll never again take more than one small glass at one sitting."

"I swear it, Malcolm," said the factor.

"It's easy to swear now, but when you're up again it'll be hard to keep your oath.—Oh, Lord," spoke the youth, breaking out into an almost involuntary prayer, "help this man to keep truth with you.—And now, Mr. Crathie," he resumed, "I'm your servant, ready to do anything I can. Forgive me, sir, for laying it onto you over-hard."

"I forgive you," said the factor, delighted to have something to forgive.

"I thank you from my heart," answered Malcolm, and again they shook hands.

"But, Malcolm," he added, "how will I ever show my face again?"

"Oh, folks are terrible good-natured," returned Malcolm eagerly, "when you allow that you're in the wrong. I do believe that when a man confesses to his neighbor and says he's sorry, he thinks more of him than he did before. You see, we all know we have done wrong, but we haven't usually confessed it. And it's a funny thing, but a man will think it grand of someone else to confess, but when the time comes when there's something he needs to repent of himself, he hesitates for fear of the shame of having to confess it. To me the shame lies in *not* confessing after you know you're in the wrong. You'll see, sir, the fisherfolk will mind what you say to them a heap better now."

"Do you really think so?" sighed the factor.

"I do, sir. Only when you grow better you mustn't let Satan tempt you into thinking that this repenting was but a weakness of the flesh instead of an enlightenment of the Spirit."

"I'll bind myself to it!" cried the factor eagerly. "Go and tell them all in my name that I take back every notice I gave. Do you think it would be good to take a pound note apiece to the two women?"

"I wouldn't do that, sir," answered Malcolm. "For your own sake, I wouldn't to Mistress Mair, for nothing would make her take it; it would only affront her. You'll have many a chance of making it up to them both, ten times over, before you and them part ways."

"I must leave the country, Malcolm."

"Indeed, sir, you'll do nothing of the kind! The fishers themselves would rise up to prevent you from doing that, as they did with Blue Peter. As soon as you're able to be out and about again, you'll see plain enough that there's no occasion for anything like that. Portlossie wouldn't know itself without you. Just give me a commission to say to the two honest women that you're sorry for what you did, and that's all that need be said between you and them, or their men either."

The result showed that Malcolm was right, for the very next day, instead of looking for gifts from him, the two injured women came to the factor's door with the offering of a few fresh eggs and a great lobster.

32   The Understanding

Malcolm's custom was, immediately after breakfast, to give Kelpie her airing—and a tremendous amount of air she wanted for the huge animal furnace of her frame and the fiery spirit that kept it alight. Then, returning to the Seaton, to change the dress of a groom, in which he always appeared about the House lest by chance his mistress should want him, for that of a fisherman so that he could help with the nets or boats or with whatever else was going on. As often as he might he went also to the long shed where the women prepared the fish for salting, took a knife and wrought as deftly as any of them, throwing a rapid succession of cleaned herrings into the preserving brine. It was no wonder he was a favorite with the women. Although the place was malodorous and the work dirty, Malcolm had been accustomed to the sight and smell from earliest childhood. Still it was work most men would not do. He had such a chivalrous humanity that it could not bear to see man or woman at anything scorned except that he bore a hand in it himself. He did it half in love, half in terror of being unjust.

He had gone to Mr. Crathie in his fisher-clothes and the nearest way led him past a corner of the House overlooked by one of the drawing-room windows. Clementina saw him pass and, judging by his garb that he would probably return presently, went out in hope of meeting him. As he was going back to his net by the sea gate, he caught sight of her on the opposite side of the burn, accompanied only by a book. He walked through it, climbed the bank, and approached her.

It was a hot summer afternoon. The burn ran dark and brown and cool in the deep shade, but the sea beyond was glowing in light. No breath of air was stirring; no bird sang. The sun was burning high in the west.

Clementina stood awaiting him. "Malcolm," she said, "I have been watching all day, but have not found a single opportunity of speaking to your mistress as you wished. But to tell the truth, I am not sorry, for the more I think about it the less I see what to say. That another does not like a person can have little weight with one who does, and I *know* nothing against him. I wish you would release me from your request. It is such an ugly thing to speak to one's hostess to the disadvantage of a fellow guest!"

"I understand," said Malcolm. "It was not a right thing to ask of you."

"Thank you. Had it been before you left London! Lady Lossie is very kind, but does not seem to put the same confidence in me as before. She and Lady Bellair and that man make a trio, and I am left outside. I almost think I ought to go. Even Caley is more of a friend than I am. I cannot get rid of the suspicion that something not right is going on. There seems a bad air about the place. Those two are playing their game with the inexperience of that poor child, your mistress."

"I know that very well, may lady, but I hope yet they will not succeed," said Malcolm.

By this time they were near the tunnel.

"Could you let me through the other way—to the shore?" asked Clementina.

"Certainly, my lady. I wish you could see the boats go out. They will all be starting together as soon as the tide turns."

"Could I not go with you—for one night—just for once, Malcolm?"

"My lady, it would hardly do, I am afraid. If you knew the discomforts to one unaccustomed, I doubt you would want to go. You would need to be a fisherman's sister—or wife—I fear, my lady, to get through it."

Clementina smiled gravely, but did not reply. Malcolm, too, was silent, thinking. "Yes," he said at last, "I see how we could manage it. You shall have a boat for your own use, my lady, and—"

"But I want to see just what you see and feel what you feel. I don't want a rose-leaf notion of the thing. I want to understand what you fishermen encounter and experience."

"But look what clothes, what boots, we fishers must wear to be fit for our work! But I suppose you could have a true idea—as far as it reaches. All right, you shall go in a real fishing boat with a full crew and all the nets, and you shall catch real herrings. Only you shall not be out any longer than you please. But there is hardly time to arrange it for tonight, my lady."

"Tomorrow, then?"

"Yes, I have no doubt I can manage it by then."

"Oh, thank you!" said Clementina. "It will be a great delight."

"And now," suggested Malcolm, "would you like to go through the village and see some of the cottages, and how the fishers live?"

"If they would not think me intrusive," answered Clementina.

"There is no danger of that," rejoined Malcolm. "If it were someone such as Lady Bellair who would patronize them and then blame what she might call their poverty on sin and childishness as if she were their spiritual and social superior, they might very likely think it rude. The whole question reminds me of what Mr.

Graham said: that in the kingdom of heaven to rule is to raise; a man's rank is in his power to uplift."

"I would I were in the kingdom of heaven if it be as you and Mr. Graham take it for!" said Clementina.

"You must be in it, my lady, or you couldn't wish it to be such as it is."

"Can one be in it and yet seem to himself to be out of it, Malcolm?"

"So many are out of it that seem to be in it, my lady, that one might well imagine it the other way around with some."

"That seems an uncharitable thing to say, Malcolm."

"Our Lord speaks of many coming up to His door confident of admission, whom He yet sends away. Faith is obedience, not confidence."

"Then I do well to fear."

"Yes, my lady, so long as your fear makes you knock the louder."

"But if I be in, as you say, how can I go on knocking?"

"There are a thousand more doors to knock at after you are in, my lady. No one content to stand just inside the gate will be inside it long. It is one thing to be in and another to be satisfied that we are in. Such a satisfying as comes from our own feelings may, you see from what our Lord says, be a false one. He who does what the Lord tells him *is* in the kingdom, even if every feeling of heart and brain told him otherwise."

During their talk they reached the Seaton, and Malcolm took her to see his grandfather.

"Tall and faer, chentle and coot!" murmured the old man as he held her hand for a moment in his. "She'll not pe a Cawmill, Malcolm?"

"No, no, Daddy—far from that," answered Malcolm.

"Then my laty will pe right welcome to Tuncan's heart," he replied and, taking her hand, led her to a chair.

When they left they visited the Partaness. Clementina's heart was drawn to the young woman who sat in a corner rocking her child in its wooden cradle, never lifting her eyes from her needle-work. She knew her for the fisher-girl of Malcolm's picture.

From house to house he took her, and wherever they went they were welcomed. The fishers and their wives did the honors of their poor houses in a homely and dignified fashion. "What would you do now if you were lord of the place?" asked Clementina as they left and walked toward the sea gate. "What would be the first thing you would do?"

"As it would be my business to know my tenants that I might rule them," he answered, "I should be in no hurry to make changes, but would talk openly with them, understand them, and try to be worthy of their confidence. Of course I would see a little better to their houses and improve their harbor; and I would build a boat for myself to show them a better kind. But I would spend my best efforts to make them follow Him whose first servants were the fishermen of Galilee."

A pause followed.

"Don't you sometimes find it hard to remember God all through your work?" asked Clementina.

"I don't try to consciously remember Him every moment. For He is in everything, whether I am thinking of it or not. When I go fishing, I go to catch God's fish. When I take Kelpie out, I am teaching one of God's wild creatures. When I read the Bible or Shakespeare, I am listening to the word of God, uttered in each after its own kind. When the wind blows on my face, it is God's wind."

After a little pause, "And when you are talking to a rich, ignorant, proud lady?" said Clementina, "what do you feel then?"

"That I would it were my Lady Clementina instead," answered Malcolm with a smile.

She held her peace.

When he left her, Malcolm hurried to Scaurnose and arranged with Blue Peter for his boat and crew the next night. Returning to his grandfather, he found a note waiting him from Mrs. Courthope to the effect that, as Miss Caley had preferred another room, there was no reason why, if he pleased, he should not reoccupy his own.

33   The Sail

The next morning the sun dawned crisp and warm as the boats slipped slowly back with a light wind to the harbor of Portlossie. Malcolm did not wait to land the fish, but having changed his clothes and taken his breakfast with Duncan, who was always up early, went up to the House to look after Kelpie. When he had done with her, finding some of the household already in motion, he went through the kitchen and up the old corkscrew stairs to his room, to have the sleep he generally had before breakfast. Presently came a knock at his door, and there was Rose. She had either been watching for him or had learned from Mrs. Courthope that he might be returning to the House.

The girl's behavior to Malcolm was changed. The conviction had been growing in her that he was not what he seemed, and she regarded him now with a vague awe. But there was a fear in her eyes now. She looked this way and that and timidly followed him to the door to tell him, once out of sight of the other servants, that she had seen the woman who gave her the poisonous philtre talking to Caley the night before at the foot of the bridge, after everybody else was in bed. She had been miserable until she could warn him. He thanked her heartily and said he would be on his guard. She crept softly away. He secured his door, lay down and, trying to think, fell asleep.

When he awoke, his brain was clear. The very next day, whether Lenorme came or not, he would declare himself. That night he would go fishing with Lady Clementina, but not one day longer would he allow those people to be about his sister. Who could tell what might not be brewing, or into what abyss, with the help of her friends, the woman Catanach might plunge Florimel?

He rose, took Kelpie out, and had a good gallop. On his way back he saw, in the distance, Florimel riding with Liftore. The earl was on his father's bay mare. He could not endure the sight and dashed home at full speed.

Learning from Rose that Lady Clementina was in the flower garden, he found her at the swan basin feeding the goldfish.

"My lady," he said, "I have got everything arranged for to-night."

"And when shall we go?" she asked eagerly.

"At the turn of the tide, about half-past seven. But seven is your dinner hour."

"It is of no consequence. But could you not make it half an hour later, and then I should not seem rude?"

"Make it any hour you please, my lady, so long as the tide is falling."

"Let it be eight, then, and dinner will be almost over. Shall I tell them where I am going?"

"Yes, my lady. It will be better. They will look amazed, for all their breeding."

"Whose boat is it, that I may be able to tell them if they should ask me?"

"Joseph Mair's. He and his wife will come and fetch you. Annie Mair will go with us—if I may say us. Will you allow me to go in your boat, my lady?"

"I couldn't go without you, Malcolm."

"Thank you, my lady. Indeed, I don't know how I could let you go without me. Not that there is anything to fear, or that I could make it the least safer, but somehow it seems my business to take care of you."

"Like Kelpie?" said Clementina, with a merrier smile than he had ever seen on her face before.

"Yes, my lady," answered Malcolm, "if to do for you all and the best you will permit me to do is to take care of you like Kelpie."

Clementina gave a little sigh.

"Mind you don't scruple, my lady, to give what orders you please. It will be *your* fishing boat for tonight."

Clementina bowed her head in acknowledgment.

The evening came, and the company at Lossie House was still seated at the table, Clementina heartily weary of the vapid talk that had been going on all through the dinner, when she was informed that a fisherman of the name of Mair was at the door, accompanied by his wife, saying they had an appointment with her. She had already acquainted her hostess with her arrangements for going fishing that night; now she rose and excused herself. Clementina hurriedly changed her dress, hastened to join Malcolm's messengers, and almost in a moment had made the two childlike people at home with her by the simplicity and truth of her manner. They had not been with her five minutes before thy said in their hearts that here was the wife for the marquis if he could get her.

They took the nearest way to the harbor—through the town. All in the streets and at the windows stared to see the grand lady from the House walking between a Scaurnose fisherman and his wife, chatting away with them as if they were all fishers together.

"I'm glad to see the young woman—and a pretty lass she is— in such good company," said Miss Horn to herself. "I'm thinking the hands of the marquis must be in this!"

The boat and crew were all ready to receive her. On the shore stood Malcolm with a young woman whom Clementina recognized at once as the girl she had seen at the Findlays.

"My lady," he said, approaching, "would you do me the favor to let Lizzy go with you. She would like to attend to your ladyship, because, being a fisherman's daughter, she is used to the sea, and Mrs. Mair is not so much at home upon it, being a farmer's daughter from inland."

Receiving Clementina's thankful assent, he turned to Lizza and said, "Mind you, tell my lady what reason you know why my mistress at the House shouldn't be married to Lord Liftore—he that was Lord Meikleham. You can speak to my lady there as you would to myself."

Lizza blushed a deep red and glanced at Clementina, but there was no annoyance in her face. Malcolm hoped that if she heard, or guessed, Lizza's story, Clementina might yet find some way of bringing her influence to bear on his sister even at the last hour of her chance; from which, for her sake, he shrank the more the nearer it drew. Clementina held out her hand to Lizza and again accepted her offered service with kindly thanks. Peter took his wife in his arms and, walking through the few yards of water between, lifted her into the boat. Malcolm and Clementina turned to each other. He was about to ask leave to do her the same service, but she spoke before him. "Put Lizzy on board first," she said.

He obeyed and when, returning, he again approached her, "Are you able, Malcolm?" she asked. "I am very heavy."

He smiled, took her in his arms like a child, and had placed her on the cushions before she had time to contest the mode of her transference. Then taking a stride deeper into the water, he scrambled on board. The same instant the men gave way and away glided the boat out into the measureless north with the tide, where the horizon was now dotted with the sails that had preceded it.

No sooner were they afloat than a kind of enchantment enwrapped and possessed the soul of Clementina. Everything seemed all at once changed utterly. The cliffs, the rocks, the sands, the dune, the town, the very clouds that hung over the hill above Lossie House were all transfigured. Out they rowed and drifted till the coast began to open up beyond the headlands on either side. There a light breeze was waiting them. Up went three short masts, and three darkbrown sails shown red in the sun. Malcolm came aft, over the great heap of brown nets, and got down in a little well, there to sit and steer the boat. For now, obedient to the wind in its sails, it went frolicking over the sea.

The slow twilight settled into night. The nets were thrown out and sunk straight into the deep, stretched between leads below and floats and buoys above, and the sails were brought down. The boat was still, anchored, as it were, by hanging acres of curtain, and all was silent. Most of the men were asleep in the bows of the boat; all were lying down but one. That one was Malcolm. The boat rose and sank a little, just enough to rock the sleeping children a little deeper into their sleep. Malcolm thought all slept. He did not see how Clementina's eyes shone as she gazed at the vault of stars in the heavens. She knew that Malcolm was near her, but she would not speak, she would not break the peace. Then softly woke a murmur of sound that strengthened and grew and swelled at last into a song. She feared to stir lest she should interrupt its flow.

There was an auld fisher—he sat by the wa',
    An' luikit oot ower the sea:
The bairnies war playin'; he smilit on them a',
    But the tear stude in his e'e.
        An' it's oh to win awa', awa'!

Refrain:

    An' it's oh to win awa'
Whaur the bairns come home, an' the
    wives they bide,
    An' God is the Father o' a'!

Jocky an' Jeamy an' Tammy oot there,
    A'i' the boatie gaed doon;
An' I'm ower auld to fish ony mair,
    An' I hinna the chance to droon.
        An' it's oh to win awa', awa'! (Repeat refrain)

An' Jeanie she grat to ease her hert,
    An' she easit hersel' awa';
But I'm ower auld for the tear to stert,
    An' sae the sighs maun blaw.
        An' it's oh to win awa', awa'! (Repeat refrain)

Lord, steer me hame whaur my Lord has steerit,
    For I'm tired o' life's rockin' sea;
An' dinna be lang, for I'm nearhan' fearit
    'At I'm maist ower auld to dee.
        An' it's oh to win awa', awa'! (Repeat refrain)

Again the stars and sky were everything, and there was no
sound but the slight lapping of the water against the edge of the
boat. Then Clementina said, "Did you make that song, Malcolm?"

"Yes, my lady."

"I didn't know you could enter like that into the feelings of an
old man."

"And why not, my lady? I never can see a living thing without
asking how it feels. I've often, when out like this, tried to fancy
myself a herring caught by the gills in the net down below, instead

of the fisherman in the boat above going to haul him out."

"And did you succeed?"

"Well, I fancy I came to understand as much of him as he does himself. But would you not like to sleep, my lady?"

"No, Malcolm. I would much rather hear you talk. Could you not tell me a story now. Lady Lossie mentioned one you told her once about an old castle not far from here."

"Eh, my lady," broke in Annie Mair, who had waked up while they were speaking. "I wish you would make him tell you that story, for my man's heard him tell it and he says it is terrible gruesome. I would sure like to hear it—Wake up, Lizzy," she went on, in her eagerness waiting for no answer, "Malcolm's going to tell the tale of the old Colonsay castle."

Malcolm could see no reason not to tell the strange and wild story requested of him and thereupon commenced it, but modified the Scotch considerably for the sake of unaccustomed ears.

When it was ended, Clementina said nothing. All was silent for a time.

When the time was right, up sprang the men and went each to his place. As they pulled in the nets a torrent of gleaming fish poured in over the gunwale of the boat. Such a take it was! A light westerly wind was blowing and all the boats were now ready to seek the harbor. Heavy-laden, they crept slowly to the land. As she lay snug and warm, with the cool breath of the sea on her face, a half sleep came over Clementina. No word passed between her and Malcolm all their homeward way. Each was brooding over the night and its joy that enclosed them together. Clementina also had in her mind a scheme for attempting what Malcolm had requested of her. The next day she must try it, thinking that, if she failed, she must leave at once for England.

They glided once more through the harbor. When Clementina's foot touched the shore, she felt like one waked out of a dream. She turned away from the boat and its crew and with Malcolm and Lizza passed along the front of the Seaton. Arriving at the entrance of her home, Lizza bade them good-night, and Clementina and Malcolm were left. Now drew near the full power, the culmination of the mounting enchantment of the night, for

Malcolm. When the Scaurnose people should have passed them, they would be alone. There would not be a living soul on the shore for hours. From the harbor, the nearest way to the House was by the sea gate, but where was the haste with the lovely night around them, private as a dream shared only by two? Instead, therefore, of turning up by the side of the stream where it crossed the shore, he took Clementina once again in his arms unforbidden and carried her over. Then the long sands lay open to their feet.

Presently they heard the Scaurnose party behind them. As by common resolve they turned to the left and, crossing the end of the dune, resumed their former direction. The voices passed on the other side, and they heard them slowly fade into the distance. At length Malcolm knew his friends were winding the red path to the top of this cliff. And now the shore was bare of any presence, bare of sound except the rush of the rising tide. But behind the long sandhill, for all they could see of the sea, they might have been in the heart of a continent.

"Who could imagine the ocean so near us, my lady?" said Malcolm after they had walked for some time without word spoken.

"Who can tell what may be near us?" she returned.

"True, my lady. Our future is near us, holding thousands of things unknown."

As they spoke they came opposite the tunnel, but Malcolm turned from it and they ascended the dune. Far in the east lurked a suspicion of dawn. They descended a few paces and halted again.

"Did your ladyship ever see the sunrise?" asked Malcolm.

"Never in open country," she answered.

"Then stay and see it now, my lady. He'll rise just over yonder. A more glorious chance you could not have."

Clementina slowly sank on the sand of the slope. Malcolm took his place a little below, leaning on his elbow and looking at her. Thus they waited the sunrise.

Was it minutes or only moments passed in that silence, whose speech was only the soft ripple of the sea on the sand? Neither could have answered the question. At length said Malcolm, "I am thinking of changing my service, my lady."

"Indeed, Malcolm?"

"Yes, my lady. My—mistress does not want to turn me away, but she is tired of me and does not want me any longer."

"But you would never think of forever forsaking a fisherman's life for that of a servant, surely, Malcolm?"

"What would become of Kelpie, my lady?" rejoined Malcolm, smiling to himself.

"Ah!" said Clementina. "I had not thought of her. But you cannot take her with you," she added.

"There is nobody about the place who could, or rather who would, do anything with her. They would sell her. I have enough to buy her, and perhaps somebody might not object to the encumbrance, but hire me and her together . . . *your* groom wants to find a coachman's place, my lady."

"Oh, Malcolm! Do you mean you would be *my* groom?" cried Clementina, pressing her palms together.

"If you would have me, my lady; but I have heard you say you would have none but a married man."

"But, Malcolm, don't you know anybody that would . . . Could you not find someone—women lady that . . . I mean, why shouldn't you be a married man?"

"For a very good and, to me, rather sad reason, my lady. The only woman I could marry or should ever be able to marry would not have me. She is very kind and very noble, but . . . it is preposterous, the thing is too preposterous. I dare not have the presumption to ask her."

Malcolm's voice trembled as he spoke and a few moments' pause followed, during which he could not lift his eyes. The whole heaven seemed pressing down upon him.

But his words had raised a storm in Clementina's bosom. A cry broke from her, but she called up all the energy of her nature and stilled it that she might speak. The voice that came was little more than a sob-scattered whisper, but to her it seemed as if all the world must hear. "Oh, Malcolm," she panted, "I *will* try to be good and wise. Don't marry anybody else—*anybody*, I mean; but come with Kelpie and be my groom, and wait and see if I don't grow better."

Malcolm leaped to his feet and threw himself at hers. He had heard but in part and he *must* know all. "My lady," he said with intense quiet, "take me for fisherman, groom, or what you will. I offer the whole sum of service that is in me."

Slowly, gently, Clementina knelt before him. In clear, unshaken tones, for she feared nothing now, she said, "Malcolm, I am not worthy of you. But take me—take my very soul if you will, for it is yours."

The two entranced souls looked at each other. Clementina rose, and they stood hand in hand, speechless.

"Ah, my lady," said Malcolm at length, "what is to become of this delicate smoothness in my great rough hand? Will it not be hurt?"

"You don't know how strong it is, Malcolm. There!" she said and squeezed his hand tightly.

"I can scarcely feel it with my hand, my lady; it goes through to my heart. It shall lie in mine as the diamond in the rock."

"No, no, Malcolm! Now that I am going to be a fisherman's wife, it must be a strong hand—it must work. What will you have me do to rise a little nearer your level? Shall I give away my lands and money? Shall I live with you in the Seaton or will you come and fish at Wastbeach?"

"Forgive me, my lady. I can't think of those things now—even with you in them. Let us not now, when your love makes me happier than ever I was, talk of times and places."

A silence fell. But he resumed: "My lady, I know I shall never love you aright until you have made me better. When the face of the least lovely of my neighbors needs but to appear to rouse in my heart a divine tenderness, then it must be that I shall love you better than now. Now, alas! I am so swayed toward wrong, so fertile of resentments and indignation! You must help cure me, my divine Clemency. But am I a poor lover to talk, this first glorious hour, of anything but my lady and my love?"

"Alas! I am beside you but a block of marble," said Clementina. "You are so eloquent, my—"

"New groom," suggested Malcolm, gently.

Clementina smiled. "But my heart is so full," she went on, "that

I cannot think the smallest thought. I hardly know that I feel. I only know that I want to weep."

All at once they became aware that an eye was upon them. It was the sun. He was ten degrees up the slope of the sky, and they had never seen him rise. And with the sun came a troubled thought. It suddenly occurred to Clementina that she would rather not walk up to the door of Lossie House with Malcolm at this hour of the morning. Yet neither could she well appear alone.

Before she had spoken her anxiety, Malcolm rose. "You won't mind being left, my lady," he said, "for a quarter of an hour or so, will you? I want to bring Lizzy to walk home with you."

He went, and Clementina sat alone on the dune. She watched the great strides of her fisherman as he walked along the sands. She was a little weary, laid her head own upon her arm, and slept. In a moment, it seemed, she opened her eyes, calm as a child, and there stood her fisherman.

"I have been explaining to Lizzy, my lady," he said, "that your ladyship would rather have her company up to the door than mine. Lizzy is to be trusted, my lady."

Clementina rose and they went straight to the door in the bank, through the tunnel and young wood and along the lovely path—the three together. When they drew near the House, Malcolm left them. After they had rung a good many times, the door was opened by the housekeeper, looking just a little scandalized.

"Please, Mrs. Courthope," said Lady Clementina, "will you give orders that when this young woman comes to see me today, she shall be shown up to my room?"

Then she turned to Lizza and thanked her for her kindness, and they parted—Lizza to her baby, and Clementina to yet a dream or two. Long before her dreams were sleeping ones, however, Malcolm was out in the bay in the *Psyche*'s dinghy catching mackerel—some should be for his grandfather, some for Miss Horn, some for Mrs. Courthope, and some for Mrs. Crathie.

34   The Announcement

When Malcolm had caught as many fish as he wanted, he rowed to the other side of Scaurnose. There he landed, left the dinghy in the shelter of the rocks, climbed the steep cliff, and sought Blue Peter at his home. Though the sun was up, the brown village was yet quiet as a churchyard. Some of the men had not yet returned from the night's fishing, others were asleep. But he was the only one awake; on the threshold of Peter's cottage sat little Phemy.

"Are you already up, Phemy?" asked Malcolm, smiling as he approached.

"Ay, for some time," she said.

"Would you tell your father I would like to see him?"

In a few minutes Blue Peter appeared, rubbing his eyes.

"I'm sorry to have to wake you, friend Peter," began Malcolm, "but I had to talk to you. I'm going to speak out today, declare myself."

"Well, I am glad of that, Malcolm!—I beg your pardon, my lord, I should say—Annie!"

"Keep it quiet though, man. I don't want it out in Scaurnose first. I've come to ask you to stand by me when the time comes."

"I will do that, my lord."

"Well, go and gather your boat crew and fetch them down to the cove. I'll tell them, and maybe they'll stand by me too."

"There's little fear of them letting you down, if I know my men," answered Peter and went off, nearly only half dressed, while Malcolm went back down the path and waited by his boat.

At length six men appeared coming down the winding path. All but Peter were no doubt wondering why they were called so soon from their beds on such a peaceful morning after being out the night before.

Malcolm went to meet them. "Friends," he said, "I'm in need of your help."

"Anything you like, Malcolm, except it be to ride your mare," answered one.

"It's not that," returned Malcolm. "It's nothing so fearsome or hard. The hard part will be to believe what I'm going to tell you. But first you must promise to hold your tongues for half a day."

"Ay, we'll not tell," said one. "We'll hold our tongues," said another; "you can depend on us!"

"Well," said Malcolm, "my name's not Malcolm MacPhail, but—"

"We all know that," said one, rather sarcastically.

"And what more do you know?" asked Blue Peter with some anger at his interruption.

"Well, nothing much," the man answered.

"Then you know little!" said Peter, and the others laughed.

"My name's Malcolm Colonsay," resumed Malcolm quietly, "and I'm the next marquis of Lossie."

A dead silence followed, and in doubt and astonishment two or three of them had to suppress a strong inclination to laugh. But after a few moments first one, then another, looked at Blue Peter and, perceiving that the matter was to him not only serious but evidently no news, each began slowly to come to his senses.

"You mustn't take it hard, my lord," said Peter, "if the lads be a bit taken aback with the news. It is a sudden shift in the wind for them."

"I wish your lordship well," thereupon said one and held out his hand.

"Long life to your lordship!" said another, and the rest followed. Each spoke a hearty word and shook hands with him after which followed a good deal of laughter and many questions from all around.

"Time enough later to clear it all up," said Malcolm laughing. "It is enough for now that you believe me and trust me. And that I am able to trust you. For serious matters must be attended to today, and I need you to stand with me should things go difficult with certain things I must do."

"We are with you, my lord," they seemed to answer in unison. "We are at your service."

With the understanding that they were to be ready at his call and that they should hear from him in the course of the day, Malcolm left them and rowed back to the Seaton. There he took his basket of fish on his arm which he went and distributed according to his purpose, ending with Mrs. Courthope at the House. Leaving there he spent thirty minutes with Miss Horn.

Then he fed and dressed Kelpie, saddled her, and galloped to Duff Harbor where he found Mr. Soutar at breakfast and arranged with him to be at Lossie House at two o'clock. On his way back he called on Mr. Morrison and requested his presence at the same hour. Skirting the back of the House and riding as fast as he could, he then made straight for Scaurnose and appointed his friends to be near the House at noon, so placed as not to attract attention and yet within hearing of his whistle from door or window in the front. Returning to the House, he put up Kelpie, rubbed her down, and fed her. Then, finding there was yet some time to spare, paid a visit to the factor. He was cordial and, to Malcolm's great satisfaction, much recovered. He had a better than pleasant talk with him.

While they were out in the fishing boat together, Lizza had told Clementina her story, and Clementina, in turn, had persuaded Lizza to tell Lady Lossie her secret. It was in the hope of an interview with her false lover that the poor girl had consented so easily. A great longing had risen within her to have the father of her child acknowledge him—even if only to her—taking him just once in his arms. That was all. She had no hope for herself. With trembling hands, and heart beating wildly, she dressed her baby and herself as well as she could and about one o'clock went to the House.

Nothing could have better pleased Lady Clementina than that Liftore and Lizza should meet in Florimel's presence, but she recoiled altogether from the small stratagems, not to mention the lies necessary, to bring about such a confrontation. So she had to content herself with bringing the two girls together. After Lizza's arrival, they sat together for a few moments while Lizza calmed herself and then Clementina went to look for Florimel. She found her in a little room adjoining the library where she often went. Liftore had, if not quite complete freedom of the spot, yet privileges there; but at that moment Florimel was alone. Clementina informed her that a fisher-girl with a sad story which she wanted to tell her had come to the House. Florimel, who was not only kindhearted, but relished the position she imagined herself to occupy as lady of the place, at once assented to her proposal to bring the young woman to her there.

When Clementina entered with Lizza carrying her child, Florimel instantly suspected the truth, both as to who she was and as to the design of her appearance. Her face flushed and her heart filled with anger, chiefly against Malcolm, but against the two women as well, who, she did not doubt, had lent themselves to his designs, whatever they might be. She rose, drew herself up, and stood prepared to act both for Liftore and herself.

Scarcely, however, had the poor girl opened her mouth to speak when Lord Liftore, daring an entrance without warning, opened the door and walked into the room. Looking about, he stopped and began an apology almost at once. But Lizza, hearing his voice, turned with a cry and fell at his feet and held up her child imploringly. Taken altogether by surprise, the earl stared for a moment and then fell back on the pretense of knowing nothing about her.

"Well, young woman," he said, "what do you want with me? I didn't advertise for a baby. Pretty child, though."

Lizza turned white as death, and her whole body seemed to give a heave of agony. Clementina had just taken the child from her arms when she sank motionless at his feet. Florimel went to the bell.

But Clementina prevented her from ringing. "I will take her away," she said; "do not expose her to your servants." Then gathering her courage, she went on: "Lady Lossie, Lord Liftore is the father of this child. If you can marry him after the way you have seen him use its mother, you are not too good for him, and no one will trouble themselves about you any longer!"

"I know the author of this false accusation!" cried Florimel. "You have been listening to the inventions of an ungrateful dependent. You slander my guest. What right do you have—"

"Is it a false accusation, my lord? Do I slander you?" said Clementina, turning sharply upon the earl. He made her a cool, obeisant bow, but said nothing.

Clementina ran into the library, laid the child in a big chair, and returned for the mother. She led her from the room, but from the doorway turned and said, "Good-bye, Lady Lossie. I thank you for your hospitality, but I can, of course, remain as your guest no longer."

"Of course not!" Florimel responded with the air of a woman of forty.

"Florimel, you will curse the day you marry that man!" she cried and closed the door.

As they left the House, they immediately came upon Malcolm walking toward it from the factor's. He immediately surmised the scope of Clementina's plot.

"Malcolm," groaned the poor girl, holding out the baby, "he won't admit to it. He won't allow that he knows anything about me or the child."

"He's a rascal, Lizzy! But don't worry, we'll take care of your child," he said, and bent over to kiss it tenderly.

At that very moment he lifted his eyes to the House where, leaning from the window above them, he saw Florimel and Liftore. Liftore turned to Florimel with a smile that seemed to say, "There! I told you so; he's the father himself!"

Malcolm strode toward the House.

Lizza ran after him, "Malcolm, Malcolm!" she cried, "don't hurt him. For my sake. He's the father of my child!"

"I won't lay a hand on him, Lizzy."

When the earl saw Malcolm coming, although he was no coward, for the next few seconds his heart doubled its beats. But of all things he must not show fear before Florimel. "What can the fellow be after now?" he said. "I'll go down to him."

"No, no! Don't go near him. He may be violent," objected Florimel. "He is a dangerous man!"

Malcolm reached the top of the flight of stairs just as Liftore was emerging from the drawing room, followed closely by Florimel, fearful of what was about to happen.

"MacPhail," she said like an indignant goddess as she hastened toward them, "I discharge you from my service. Leave this house instantly!"

Malcolm turned immediately, flew down the stairs and outside for a brief parley with Peter who had all the time been close by. Returning through the hall he saw Rose, who had been waiting anxiously in the kitchen. "Come with me," he said without stopping and again approached the stairs.

He entered the drawing room. The earl had Florimel's hand in his and their tone was quiet as he burst suddenly through the door.

"For heaven's sake, my lady!" cried Malcolm, "hear me one word before you promise that man anything."

The earl retreated from Florimel and turned upon Malcolm in a fury. But now he did not have the advantage of the stairs as a moment ago and hesitated. Florimel's eyes filled with wrath.

"I tell you for the last time, my lady," said Malcolm, "if you marry that man, you will marry a liar and a scoundrel."

Liftore laughed, and his imitation of scorn was wonderfully successful, for he felt sure of Florimel, now that she had thus taken his part. "Shall I ring for the servants, Lady Lossie, to put the fellow out?" he said. "That man is as mad as a March hare."

Clementina and Lizza, having reentered the house after Malcolm, followed Rose up the stairs after him, and the three of them listened, from the landing, in fear and anticipation of the proceedings inside the drawing room. Lizza, fearing what might happen, suddenly opened the door and reentered the room.

"So," cried Florimel, "this is the way you keep your promise to my father?"

"It is, my lady. To associate the name of Liftore with his would be a blot on his memory. My lady, I beg a word with you in private."

"You insult me!"

"I beg of you, my lady, for your own dear sake."

"Once more I order you to leave my house, and never set foot in it again!" she said and rang the bell for the servants.

"You hear her ladyship!" cried Liftore; "Get out!" He approached threateningly.

"Stand back," said Malcolm. "If it were not that I promised the poor girl carrying your baby, I would soon—"

It was unwisely said, for the earl came on all the bolder, and it was all Malcolm could do to parry, evade, or stop his blows. He had already taken several severe ones when the voice of Lizza came in agony from next to the door, "Defend yourself, Malcolm! I can't stand it, I give you back your promise."

"We'll manage yet, Lizzy," said Malcolm and kept warily retreating toward a window. He continued holding off Liftore as best he could. Suddenly he dashed his elbow through a pane of glass and gave a loud shrill whistle and at the same moment received a blow over his eye. Blood followed. But already Clementina and Rose had darted between them, and full of rage as he was, Liftore was compelled to restrain himself.

The few menservants now came hurrying all together into the room.

"Take that rascal there and put him under the pump," said Liftore. "He is mad."

"My fellow servants know better than to touch me," said Malcolm.

The men looked to their mistress. "Do as my lord tells you," she said, "and instantly!"

"Men," said Malcolm, "I have spared that foolish lord there for the sake of this fisher-girl and his child, but don't one of you touch me."

Stoat was a brave enough man and not a little jealous of Malcolm, but he dared not obey his mistress.

And now came the tramp of many feet along the landing and six fishermen entered.

Forimel started forward. "My brave fishermen!" she cried. "Take that mad man, MacPhail, and put him out of my grounds."

"I can't do that, my lady," answered their leader.

"Take Lord Liftore," Malcolm said to them, "and hold him while I make him acquainted with a fact or two which he may judge of consequence to him."

The men walked straight up to the earl. He struck right and left, but was overpowered and in a moment held fast.

Then Malcolm stepped into the middle of the room, approaching his sister.

"I tell you to leave this House!" Florimel shrieked, beside herself with fury.

"Florimel!" said Malcolm solemnly, calling his sister by her real name for the first time.

"You insolent wretch!" she cried. "What right have you, if you be, as you say, my baseborn brother, to call me by my name?"

"Florimel!" repeated Malcolm—and the voice was like the voice of her father—"I have done what I could to serve you."

"And I want no more such service," she returned, beginning to tremble.

"But you have driven me almost to extremities," he went on, heedless of her interruption.

"Will nobody take pity on me?" said Florimel imploringly, looking about the room. Then finding herself ready to burst into tears, she gathered all her pride, stepped up to Malcolm, looked him in the face, and said:

"Pray, sir, is this House yours or mine?"

"Mine," answered Malcolm. "I am the marquis of Lossie, and while I am your elder brother and the head of the family, you shall never with my consent marry that man."

Liftore uttered a fierce imprecation.

"If you dare give breath to another such word, I will have you gagged," said Malcolm. "If my sister marries that man," he continued and then turned again to Florimel, "not one shilling shall she take with her beyond what she may happen to have in her purse at that moment. She is in my power and I will use it to the utmost to protect her from him."

"What are you saying, MacPhail?" cried Florimel, a tear issuing from her pale and dilated eyes. "You are mad!" But even as she uttered it, she sought a chair. The fight was ebbing from her body; something in her soul told her Malcolm's words were true.

"Proof!" exclaimed Liftore.

"To my sister I will give all the proof she may require," answered Malcolm. "But to you, my lord, I owe none. Stoat, order horses for Lady Bellair and his lordship."

"I will go with Lady Bellair," said Florimel. Then turning to Liftore, "Let us leave this place at once."

Malcolm took her by the arm. For a moment she struggled, but finding no one dared interfere, submitted and was led from the room like a naughty child.

"Keep his lordship there till I return," he said as they went.

He led her into an adjoining room and when he had shut the door, he said, "Florimel, I have striven to serve you the best way I knew. I loved my sister and longed for her goodness. But she has foiled all my attempts. She has not loved or followed the truth. She has been proud and disdainful and careless of right. You have cast from you the devotion of a gifted and large-hearted painter for a small and vile man. You have wronged the nature and the God of women. Once more, I pray you to give up this man—let your true self speak and send him away."

"Sir, I go with my Lady Bellair, driven from my father's house by one who calls himself my brother. My lawyer shall make inquiries."

She would have left the room but he prevented her.

"Florimel! You are casting the pearl of your womanhood before a swine. He will trample it under his feet and turn against you!"

"Let me go!"

"You shall not go until you have heard all the truth."

"What! More truth still? Your truth is anything but pleasant."

"It is more unpleasant than you yet think. Florimel, you have driven me to it. I would have prepared you a shield against the shock which must come, but you compel me to wound you to the quick. I would have had you receive the bitter truth from lips you loved, but you drove those lips of honor from you. Now there are left to utter it only lips that you hate. Yet you shall receive the truth. It may help to save you from weakness, arrogance, and falsehood. Our father married my mother; therefore I am the marquis.

But, sister, your mother was never Lady Lossie."

"You lie! I know you lie! Because you wrong me, you would brand me with dishonor to take from me, as well, the sympathy of the world. But I defy you!"

"Alas, there is no help, sister. Your mother indeed passed as Lady Lossie, but my mother, the true Lady Lossie, was alive the whole time and only died last year. For twenty years my mother suffered in silence. In the eye of the law you are no better than the little child Liftore denied a short while ago. Give that man his dismissal, or he will give you yours when he learns of this. Never doubt that he would do it. Refuse me again, and I will go from this room to publish the fact that you are neither Lady Lossie nor Lady Florimel Colonsay. You have no right to any name but your mother's. You are Miss Gordon."

She gave a great gasp.

"All that is now left you," concluded Malcolm, "is the choice between sending Liftore away or being abandoned by him. That choice you must now make."

The poor girl tried to speak, but could not. Her fire was burning out, her strength fast failing her.

"Florimel," said Malcolm, and knelt on one knee and took her hand. "Florimel, I will be your true brother. I am your brother, your very own brother, to live for you, love you, fight for you, watch over you until a true man takes you for his wife." Her hand quivered.

"Send him away," she breathed rather than said and sank to the floor.

He lifted her, laid her on a couch, and returned to the drawing room.

"My Lady Clementina," he said, "will you oblige me by going to my sister in the next room?"

"I will, my lord," she said and went.

Malcolm walked up to Liftore. "My lord," he said, "my sister takes her leave of you."

"I must have my dismissal from her own lips."

"You shall have it from the hands of my fishermen. Take him away!"

As he turned from him, he saw Caley behind the little group of servants gathered just outside the door. He walked toward her. She attempted to slip inconspicuously away, but he laid his hand on her shoulder and whispered a word in her ear. She grew white and stood stock-still.

Just then, as the fishermen, with Liftore in tow, approached the top of the stairs, Mr. Morrison and Mr. Soutar entered the House and quickly made their way to the top.

"My lord!" said the lawyer coming up hastily to him, "surely there cannot be occasion for such—such—measures?"

But then catching sight of Malcolm's wounded forehead, he added a low exclamation of astonishment and dismay—the tone saying almost as clearly as the words, "How ill and foolishly everything is managed without a lawyer!"

Malcolm only smiled, went up to the magistrate whom he led into the middle of the room, saying, "Mr. Morrison, everyone here knows you. Tell them who I am."

"The marquis of Lossie, my lord," answered Morrison, "and from my heart I congratulate your people here that at length you assume the rights and honors of your position."

A murmur of pleasure arose in response. But before it ceased, Malcolm started and sprang to the door. There stood Lenorme! He seized him by the arm and without a word of explanation hurried him to the room where his sister was. He called Clementina, half drew her from the room, pushed Lenorme in, and closed the door.

He asked Mrs. Courthope to see that everyone was served luncheon, and then begged them to excuse him for a while and ran down the hill to his grandfather. He dreaded lest any other tongue than his own should tell him the opened secret. He was just in time, for already the town was in a tumult, and the spreading ripples of the news were fast approaching Duncan's ears.

Malcolm found him expectant and restless. When he disclosed himself, he showed little astonishment, only took him in his arms and pressed him to his bosom, saying, "Ta Lort pe praised, my son!" Then he broke out in fervent ejaculation of Gaelic, during which he instinctively turned to his pipes as the only sure way of escape for his imprisoned feelings.

While he played, Malcolm slipped out and hurried to Miss Horn.

One word to her was enough to unlock the months of pent-up emotion that had been hidden deep in Miss Horn's heart. The stern old woman burst into tears.

"Oh, Grizel! My Grizel! Look down from your house among the stars and see the great lad you left behind, and praise the Lord you have such a son!"

She sobbed for a moment and wept without restraint.

Then she stopped suddenly, dabbed her eyes indignantly, and cried, "Hoot! I'm an old fool. Somebody might think I had feelings after all!"

Malcolm laughed, and she could not help joining him.

On his way back to the House, he knocked at Mrs. Catanach's door and said a few words to her which had a remarkable effect on the expression of her plump countenance and deep-set black eyes.

When Malcolm reached the House, he ran up the main staircase, knocked at the first door, opened it, and peeped in. There sat Lenorme on the couch with Florimel on his knees nestling her head against his shoulder, like a child that has been very naughty but was fully forgiven. Her face was blotted with tears, and her hair was everywhere, but there was a light of dawning goodness all about her.

She did not move when Malcolm entered—more than to just bring the palms of her hands together and look up in his face.

"Have you told him all, Florimel?" he asked.

"Yes, Malcolm," she answered, "I told him *all*—and he loves me yet! He has taken the girl without a name to his heart."

"No wonder," said Malcolm, "when she brought it with her."

"Yes," said Lenorme, "I could dare the angel Gabriel to match happiness with me."

Poor Florimel, for all her worldly ways, was but a child. Bad associates had filled her with worldly maxims and words and thoughts and judgments. She had never loved Liftore; she had only taken delight in his flatteries.

"Will you come to your brother, Florimel?" said Malcolm tenderly, holding out his arms.

Lenorme raised her. She went softly to him and laid herself on his chest. "Forgive me, brother," she said, and looked up to him.

He kissed her and turned to Lenorme. "I give her to you," he said.

With that he left them and sought Mr. Morrison and Mr. Soutar. An hour of business followed in which, among other matters, they talked about the necessary arrangements for a dinner for his people, fishers and farmers and all. After the gentlemen took their leave, nobody saw him for hours. Till sunset approached he remained alone, shut up in the Wizard's chamber, the room in which he was born. Part of the time he occupied in writing to Mr. Graham.

As the sun fell behind the sea, Malcolm ascended the sandhill from the shore where he had been walking. From the other side, Clementina ascended but a moment later. On the top they met in the red light of the sunset. They clasped each other's hand and stood for a moment in silence.

"Ah, my lord," said the lady, "how shall I thank you that you kept your secret from me? But my heart is sore to lose my fisherman."

"My lady," returned Malcolm, "you have only found your groom."

35   The Assembly

That same evening Duncan, in full dress, claymore and dirk at his sides and carrying the great Lossie pipes, marched first through the streets of the upper and then the lower town, followed by the bellman. At the proper stations Duncan blew a rousing pil-broch, after which the bellman proclaimed aloud that Malcolm, marquis of Lossie, desired the presence of each and every one of his tenants in the royal burgh of Portlossie, both Newton and Seaton, in the townhall of the same, at seven o'clock upon the evening following. The proclamation ended, the piper sounded one note three times, and they passed to the next station. When they had gone through the Seaton they entered a carriage waiting for them at the sea gate and were driven to Scaurnose, and from there again to the several other villages on the coast belonging to the marquis, making at each the same manner of announcement.

Portlossie was in a ferment of wonder, satisfaction, and pleasure. In the shops, among the nets, in the curing sheds, in the houses and cottages, nothing else was talked about. Stories and reminiscences innumerable were brought out to prove that Malcolm had always appeared likely to turn out somebody, the narrator not seldom modestly hinted at a glimmering foresight on his own part of what had now been revealed. His friends were jubilant. The men crowded around Duncan, congratulating him and asking a hundred questions. But the old man maintained a calm and stately pomp and grace and would not, by word or gesture or tone confess to any surprise, but behaved as if he had known it all the time.

Davy, in his yacht uniform, was the next morning appointed the marquis' personal attendant. Almost the first thing that fell to him in his office was to show into his master's room a pale, feeble man, bowed by the weight of a huge brass-clasped volume under each arm.

His lordship rose and met him with outstretched hand. "I am glad to see you, Mr. Crathie," he said, "but I fear you are out too soon."

"I am quite well since our talk of yesterday, my lord," returned the factor. "Your lordship's accession has made a young man of me again. I am here to render account of my stewardship."

"I want none, Mr. Crathie—nothing, that is, beyond a summary statement of how things stand with me."

"I should like to satisfy your lordship that I have dealt honestly"—here the factor paused for a moment, then with an effort added—"by you, my lord."

"One further word, then," said Malcolm, "the last of the sort, I believe, that will ever pass between us. Thank God we had it made up before yesterday. If you have ever been hard upon any of my tenants, not to say unfair, you have wronged me far more than had you taken from me. So now, if any man thinks he has cause of complaint, I leave it to you, with the help of the new light that has been given you, to reconsider the matter and, where needful, to make reparation. As to your loyalty to my family and its affairs, of that I never had a shadow of suspicion." And with that Malcolm held out his hand.

The factor's trembled in his strong grasp.

"Mistress Crathie is sorely vexed at herself, my lord," he said, rising to take his leave.

Malcolm laughed. "Give Mrs. Crathie my best wishes," he said, "and tell her that if she will, after this, greet every honest fisherman as if he might possibly turn out a lord, she and I will be more than even."

The next morning he carried her again a few mackerel he had just caught, and she never forgot the lesson given her.

When the evening came, the town hall was crammed to such an extent that Malcolm proposed they should occupy the square in front. A fisherman in garb and gesture, not the less a gentleman and a marquis, he stood on the steps of the hall and spoke to his people. They received him with wild enthusiasm.

"The open air is better for everything," he began. "Fishers, I have called you first, because you are my own people. I am and shall be a fisherman. How things have come about I will tell you later. I would like all of you to come and dine with me as soon as preparations can be made, and you shall then hear enough to satisfy your curiosity. At present my care is that you should understand the terms of what I intend to do. I would gladly be a friend to all and will do my best to that end.

"You of Portlossie shall have your harbor cleared without delay.

"You of Scaurnose shall hear the blasting necessary for your harbor commence within two weeks, and every house shall before long have a small piece of land allotted it. I feel bound to mention that there may be some among you whom I will have to keep an eye on. I give fair warning that whoever shall hereafter disturb the peace or liberty of my people shall assuredly be cast out of my borders.

"I shall take measures that all complaints shall be heard and all except foolish ones heeded. As much as lies in my power I will execute justice. Whoever oppresses or wrongs his neighbor shall have to do with me. And to aid me in doing justice I pray the help of every honest man. I am set to rule, and rule I will. He who loves right will help me to rule; he who does not love it shall be ruled or depart."

The address had been every now and then interrupted by a hearty cheer. At this point the cheering was greatly prolonged, and after it, he went on:

"And now I am about to give you proof that I mean what I say and that evil shall not come to light without being noted and dealt with.

"There are in this company two women. One of them is already well known to you all. Her name, or at least that by which she goes among you, is Barbara Catanach. The other is an Englishwoman by the name of Caley."

All eyes were turned upon the two. Even Mrs. Catanach was cowed by the consciousness of the universal stare.

"Well assured that if I brought a criminal action against them it would hang them both, I trust you will not imagine it revenge that moves me to thus expose them. In refraining from prosecuting them I bind myself of necessity to see that they work no more evil. In giving them time for repentance I take the consequences upon myself. Therefore, these women shall not go forth to pass for harmless members of society in some other place, but shall live here, in this town, thoroughly known and absolutely distrusted. That they may be thus known, I publicly declare that I hold proof against these women of having conspired to kill me. From the effects of the poison they succeeded in giving me, I fear I shall never altogether recover. There are also mischiefs innumerable upon their lying tongues. If I wrong them, let them accuse me. Only if they bring suit against me and lose, it will compel me to bring my accusations against them.

"Hear, then, what I have determined concerning them. The woman Catanach shall take to her cottage the woman Caley. That cottage they shall have rent free. I will appoint them also a sufficiency for life and maintenance, bare indeed, for I would not have them comfortable. But they shall be free to work if they can find any to employ them. If, however, either shall go beyond the bounds I set, she shall be followed the moment she is missed with a warrant for her apprehension. And I beg all honest folk to keep an eye on them. According as they live shall their lives be. If they come to repentance, they will bless the day I resolved upon such severe measures on their behalf. Now, let them go to their place."

I will not try to describe the devilish look of contempt and hate that possessed the countenance of the midwife as she obeyed the command. Caley, white as death, trembled and tottered, not daring once to look up as she followed her companion. Before many months had gone by, stared at and shunned by all, even Miss Horn's Jean, and totally deprived of every chance of indulging her dominant passion for mischievous influence, the midwife's face began to tell such a different tale that Malcolm began to hold a feeble hope that within a few years Mrs. Catanach might get so far as to begin to suspect that she was a sinner—that she had actually done things she ought not to have done.

Duncan was formally recognized as piper to the marquis of Lossie. His ambition reached no higher. Malcolm himself saw to his perfect equipment, heedful especially that his kilt and plaid should be of Duncan's own tartan of red and blue and green. His dirk and broadsword he had newly sheathed, with silver mountings. And whenever Malcolm had guests they had to endure, as long as Duncan continued able to fill the bag, as best they might, two or three minutes of uproar and outcry from the treble throat of powerful Lossie pipes between each course at every dinner. A lady guest would now and then venture to hint that the custom was rather a trying one for English ears. By his own desire, the piper had a chair and small table set for him behind and to the right of his chief, as he called him. There he ate with the family and guests, waited upon by Davy.

Malcolm was one of the few who understood the shelter of light, the protection to be gained by the open presentation of the truth. To Malcolm it was one of the promises of the Kingdom that there is nothing covered that shall not be revealed. He was anxious, therefore, to tell his people at the coming dinner the main points of his story, certain that such openness would also help to lay the foundation of confidence between him and them. The one difficulty in the way was the position of Florimel. But that could not fail to appear in any case; and he was satisfied that even for her sake it was far better to speak openly, for then the common heart would take her in and cover her. He consulted, therefore, with Lenorme, who went to find her. She came and begged him to say whatever he thought best.

This time the tables were not set in different parts of the grounds, but gathered upon the level of the drive and adjacent lawn spaces between the house and the trees. Malcolm, in full highland dress as chief of his clan, took the head of the central table, with Florimel in the place of honor at his right and Clementina on his left. Lenorme sat next to Florimel and Annie Mair next to Lenorme. On the other side, Mr. Graham sat next to Clementina, Miss Horn next to him, and Blue Peter next to Miss Horn. He set Mr. Morrison to preside at the farmers' table and had all the fisher-fold about himself.

When the main part of the dinner was over, he rose and, with as much circumstance as he thought desirable, told his story, beginning with the parts in it his uncle and Mrs. Catanach had taken. It was, however, he said, a principle in the history of the world that evil should bring forth good. Had he not been taken to the heart of one of the noblest and simplest of men who had brought him up in honorable poverty and rectitude? When he had said this he turned to Duncan who sat at his own table behind him with his pipes on a stool. "You all know my grandfather," he went on, "and all respect him."

At this rose a great shout.

"I thank you, my friends," he continued. "My desire is that

every soul here should carry himself to Duncan MacPhail as if he were in blood what he is in deed and in truth—my grandfather."

A second great shout arose.

He went on to speak of the privileges he alone of all his race had ever enjoyed—the privileges of toil and danger, of human dependence and divine aid, the privilege of the confidence and companionship of honorable men and the understanding of their ways and thoughts and feelings, and the privilege of the friendship and instruction of the schoolmaster to whom he owed more than eternity could reveal.

Then he turned again to his narrative and told how his father, falsely informed that his wife and child were dead, married Florimel's mother; how his mother, out of compassion for both of them, held her peace, how for twenty years she had lived with her cousin Miss Horn and held her peace even from her; how at last, when having succeeded to the property, she heard he was coming to the House, the thought of his nearness yet unapproachableness so worked upon a worn and enfeebled frame that she died.

Then he told how Miss Horn, after his mother's death, came upon letters revealing the secret which she had all along known must exist which, from love and respect for her cousin, she had never inquired into.

Last of all he told how, in a paroxysm of rage, Mrs. Catanach had let the secret of his birth escape her; how she afterward made affidavit concerning it, and how his father upon his deathbed, with all necessary legal observances, acknowledged him as his son and heir.

"And now, to the mighty gladness of my soul," he said, looking on Florimel at his side, "my dearly loved and honored sister has accepted me as her brother. And I do not think she greatly regrets the loss of the headship of the house she has passed over to me. She will lose little else. And of all women, it may well be to her a small matter to lose a mere title, seeing she is so soon to change her name for one which will bring her honor of a more enduring reality. For he who is about to become her husband is not only a nobleman but a man of great talent whose praises she will hear on all sides. One of his works, the labor and gift of love, you shall see when we rise from the table. It is a portrait of your late landlord, my father, painted partly from a miniature, partly from my sister, and partly, I am happy to think, from myself. And you will remember that Mr. Lenorme never saw my father. I say this not to excuse, but to enhance his work.

"My tenants, I will do my best to give you fair play. My friend and factor, Mr. Crathie, has confided to me his doubts whether he may not have been a little hard; he is prepared to reconsider some of your cases. Do no imagine that I am going to be a careless man of business. I want money, for I have enough to do with it, if only to set right much that is wrong. But let God judge between you and me.

"My fishermen, every honest man of you is my friend and you shall know it. Between you and me that is enough. But for the sake of harmony and right and order, and that I may keep near you, I shall appoint three men of yourselves in each village to whom any man or woman may go with request or complaint. If two of those three judge the matter fit to refer to me, the probability is that I shall see it as they do. If any man think them unjust toward him, let him come to me. Should I find myself in doubt, I have here at my side my loved and honored master to whom to apply for counsel. Friends, if we be honest with ourselves, we shall be honest with each other.

"And, in conclusion, I want you to hear from none but my own lips that this lady beside me, the daughter of an English earl of ancient house, has honored the house of Lossie by consenting to become its marchioness. Lady Clementina Thornicroft possesses large estates in the south of England, but not for them did I seek her favor, and it was while my birth and position was yet unknown to her—she never dreaming that I was other than only a fisherman and a groom—that she accepted me for her husband."

With that he took his seat. After hearty cheering, a glass or two of wine and several speeches, all rose and went to look at the portrait of the late marquis.

36 The Wedding

Lady Clementina had to return to England to see her lawyers and arrange her affairs. So the *Psyche* was launched. Lady Clementina, Florimel, and Lenorme were the passengers; Malcolm, Blue Peter, and Davy the crew. There was no room for servants, yet there was no lack of service. They had rough weather part of the time and neither Clementina nor Lenorme was altogether comfortable, but they made a rapid voyage and were all well when they landed at Greenwich.

Knowing nothing of Lady Bellair's proceedings, they sent Davy to reconnoiter in Portland Place. He brought back word that there was no one in the house but an old woman. So Malcolm took Florimel there. Everything belonging to their late visitors had vanished and nobody knew where they had gone.

Searching the drawers and cabinets, Malcolm found, to his unspeakable delight, a miniature of his mother along with one of his father—a younger likeness than he had yet seen. Also he found a few letters of his mother—mostly were notes written in pencil—but neither these nor those of his father which Miss Horn had given him would he read. Lovingly he laid them together and burned them to dustflakes. "My mother shall tell me what she pleases when I find her," he said. "She shall not reprove me for reading her letters to my father."

They were married at Wastbeach, both couples in the same ceremony. Immediately after the wedding the painter and his bride set out for Rome, and the marquis and marchioness went on board the *Psyche*. As it was the desire of each to begin their married life at home, they sailed direct to Portlossie. After a good voyage, however, they landed, in order to reach home quietly, at Duff Harbor, took horses from there, and arrived at Lossie House late in the evening.

Before the return voyage Malcolm wrote to the housekeeper

to prepare for them the wizard's chamber, but to alter nothing on walls or in furniture. That room, he resolved, should be the first he occupied with his bride, and it was there he told her the long story of his history which she hungered to hear. Mrs. Courthope was scandalized at the idea, but she had no choice and therefore contented herself with doing all that lay in the power of woman, under such severe restrictions, to make the dingy old room cheerful. Malcolm kept that chamber just as it was ever after, and often retired to it for meditation. He never restored the ruinous parts of the concealed stairway and kept the door at the top carefully closed. But he cleared out the rubbish that choked the place where the stairs had led lower down, came upon it again in tolerable preservation a little beneath, and followed it into a passage that ran under the burn. Doubtless there was some foundation for the legend of Lord Gernon.

There, however, he abandoned the work, thinking of the possibility of a time when employment would be scarce and his people in want of all he could give them. And when such a time did arrive within a couple of years, an even more important undertaking was in the making which was needful to employ the many who must either work or starve—the rebuilding of the ancient castle of Colonsay. Its vaults were emptied of rubbish and ruin, the rock faced afresh, walls and towers and battlements raised, until at last when its loftiest tower seemed to have reached its height, it rose yet higher, crowned by a splendid beacon lamp to shine far into the northern night to guide the fishermen when their way was unsure. Every summer for years, Florimel and her husband spent weeks in the castle and many a study the painter made there of the everchanging face of the sea.

Malcolm had such a strong feeling for good and truth that nothing would suit him but that Mr. Graham be reinstated. He told the presbytery that if it were not done, he would himself build a schoolhouse for him, with the consequence that they reversed their former position. The young man they had put in his place was willing to act as his assistant, keeping the cottage and his same salary, with the understanding that when he found he could no longer conscientiously further the endeavors of Mr. Graham, the marquis would procure him another appointment.

Mr. Graham thenceforward lived in the House, a spiritual father to the whole family. There was an ancient building connected with the House, divided for many years into barn and dairy, but evidently originally the chapel of the monastery. This Malcolm soon set about reconverting. It made a lovely chapel—too large for the household, but not too large for its Wednesday evening congregation, when many of the fisher families, farm people from the neighborhood, and a number of the inhabitants of the upper town gathered to listen to the master.

Clementina adopted Lizza as her personal attendant. As Lizza's young boy was about her nearly always, by the time she had children of her own she had some notion of what could and ought to be done for the development of the divine germ that lay deep inside every human heart. Kelpie had a foal and apparently, in consequence, grew so much more gentle that at length Malcolm consented that Clementina should mount her. After a few attempts to unseat her, not of the most determined kind, however, Kelpie consented to carry her and ever after seemed proud of having a mistress that could ride.

It was not long before people began to remark that no one now ever heard the piper utter the name Campbell. An ill-bred youth once—it was well for him that Malcolm was not near—dared the evil word in his presence. A cloud swept across the old man's face, but he held his peace, and to the day of his death, which arrived in his ninety-first year, it never crossed his lips. He died with the Lossie pipes on his bed and Malcolm by his side.

Malcolm's relations with the fisher-fold, founded as they were in truth and open uprightness, were not in the least injured by his change of position. He made it a point to always be at home during the herring fishing. And when he was at home he was always out amongst the people. Almost every day he would look in at some door in the Seaton and call out a salutation to the busy housewife—perhaps go in and sit down for a minute. Now he would be walking with this one, now talking with that—oftenest with Blue Peter.

In the third year he launched a strange vessel. Her tonnage

was two hundred, but she was built like a fishing boat. She had great stowage forward and below; if there was a large take, boat after boat could empty its load into her and go back and draw its nets again. But this was not the original design for her. The half of her deck, parted off with a light rope-rail, was kept as white as stone could make it and had a brass-railed bulwark. She was steered with a wheel, for more room; the top of the binnacle was made sloping, to serve as a lectern; and there were seats all round the bulwarks. She was called the *Clemency*.

For some time Malcolm had provided musical training for the most able of the youths he could find amongst the fishers, and now he had a pretty good band able to give back to God a shadow of His own music. And now, every Sunday evening the great fishing boat, with the marquis, and almost always the marchioness on board, led out from the harbor such of the boats as were going to spend the night on the water.

When they reached the ground, all the other boats gathered around the great boat and the chief men came on board. Malcolm then stood up to read, generally from the words of Jesus; talking to them, striving to get the truth alive into their hearts, after which a prayer and several numbers by the band sent the men dropping into their boats and the fleet scattering wide over the waters to search them for their treasure.

If ever a boat wanted help or the slightest danger arose, the first thing was to call the marquis. He was on deck in a moment, taking the situation in hand. In the morning, when a few of the boats had gathered, they would make for the harbor again, with a full blast of praising trumpets and horns, the waves seeming to dance to the well-ordered noise divine.

For such Monday mornings Malcolm wrote a little song for the band, the last stanza of which follows:

> Like the fish that brought the coin,
> We in ministry will join—
> Bringing what pleases Thee the best:
> Help from each to all the rest.